WORDSWORTH CLASSICS
OF WORLD LITERATURE

General Editor: Tom Griffith

THE TRIAL

FRANZ KAFKA

The Trial

*Translated, with an introduction,
by John Williams*

**WORDSWORTH CLASSICS
OF WORLD LITERATURE**

In loving memory of
MICHAEL TRAYLER
the founder of Wordsworth Editions

2

For customers interested in other titles from
Wordsworth Editions visit out website at
www.wordsworth-editions.com

For our latest list and a full mail order service contact
Bibliophile Books, Unit 5 Datapoint,
South Crescent, London E16 4TL
Tel: +44 0207 515 9222
Fax: +44 0207 538 4115
e-mail: orders@bibliophilebooks.com

This edition published 2008 by Wordsworth Editions Limited
8B East Street, Ware, Hertfordshire SG12 9HJ

ISBN 978 1 84022 097 1

Typeset in Great Britain by Roperford Editorial
Printed and bound by Clays Ltd, St Ives plc

CONTENTS

INTRODUCTION

Rather like 'Orwellian', the term 'Kafkaesque' has come to be used, often by those who have not read a word of Kafka, to describe what are perceived as typically or even uniquely modern traumas: existential alienation, isolation and insecurity, the labyrinth of state bureaucracy, the corrupt or whimsical abuse of totalitarian power, the impenetrable tangle of legal systems, the knock on the door in the middle of the night (or, in Josef K.'s case, just before breakfast). Kafka appears to have articulated, and indeed to have prefigured, many of the horrors and terrors of twentieth-century existence, the *Angst* of a post-Nietzschean world in which God is dead, in which there is therefore no ultimate authority, no final arbiter of truth, justice or morality. Ironically, for all his own debilitating diffidence and his reported instructions to have all his unpublished works destroyed after his death, Kafka has become established as a towering, 'iconic' figure of twentieth-century literature.

There have, of course, been dissenting voices. For much Marxist orthodoxy, Kafka was a negative exemplar of self-absorbed bourgeois defeatism, burdening posterity with his own neuroses, unproductive and enfeebling. His works were banned in Nazi Germany (he was both Jewish and a 'degenerate' modernist), and met with official disapproval in post-war Eastern Block countries, including his own country Czechoslovakia. Only occasionally were there defiant attempts to revive official interest, notably in the Prague Spring of 1968; but it was not until after 1989 that his works were freely available in most of Eastern Europe. From a quite different direction, the American critic Edmund Wilson characterised Kafka memorably and provocatively as a 'Brocken Spectre'. This is a phenomenon occasionally glimpsed by mountaineers when a low sun throws the climber's shadow across cloud or mist in a valley or corrie below; the shadow appears impressively huge, with an iridescent halo around its head. The point of Wilson's analogy is that the size of the shadow is an illusion; in physical reality it is far smaller than it appears – as is the shadow cast by Kafka over modern literary consciousness.

Franz Kafka was born in Prague in 1883, the son of Hermann Kafka, an itinerant Jewish trader from provincial Bohemia who established a successful haberdashery business in the capital shortly before Franz's birth, and of Julie Löwy, who came from a prosperous family of more orthodox, but culturally and professionally assimilated German-Jewish origins. Under the Austro-Hungarian Empire, German was the official language of the future Czechoslovakia; the language of the Kafka household was German, and Franz was given a German education. For all his strange uniqueness, he belongs firmly and consciously within a German literary and cultural tradition – though Kierkegaard was also a profound influence; but he also learned to write in Czech, knew Yiddish and taught himself some Hebrew. A lonely childhood, a delicate constitution and progressive ill health (which Kafka attributed to, or at least regarded as a manifestation of, a psychic or spiritual sickness), the consciousness of being part of a minority in two senses (a Jew in Austro-Hungary, a German in Czech Bohemia), and above all an extremely fraught and problematic relationship with an overbearing, philistine, and opinionated father – all these factors must have conspired to mark Kafka as a writer who articulated the vision of a fragile, insecure and vertiginous existence.

Kafka's relationship with his father haunts much of his writing; but it is expressed most vividly and devastatingly in two accounts, one presented as autobiography and one as fiction. Though neither can be read as straightforward biography, there can be little doubt that they reflect, at least obliquely, his own anguished filial feelings of *pietas* and fear, respect and resentment, obedience and rebellion. The relation between biography and imagination in Kafka's work is too wide a subject to go into here; but the many parallels are striking and tantalising – Kafka seems to invite identification in many details of his work, even naming the figures of his principal novels Josef K. or, in *The Castle*, simply K.

In the *Letter to my Father*, written when he was thirty-six (this is no adolescent outburst), he even states: 'All my writing was about you.' The letter appears to be an attempt at cathartic self-analysis, an ambivalent acknowledgement that his father had driven him into a situation where he can only retreat into the isolation of the imaginative artist. Instead of stability, encouragement and guidance, his father, who 'ruled the world from his armchair', had used abuse, threat, sarcasm and mockery to rob his son of all security and self-confidence. In the even more disturbing short story *The Judgement*, a physically feeble, toothless and ailing father, who nevertheless dominates his son as a 'giant' figure of paternal authority, sentences the son to death by drowning. The son throws himself from a bridge with the words: 'Dear parents, I really have always loved you.'

For all the nightmarish insecurities of his imaginative work and his own inner life, Kafka's professional career was, by contrast, remarkably ordered (though increasingly disrupted by sickness) – as Josef K.'s life was, we may infer, as he worked his way up to a senior position in a bank before his arrest shattered his unremarkable existence. In 1903 Kafka took a law degree at the German University of Prague, and in 1908 joined the clerical staff of the Workers' Accident Insurance Institute, working diligently and conscientiously until 2.00 p.m., when he would devote himself to writing, frequently into the night. He occupied a responsible post before taking early retirement on grounds of ill health in 1922. A move to Berlin in 1923 to live with Dora Dymant – the last in a series of emotionally fraught and ill-fated sexual relationships – ended when he was admitted to a sanatorium near Vienna, where he died of laryngeal tuberculosis in 1924.

Kafka instructed his friend and literary executor Max Brod to burn all his unpublished work – only some stories, among them *The Judgement*, *Metamorphosis*, and *In the Penal Colony*, had been published in his lifetime. Instead, Brod preserved the manuscripts, many of them unfinished; he collated and edited them himself, which has led to some uncertainty about the authentic versions – both *The Trial* and *The Castle* are incomplete, and the intended order of the chapters in *The Trial* is uncertain. This is not, in the final instance, a great drawback. Kafka may well have planned to add more material to *The Trial* (chapter eight, for example, is incomplete, and the wandering, inconclusive interviews between Josef K. and his mentors could have been extended and elaborated almost indefinitely); in *The Castle*, K. fails to gain the access or acceptance he craves, and almost certainly was never meant to.

Kafka frequently expressed himself through aphorism and parable, and some of these brief accounts distil the main themes of his work with chilling brevity – though not therefore necessarily with clarity, since they are as oblique and enigmatic as any of the longer works. Many express remoteness, hopelessness, the impossibility of access to sources of authority or certainty, or what in German is termed *Ausweglosigkeit* – the impossibility of escape or release from a labyrinth of false trails and frustrated hopes. *The Cat and the Mouse*, a 'little fable', tells of a mouse who complains to a cat that the world is getting smaller every day. Wherever it runs, walls are closing in on it; it has already reached the last room, and in the corner stands the trap it is heading for. 'You only have to change direction,' replies the cat before it eats up the mouse. In *Give it up*, a stranger hurrying to the station notices that it is much later than he had thought. Unsure of the way, he asks a policeman, who says: 'Do you expect me to tell you the way?' 'Of course,' replies the stranger, 'since I cannot find it myself.' 'Give it up, give it up,' says the policeman, laughing and turning away 'like someone who wishes to be alone with his laughter'.

An Imperial Messenger is a more elaborate parable on the impossibility of access to ultimate authority, on the infinity of obstacles that hinder the transmission of any message of comfort or reassurance; it could almost be entitled 'God is dead'. As the Emperor of China was dying, a humble subject is told, he summoned a messenger to his deathbed and whispered to him a message meant only for you, an insignificant subject at the furthest remove from the imperial sun. The Emperor makes the messenger repeat the message to him to ensure its accuracy, and the messenger sets out. A vigorous, tireless man, he fights his way through the crowds gathered around the dying Emperor; the imperial emblem of the sun on his breast gives him passage, he makes progress as no one else could. But there are so many people in his way; he gets no further than the inner halls of the palace. And even if he did, how many halls, staircases, courtyards and palaces would there be to struggle through – and so on, 'through millennia'. No one could get through, even with a dead man's message; but you sit at your window in the evening and dream the message to yourself.

A similar infinity of obstacles, a vanishing perspective of impossibilities, informs the parable of the doorkeeper at the gates of the law in *The Trial*. Access to the law, the source of supreme authority or truth, is through a series of doors guarded by a series of ever more fearsome doorkeepers. The man from the country who seeks admittance to the law spends his whole life waiting to be let in; only in his dying moment is he told by the doorkeeper that this door was provided uniquely for him – and it is now going to be closed. For all the specious and casuistic interpretations of the priest who tells the story, the parable is a stark expression of the impossibility of admittance. At the end the dying man glimpses an 'inextinguishable radiance' that streams from within; but that light of possible assurance or redemption is itself inaccessible.

The Trial has the structure of a quest by Josef K. – evidently also a quest for what is inaccessible; but it has the narrative quality of a nightmare. Guilt appears to be an innate part of the human condition, but it is undefined, unquantifiable. A series of unreliable and at times ludicrous mentors, who contradict themselves and each other, offer him dubious guidance on his quest – the uncle, the advocate, the painter, the priest; his hopes are invested in elusive and sporadic female figures who do not advance his cause (or his 'case') in the slightest – Fräulein Bürstner, the washerwoman at the court, Leni. The atmosphere of the court chambers, of any of the legal institutions, is oppressive, claustrophobic, suffocating; Kafka spoke of experiencing feelings of nausea like 'a seasickness on dry land' – a panic loss of psychic equilibrium that is expressed most vividly towards the end of chapter three, when the corridor of the court chambers pitches and heaves under Josef K. like a ship in a storm.

There are innumerable elements in the narrative that have the inexplicable sequence (or lack of sequence) of a dream, the lurching perspectives of a nightmare. The mysterious figures who appear at windows, watching; K.'s perception of the deputy manager and the manufacturer looming huge over him – a prefiguration of the two executioners passing the butcher's knife to each other over his head; the unnerving laughter of the information officer and the deputy manager; the discovery of the flogging scene in a lumber-room of Josef K.'s bank; the startling revelation that there are apparently court chambers in every attic in every part of the city; the situation of these chambers in squalid blocks of tenements in impoverished areas of the city; the inconclusive appearance of a figure who may or may not be Fräulein Bürstner on K.'s final journey; the glimpse of a man reaching out from the upper storey of a house immediately before his execution; the appearance of strange figures – the Italian, the sacristan – who seem to be guiding him towards significant encounters that lead nowhere except to his final moment – these and many other devices can only be read as the narrative of a nightmare.

We are told that when Kafka read his stories to his friends – specifically *Metamorphosis*, surely one of his most disturbing works – he would frequently laugh or giggle; it is also reported that in his private life Kafka, for all his many desolate or depressive pronouncements, at times showed a quiet sense of humour. If this is true, and if it was not a nervous tic like that of the clerk Kaminer, it seems at first astonishing. And yet, for all the gruesome details and the overall horror and helplessness of the predicament of Kafka's victims, it is possible to detect a certain bizarre humour, even hilarity, in his work. The inept courtesies of the guards Franz and Willem or of the second-rate 'actors' or 'tenors' who come to fetch K. at the end, the crazed hubbub of the first investigation, the grotesque figure of the student, the breathless clumsiness of K.'s uncle, the 'spectre from the country', the interminable prosings of the advocate Huld – above all, the anecdote of the court official who throws one advocate after another down the stairs; these may be the figures of nightmares, but they are also straw men, ludicrous and ineffectual.

Rather in the way that the Grimms' fairy tales confront the wishes, fears and insecurities of childhood, Kafka's stories are existential fables which confront the more metaphysical adult anxieties and uncertainties of the twentieth century. But they are oblique fables whose meaning is utterly elusive. They pose problems and questions that admit of no answers, and move in a strange and menacing parallel world – a world described in painstaking, one might almost say realistic detail, but a world that is alien, baffling and disturbing. They are nightmare scenarios – but they are nightmares from which, at least in the case of Josef K., the finally acquiescent, even willing, victim does not wake up in time.

JOHN R. WILLIAMS
St Andrews, 2008

TRANSLATOR'S NOTE

It has been said by a distinguished translator that Kafka poses few problems for the translator. This is true only up to a point; his stories, however alienated from everyday experience, are written in a precise and matter-of-fact language that belies (or perhaps emphasises) the bizarre dislocations of the narrative. Nevertheless, there are certain problems, semantic and syntactical. There are complex passages of reported speech – more easily identified in German by the use of the subjunctive, but less straightforward in English; there are also some shifts in perspective between an occasionally 'omniscient' narrator and Josef K.'s subjective perceptions.

The title of the novel is universally known as *The Trial*; but *Prozeß* in German also suggests a process, an interminable searching and seeking. Fortuitously, the English word 'trial' also has an ambiguity; it can denote a court case, or more widely an emotional, psychic or spiritual ordeal, and as such is entirely appropriate as an overall title. Within the narrative, however, *Prozeß* is often better understood as Josef K.'s *case*. After all, K. is never formally tried before a court; he only appears at a chaotic and inconclusive preliminary hearing before an examining magistrate (*Untersuchungsrichter*) – the burlesque and grotesque equivalent of a French *juge d'instruction*. In German, *Richter* means a judge; but I have distinguished in the translation between the inaccessible 'higher' or senior judges (whom K. never encounters except by hearsay) and the lower 'magistrates', who appear without exception to be venal, slovenly, and lecherous.

Certain characteristically German (or Austrian) formal modes of address cannot be literally translated into English: '[der] Herr Prokurist' denotes K.'s senior position at the bank, but 'Herr K.' seems a more appropriate rendering for English-speaking readers. Kafka's paragraphs frequently run to several pages, and his lengthy sentences are often structured by strings of commas. In order to make the text more reader-friendly, and risking the disapproval of specialist colleagues for interrupting the 'authentic' flow of Kafka's prose, I have broken up the text into shorter paragraphs and used semicolons more frequently than Kafka does.

SUGGESTIONS FOR FURTHER READING

Samuel Beckett, *Waiting for Godot*
Albert Camus, *The Outsider*
Elias Canetti, *Kafka's Other Trial*
Charles Dickens, *Bleak House*
Fyodor Dostoevsky, *Notes From Underground*
Nikolai Gogol, *The Nose*
Hermann Hesse, *Steppenwolf*
Franz Kafka, *The Castle*
Gustav Meyrink, *The Golem*
George Orwell, *Nineteen Eighty-Four*
Harold Pinter, *The Birthday Party*
Jean-Paul Sartre, *Nausea*

THE TRIAL

CHAPTER ONE

Arrest – Conversation with Frau Grubach – then
Fräulein Bürstner

Someone must have been spreading slander about Josef K., for one morning he was arrested, though he had done nothing wrong. The cook who worked for his landlady Frau Grubach, and who brought his breakfast towards eight in the morning, did not arrive. That had never happened before. K. waited a while, and from his pillow saw the old lady who lived opposite watching him with a curiosity quite unusual for her; but then, disconcerted and hungry, he rang the bell. At once there was a knock at the door, and a man he had never seen in this house came in. He was slim but powerfully built, and wore a close-fitting black suit which, like a travelling coat, was fitted with various pleats, pockets, buckles, buttons and a belt, and seemed extremely practical, although one could not quite say what purpose it was supposed to serve.

'Who are you?' asked K., sitting up in bed. But the man ignored the question, as if his appearance ought to be taken for granted, and simply replied: 'Did you ring?' 'Tell Anna to bring me my breakfast,' said K., then without a word studied the man carefully, trying to establish just who he was. But the man did not submit to his scrutiny for very long; he turned to the door, opened it a little, and said to someone who was evidently standing close behind it: 'He wants Anna to bring his breakfast.' This was followed by a short laugh in the next room; it was not clear from the sound whether more than one person was involved. Although the stranger could not have learned from this anything that he had not known before, he now told K., as if he were making a report: 'That is impossible.' 'I've never heard such a thing,' said K., jumping out of bed and quickly pulling on his trousers. 'I'm going to find out who those people are in the next room, and see how Frau Grubach will explain this disturbance.' At once it occurred to him that he should not have said this aloud, and that by doing so he had somehow acknowledged the stranger's right to supervise him; but for the moment it seemed unimportant. Even so, that is how the stranger took it, for he said: 'Hadn't you better stay here?' 'I do not wish to stay here, nor do I wish to be addressed by you until you have introduced yourself.' 'I was only trying to help,' said the stranger, and opened the door without demur.

K. entered the next room more slowly than he intended to; at first sight it looked almost exactly as it had the previous evening. It was Frau Grubach's sitting-room, crammed with furniture, rugs, porcelain and photographs. Perhaps today there was a little more space in the room; but this was not immediately obvious, especially since the main difference was the presence of a man who sat at the open window with a book, from which he now looked up. 'You should have stayed in your room! Did Franz not tell you to?' 'What are you doing here?' said K., turning from this new acquaintance to the one called Franz, who was still standing in the doorway, and back again. Through the open window he again caught sight of the old lady, who with all the inquisitiveness of old age had moved to the window directly opposite in order not to miss anything. 'I'm going to see Frau Grubach . . . ' said K., and made as if to tear himself away from the two men and leave, although they were standing some distance from him. 'No,' said the man at the window. He threw the book onto a small table and stood up. 'You may not leave; you see, you are under arrest.' 'So it seems,' said K. Then he asked: 'And why is that?' 'We have not been authorised to tell you that. Go and wait in your room. Proceedings are under way, and you will know everything in good time. I am exceeding my instructions by speaking to you in such a friendly way. But I hope no one hears it except Franz, and he is also in breach of regulations by being friendly to you. If you continue to be as lucky in the choice of your guards as you have been, you won't have to worry.'

K. wanted to sit down, but now he saw that there was no other seat in the room except the chair by the window. 'You will realise the truth of all this,' said Franz, as they both came towards him. The other man, in particular, was much taller than K., and frequently tapped him on the shoulder. Both of them examined K.'s nightshirt, and said he would now have to wear a shirt of far inferior quality, but that they would keep this one along with the rest of his linen; if his case should end favourably, it would be returned to him. 'It's better you should give us your things than let the depot have them,' they said, 'because there's a lot of pilfering in the depot, and besides they sell everything after a certain period of time, whether the relevant proceedings have been completed or not. And you don't know how long these cases can last, especially recently! Of course, you'd get the money from the depot in the end, but in the first place it doesn't amount to much, because what matters when things are sold is not the price offered but the size of the bribe, and besides we know from experience that the sum gets smaller as it passes through various hands from year to year.' K. scarcely paid attention to these words; he did not attach much importance to his right to dispose of his things, if he still possessed such a right. It was much more important to him to clarify his position; but in the presence of these people he could not even think. Time and again the belly of the second guard — they could only be guards — pushed against him in a perfectly friendly way, but when he looked up he caught sight of a face that did not go with this fat body at all, an impassive, bony face with a large bent nose, exchanging meaningful looks with the other guard above his head. What sort of people were they? What were they talking about? What authority did they represent? After all, K. lived in a properly constituted state where things were peaceful and the laws were upheld; who dared to ambush him in his own home? He always tended to take everything as calmly as possible, to believe the worst only when the worst happened, and not to worry about the future even when everything looked threatening. But that did not seem to apply here; of course, one could regard the whole thing as a hoax, a crude joke played on him for some unknown reason by his colleagues at the bank, perhaps because today was his thirtieth birthday; that was of course possible, perhaps he only needed somehow to laugh in the guards' faces and they would join in, perhaps they were porters off the street — they looked rather like it. All the same, on this occasion, ever since he had set eyes on the guard Franz, he was quite determined not to lose the slightest advantage he might have over these people. K. was aware of a very slight risk that he might later be accused of not being able to take a joke, but he remembered — though it had not been usual for him

to learn from experience – some incidents, insignificant in themselves, where unlike his friends he had deliberately and without
the slightest regard for the consequences, behaved rashly and had
paid for it as a result. That must not happen again, at least not this
time; if it was an act, he would play along with it.

He was still free. 'Excuse me,' he said, and quickly passed
between the guards into his room. 'It looks as if he's being
sensible,' he heard one of them say behind him. In his room, he
hurriedly pulled open the drawers of his desk; everything was in
perfect order, but in his agitation he could not at first find the
official papers he was looking for. Finally he found his bicycle
licence, intending to show it to the guards, but then he thought
this certificate too trivial, and searched further until he found his
birth certificate. As he went back into the next room, the door
opposite opened and Frau Grubach made to come in. He only
caught a glimpse of her, for as soon as she recognised K. she
clearly became embarrassed, excused herself and disappeared,
shutting the door with the utmost care. 'Do come in' was all K.
had been able to say; but now he stood with his papers in the
middle of the room still looking at the door, which was not
opened again, and he was only roused by a call from the guards,
who were sitting at the small table by the open window and, as he
now realised, were eating his breakfast. 'Why did she not come
in?' he asked. 'She is not allowed to,' said the tall guard. 'You're
under arrest, you see.' 'But how can I be under arrest? How can
you arrest me like this?' 'Don't start that all over again,' said the
guard, dipping a piece of bread and butter into the jar of honey.
'We don't answer questions like that.' 'You will have to answer
them,' said K. 'Here are my identity papers, now show me yours,
especially the warrant for my arrest.' 'Good heavens,' said the
guard. 'If you'd only accept your situation. You seem intent on
annoying us needlessly, when we are now probably closer to
you than anyone else!' 'That's true, believe me,' said Franz. He
was holding a cup of coffee in his hand, but he did not raise it to
his lips; instead, he gave K. a long, probably meaningful but
inscrutable look. Without wishing to, K. exchanged glances with
Franz; but then he tapped his papers and said: 'Here are my
official papers.' 'What have those got to do with us?' cried the tall
guard. 'You're behaving worse than a child. What do you want?

Do you think you'll get this damned case of yours over quickly by discussing your official papers and your arrest warrant with us, your guards? We are minor employees who can hardly understand official papers, and we have nothing to do with your case except to stand guard on you for ten hours a day. That's what we're paid for, that's all we are; but even so, we can still understand that the higher authorities we serve under don't proceed with such an arrest until they are very clearly informed about the reasons for the arrest and the character of the suspect. There is no mistake here. Our authorities, as far as I know them, and I only know the lowest grades, don't go looking for guilt among the population; they are, as the law puts it, drawn towards guilt and have to send us guards out. That's the law. How could there be any mistake?' 'I don't know this law,' said K. 'All the worse for you,' said the guard. 'I dare say it only exists in your heads,' said K., in an attempt somehow to infiltrate the guards' thoughts, to turn them to his advantage or establish himself in their minds. But the guard only said dismissively: 'You'll soon know about it.' Franz joined in and said: 'You see, Willem, he admits he doesn't know the law, and at the same time claims he's innocent.' 'You're quite right, but you can't make him understand anything,' said the other. K. made no further reply; why should I, he thought, let myself get even more confused by the babble of these underlings, which is what they admit they are? Besides, they are talking about things they do not understand. They are so certain only because they are so stupid. A few words with someone of my own standing will make everything incomparably clearer than any amount of talking to them. He walked up and down a few times in the free space of the room; opposite he saw the old woman, who had dragged an even older man to the window and was holding him in her arms. K. had to put an end to this performance. 'Take me to your superior,' he said.' 'When he wants to see you, not before,' said the guard called Willem. 'And now I advise you,' he added, 'to go back to your room, keep calm and wait to see what will be done about you. We advise you not to be distracted by futile thoughts, but to compose yourself; great demands will be made on you. You have not treated us in the manner our helpfulness might have deserved. You have forgotten that whoever we may be, we are at least for the moment free men compared to you, and that is no small advantage. However, we are still prepared, if you have any money, to fetch you some breakfast from the café across the road.'

Without making any reply to this offer, K. stood there for a while. Perhaps if he opened the door to the next room, or even the door into the hall, the two men would not dare to stop him, perhaps it would be the simplest way to resolve the whole matter by bringing things to a head. But perhaps they would seize him after all, and if they did overpower him he would lose any superiority he still, in a certain sense, had over them. And so, to be on the safe side, he preferred to solve things by letting them take their course, and went back into his room without a word having been uttered by him or by the guards.

He threw himself on his bed and took a single apple from the washstand, which he had chosen the previous evening for his breakfast. Now it was all the breakfast he had; but, as he assured himself with the first bite he took, it was still far better than the breakfast he might have had from the filthy all-night café through the charity of the guards. He felt well and confident; he was absent from his work at the bank this morning, but that would be readily excused given the relatively senior position he held there. Should he report the real reason? He thought he would. If they did not believe him, which was understandable in this case, he could call on Frau Grubach as a witness, or even the two old people from across the road, who were no doubt now on their way towards the window opposite. K. was surprised, at least it surprised him from the guards' point of view, that they had driven him back into his room and left him here alone, where he had a dozen means of killing himself. And yet at the same time he asked himself, this time from his own point of view, what reason he could have to do so. Perhaps because the two of them were sitting next door and had helped themselves to his breakfast? It would have been so senseless to kill himself that even if he had wished to do so, the senselessness of it would have made him unable to do it. If the limited intelligence of the guards had not been so obvious, one might have assumed that they too, for the same reason, had seen no danger in leaving him alone. They were welcome to watch him as he went to a small cupboard in which he kept a good quality schnapps, swallowed one glass instead of his breakfast, then poured another to give himself courage – the latter only as a precaution, in the unlikely event that he might need it.

Then a shout from the next room startled him so much that he hit the glass against his teeth: 'The chief wants to see you!' It was only the shout that startled him, this curt, abrupt military bark that he would not have believed the guard Franz capable of. The order itself was most welcome to him. 'At last!' he called back, locked the cupboard and went at once into the next room. The two guards, who were standing there, drove him back into his room as if it were a matter of course. 'What are you thinking of?' they shouted. 'You think you're going to appear before the chief in your shirt? He'll have you thrashed, and us too.' 'Leave me alone, damn you!' cried K., who had already been forced back towards his wardrobe. 'If you pounce on me when I'm in bed, you can't expect me to be in my best suit.' 'That won't help,' said the guards who, whenever K. shouted, became very calm, indeed almost solemn, which confused him or to some extent brought him to his senses. 'Ridiculous formalities!' he grumbled; but he was already taking a jacket from the chair, and held it up for a while with both hands, as if presenting it for the guards' approval. They shook their heads. 'It must be a dark jacket,' they said. At this, K. threw the jacket on the floor and said – he did not know himself in what sense he meant it – 'But it's not the main hearing yet.' The guards smiled, but insisted: 'It must be a dark jacket.' 'If it speeds things up, I don't mind,' said K. He opened his wardrobe, and spent some time looking through his many clothes. He chose his best dark suit with a well-cut jacket that had made quite an impression on his acquaintances, then took out another shirt and began to dress carefully. Privately he thought to himself that he had managed to expedite matters because the guards had forgotten to make him take a bath. He watched them to see whether they might still remember to do so; but of course it did not occur to them, though Willem did not forget to send Franz to the supervisor with the message that K. was getting dressed.

When he was fully dressed, he had to go, with Willem close behind him, through the empty room next door into the far room, whose double doors stood open. This room, as K. knew very well, had recently been taken by a Fräulein Bürstner, a typist who left for work very early and came back late, with whom K. had hardly exchanged more than a brief greeting. Now her bedside table had been moved into the middle of the room as an interrogator's desk, and the supervisor was sitting behind it. He had crossed his legs and draped one arm over the back of the chair.

In a corner of the room stood three young people looking at Fräulein Bürstner's photographs, which were pinned to a mat hanging on the wall. A white blouse hung from the latch of the open window. The two old people had returned to the window across the street, but now they had more company, for behind them, towering over them, stood a man wearing a shirt open at the neck, who stroked and twisted his reddish pointed beard with his fingers. 'Josef K.?' asked the supervisor, perhaps only in order to direct K.'s distracted gaze towards him. K. nodded. 'I suppose you are very surprised by this morning's events?' asked the supervisor, while with both hands he rearranged the few objects on the bedside table, the candle, a box of matches, a book and a pin-cushion, as if they were things he required for the interview. 'Of course,' said K., with a flood of relief that he was at last faced with a rational person with whom he could discuss his situation. 'Of course I am surprised, but I am by no means very surprised.' 'Not very surprised?' asked the supervisor, placing the candle in the middle of the table and arranging the other things around it. 'Perhaps you misunderstand me,' K. hastened to add. 'I mean' – at this point K. broke off and looked round for a chair. 'I suppose I may sit down?' he asked. 'It is not customary,' the supervisor replied. 'I mean,' continued K., 'I am certainly very surprised, but when one has lived for thirty years and has had to make one's own way in the world, as I have, one becomes inured to surprises and doesn't take them too seriously. Especially not this one.' 'Why especially not this one?' 'I am not saying I regard the whole thing as a joke; the arrangements that have been made seem to me to be too elaborate for that. All the people in the boarding-house would have to be involved, and all of you too; that would go beyond the limits of a joke. So I would not call it a joke.' 'Quite right,' said the supervisor, and inspected the matchbox to see how many matches it contained. 'On the other hand, however,' K. continued, turning to all of them – and he would have liked to turn to the three who were looking at the photographs – 'on the other hand, the matter cannot be of great importance. I assume this from the fact that I have been accused, but I cannot think of the slightest offence of which I could be accused. But that too is beside the point; the main question is, by whom am I accused? What authority is conducting these proceedings? Are you officials? None of you has a uniform, unless your clothes' — here he addressed Franz — 'can be called a uniform; but they look more like travelling clothes. I demand a clear explanation of these matters, and I am convinced that once they have been explained, we shall be able to part on the most cordial terms.' The supervisor banged the matchbox down on the table. 'You are greatly mistaken,' he said. 'These gentlemen here and I are of no importance whatever in your case, indeed we know hardly anything about it. We could be wearing the most official uniforms, and you would be in no worse a position. And I am quite unable to tell you that you are accused of any offence, or rather, I do not know whether you are. You are under arrest, that is correct, but more than that I do not know. If the guards have told you something different, that was just idle chatter. But even if I can't answer your questions, I can still advise you not to think so much about us, but about what is going to happen to you — you would do better to think about yourself. And don't make such a fuss about feeling innocent; it spoils the otherwise not unfavourable impression you are making. You should be altogether more careful in what you say; almost everything you have said so far, even if it was only a few words, could have been inferred from your behaviour, and besides, none of it is particularly favourable to your case.'

K. stared at the supervisor. Was he being taught lessons like a schoolboy by a man perhaps younger than himself? Was he being reprimanded for his frankness? And was he being told nothing of the reason for his arrest or who had authorised it? In a state of some agitation, he walked up and down, which no one tried to prevent, pulled back his cuffs, fingered his chest, smoothed his hair, and as he passed the three young men said: 'But it is senseless,' at which the three looked at him sympathetically but earnestly. He finally stopped again at the supervisor's desk. 'The State Attorney Hasterer is a good friend of mine,' he said. 'Can I call him?' 'Certainly,' said the supervisor, 'but I don't see the sense of that, unless you have some private matter to discuss with him.'

'You don't see the sense of it?' K. cried, more in dismay than in anger. 'Who are you, then? You look for sense and behave in the most senseless way possible? It's heartbreaking. First I'm ambushed by these gentlemen, and now they are sitting or standing around while you put me through my paces. You don't see the sense of telephoning a lawyer when I am apparently under arrest? Right, I won't call him.' 'No, go on,' said the supervisor, pointing to the hallway where the telephone was, 'please do.' 'No, I don't want to any more,' said K., and went over to the window. Across the road they were still gathered at the window, and only now, as K. appeared, did their calm attention seem to waver a little. The old couple made to get up, but the man behind reassured them. 'There are spectators over there, too!' K. cried in a loud voice to the supervisor, pointing out of the window. 'Get away from there!' he shouted across. And indeed the three at once retreated a few steps; the old couple even hid behind the man, who shielded them with his broad frame and, to judge from the movements of his lips, said something that could not be heard from that distance. They did not disappear altogether, though, but seemed to be waiting for the moment when they could once again approach the window unnoticed.

'Inquisitive, impertinent people!' said K., turning back into the room. From a sidelong glance he gave to the supervisor, it seemed to K. that he might agree with him. But it was equally possible that he had not listened at all, for he had pressed one hand firmly onto the table and seemed to be comparing the length of his fingers. The two guards sat on a chest draped with an embroidered cloth, rubbing their knees. The three young people had put their hands on their hips and were looking around aimlessly. It was as quiet as in some deserted office. 'Now, gentlemen,' cried K. – it seemed to him for a moment as if he were shouldering the responsibility for all of them – 'from the way things look, it seems my case is finished. I think it would be best not to dwell on the rights and wrongs of your behaviour and to conclude the matter amicably with a mutual handshake. If you are also of this opinion, then please' – he approached the supervisor's desk and held out his hand. The supervisor looked up, chewed his lips and looked at K.'s outstretched hand; K. still believed the supervisor would accept it. But he stood up, took a hard, round hat that lay on Fräulein

Bürstner's bed, and placed it carefully with both hands on his head, as one does when trying on a new hat. 'How simple everything seems to you!' he said to K. meanwhile; 'you thought we should conclude the matter amicably? No, no, that is simply not possible. On the other hand, I'm certainly not suggesting you should despair. No, why should you? You are only under arrest, that's all. It was my job to inform you of it; I have done that, and I have also seen how you have received it. That is enough for today, and we can say goodbye to each other — though only for the time being. I suppose you will want to go to the bank now?'

'To the bank?' asked K., 'I thought I was under arrest.' K. said this with a certain defiance, for although his handshake had not been accepted, he felt, especially since the supervisor had stood up, more and more independent of all these people. He was playing with them. If they should leave, he intended to follow them to the front door and invite them to arrest him. And so he said again: 'But how can I go to the bank when I'm under arrest?' 'Ah,' said the supervisor, who had already reached the door, 'you have mis-understood me. You are under arrest, certainly, but that does not prevent you from doing your job. Your normal way of life will not be affected.' 'Then being under arrest is not so bad,' said K., going up to the supervisor. 'I never intended to suggest otherwise,' he replied. 'In that case it seems it was not even particularly necessary to inform me of my arrest,' said K., stepping even closer. The others had also approached; they were now all gathered into a small space near the door. 'It was my duty,' said the supervisor. 'A stupid duty,' said K. implacably. 'Perhaps,' answered the super-visor, 'but we won't waste time with such talk. I had assumed that you wanted to go to the bank. Since you pay attention to every-thing that is said, I would add: I am not forcing you to go to the bank, I had only assumed you wanted to. In order to make that easier for you, and to make your arrival at the bank as unobtrusive as possible, I have placed these three gentlemen, your colleagues, at your disposal.' 'What?' cried K., and stared at the three in amazement. These insipid young men, so unremarkable, whom he had noticed only as a group around the photographs, were indeed officials from his bank — not colleagues, that was saying too much, and it indicated a flaw in the omniscience of the supervisor; but they were certainly junior clerks. How could K. not have noticed them? He must have been so preoccupied with the supervisor and the guards that he did not recognise these three! Rabensteiner, who held himself stiffly and flapped his hands, Kullich, fair-haired, with deep-set eyes, and Kaminer with his insufferable smile that was caused by a chronic muscular spasm. 'Good morning,' said K. after a pause, and offered his hand to the gentlemen as they bowed politely. 'I did not recognise you. So, let us go to our work now, shall we?' The men nodded eagerly and smiled, as if that was what they had been waiting for all the time; but when K. realised he had left his hat in his room, all three ran to fetch it, which still suggested a certain embarrassment on their part. K. stood there and watched them through the two open doors. The diffident Rabensteiner, who had merely broken into an elegant trot, was of course the last; Kaminer handed him his hat, and K. was forced to remind himself, as he had often had to at the bank, that Kaminer's smile was involuntary, indeed that he was incapable of smiling intentionally.

In the hallway Frau Grubach, who seemed to have no feelings of guilt, opened the door of the apartment for the whole company, and K. looked down, as he often did, at her apron-string, which was tied so unnecessarily tight it cut deeply into her ample body. Downstairs K., his watch in his hand, decided to take a cab to avoid any unnecessary delay; for they were already half an hour late. Kaminer ran to the corner to fetch the cab, and the other two were making obvious efforts to distract K., when Kullich suddenly pointed to the front door of the house opposite, in which the tall man with the ginger beard had just appeared. Initially somewhat embarrassed that he could now be seen at his full height, he stepped back to the wall and leaned against it. The old couple were probably still on the staircase. K. was annoyed with Kullich for drawing his attention to the man; he had already seen him, indeed, he had even expected him. 'Don't look over there!' he snapped, without realising how odd it was to speak to a grown man like that. But there was no need to explain himself, for at that moment the car arrived, they got in and drove off. Then K. remembered that he had not seen the supervisor and the guards leave; the supervisor had distracted his attention from the three clerks, and then they had distracted him from the supervisor. That did not show very much presence of mind, and K. resolved to be more observant in these matters. But he still turned round in spite of himself, and leaned over the back of the car to see if he could catch sight of the supervisor and the guards. But he turned round again at once, and leaned back comfortably in the corner of the car without even having made the effort of looking for anyone. Although he did not appear to invite it, at this point he would have welcomed some conversation. But the gentlemen seemed tired now, Rabensteiner looked out of the car to the right, Kullich to the left, and only Kaminer with his grin was available; unfortunately, K.'s better feelings did not allow him to remark on it.

That spring K. usually spent his evenings taking a short walk alone or with some colleagues after work — if he could, for more often than not he stayed in the office until nine o'clock — and then went to a small tavern, where he would sit at a reserved table with a circle of mostly older gentlemen, usually until eleven o'clock. But there were exceptions to this routine, when K. for instance was invited by the bank manager, who valued his diligence and reliability highly, for a drive in his car or to supper at his villa. Once a week K. also paid a visit to a girl called Elsa who worked through the night in a wine bar, and only received visitors from her bed during the daytime.

On this evening, however — the day had passed quickly with hard work and many flattering and friendly good wishes for his birthday — K. wanted to go straight home. He had thought about it during all the short breaks in the day's work; without knowing exactly what he meant to do, it seemed to him that the events of that morning had disrupted the whole of Frau Grubach's household, and he was the only person who could restore order. Once this had been done, all traces of those events would be removed and everything would return to normal. In particular, he had nothing to fear from the three clerks; they had been absorbed into the vast bureaucracy of the bank, and he noticed no change in their behaviour. Several times K. had called them into his office, individually and together, with no other purpose than to observe them, and each time he was able to let them go without any cause for concern on his part.

When he came home at half-past nine that evening, he met a young lad at the door who was standing in his way and smoking a pipe. 'Who are you?' asked K. abruptly, peering closely at the young man; he could not see very clearly in the gloom of the hallway. 'I am the caretaker's son, Sir,' answered the young man, taking the pipe out of his mouth and standing aside. 'The caretaker's son?' asked K., tapping his stick impatiently on the floor. 'Is there anything you need, Sir? Shall I fetch my father?' 'No, no,' said K., with a note of reassurance in his voice, as if the lad had done something wrong for which he forgave him. 'It's all right,' he said, and walked on; but before going up the stairs he turned round again.

He could have gone straight to his room, but since he wanted to talk to Frau Grubach, he went to her door and knocked. She was sitting darning a stocking; on the table in front of her lay a pile of old stockings. Embarrassed, K. excused himself for calling at such a late hour, but Frau Grubach was very friendly and brushed his apology aside. She always had time for him; he was, as he well knew, her best, her favourite lodger. K. looked around the room; everything had been put back in its place as it had been before, the breakfast things that had earlier stood on the small table by the window had also been cleared away. 'Women's hands do a lot of work unseen,' he thought; he would perhaps have smashed the crockery on the spot, and he would certainly not have been able to clear it away. He looked at Frau Grubach with some gratitude. 'Why are you working so late?' he asked. They were now both sitting at the table; now and again K. buried a hand in the stockings. 'There's a lot of work to do,' she said, 'during the day I am here for the lodgers; if I want to tidy up my own things, I only have the evenings to do it.' 'I suppose I have made an extraordinary amount of work for you today.' 'How is that?' she asked, becoming rather more agitated, and letting her work rest in her lap. 'I mean the men who were here this morning.' 'Oh,' she said, recovering her composure, 'that didn't give me much work.' K. looked on silently as she resumed her darning. She seems surprised that I mentioned it, he thought, she seems to think it's not right for me to speak about it. Then it's all the more important that I should; I can only talk about it to an older woman. 'I'm quite sure it made work for you,' he replied, 'but it will not happen again.' 'No, it can't happen again,' she said reassuringly, and smiled almost sadly at K. 'Do you really think so?' asked K. 'Yes,' she said more softly, 'but above all you mustn't take it too badly. All sorts of things happen in this world! Since you have confided in me, Herr K., I can admit I listened at the door for a while, and the two guards told me a few things as well. It's a question of your happiness, and I really have that at heart, more perhaps than I ought to, for I am only the landlady. Well now, I heard some things, but I can't say they were particularly bad. No, you are under arrest, but not like a thief is under arrest. If you are arrested like a thief, that's serious, but this arrest — it's too difficult for me, excuse me if I'm being stupid, it's something above my head that I don't understand — but then I don't have to understand it either.'

'What you have said, Frau Grubach, is not at all stupid, indeed I partly share your view; but I judge the whole thing more critically than you, and I don't think it's above your head. I think it is totally insignificant. I was taken by surprise, that's all. If I had got up as soon as I was awake, without being put out by Anna's absence, if I had gone to you and ignored anyone who stood in my way, if I had just this once had my breakfast in the kitchen and asked you to bring me my clothes from my room, if I had acted sensibly, then nothing would have happened, all these things would have been avoided. But one is so unprepared. In the bank, for example, I am prepared for everything, something like that could not possibly happen there; I have my own attendant, the public telephone and the internal telephone are on my desk in front of me, people are always coming and going, customers and colleagues, but most of all I am constantly involved in my work, so I have my wits about me. It would give me real pleasure to be faced with such a situation there. Well, it's all over now, and in fact I don't want to talk about it any further; but I just wanted to hear how you, as a sensible woman, judged the matter, and I am very glad that we agree about it. Now you must give me your hand; such an agreement must be confirmed with a handshake.'

Will she shake my hand? The supervisor did not offer me his hand, he thought, and looked at the woman in a different way, with a more searching look. She stood up because he had also risen, she was a little embarrassed because she had not understood everything K. had said. And because she was embarrassed she said something she did not mean to say, something quite inappropriate: 'Don't take it so much to heart, Herr K.,' she said tearfully, and of course forgot the handshake. 'I didn't know I was taking it to heart,' said K. He suddenly felt tired, and realised how worthless all this woman's reassurances were.

At the door he asked: 'Is Fräulein Bürstner home?' 'No,' said Frau Grubach laconically, then gave him a smile of belated but sincere sympathy. 'She is at the theatre. Do you want to see her about something? Shall I give her a message?' 'Oh, I only wanted to have a few words with her.' 'I'm afraid I don't know when she will be back; when she goes to the theatre she usually gets back late.' 'It doesn't matter,' said K.; with his head bowed he turned towards the door to leave. 'I only wanted to apologise for having taken over her room today.' 'There is no need for that, Herr K., you are too considerate, the young lady knows nothing about it, she has not been in since early this morning. Everything has been put back in order, as you can see.' She opened the door to Fräulein Bürstner's room. 'Thank you, I believe you,' said K., but all the same he went to the open door. The moon shone softly into the dark room. As far as could be seen everything was indeed in its proper place, even the blouse was no longer hanging from the window-latch. The pillows on the bed lay partly in moon-light; they seemed to be piled up remarkably high. 'The young lady often gets back late,' said K., looking at Frau Grubach as if she were responsible. 'That's how young people are!' said Frau Grubach apologetically. 'Of course, of course,' said K., 'but it can go too far.' 'It can indeed,' said Frau Grubach, 'how right you are, Herr K. That might well be the case here. I certainly don't want to speak ill of Fräulein Bürstner, she is a good girl, a nice girl, friendly, neat and tidy, hard-working too. I admire all that very much, but one thing is for sure: she should have more pride, she should not be so forward. I've seen her twice this month already in out-of-the-way streets, and each time with a different gentleman. I find it very embarrassing, I'm only telling this to you, Herr K., upon my word, but there's no way round it, I shall have to talk to Fräulein Bürstner about it. And that's not the only thing about her that makes me suspicious.' 'You are quite mistaken,' said K., scarcely able to hide his anger, 'and what's more, you have obviously misunderstood what I said about the young lady; that is not what I meant. I warn you expressly not to say anything to Fräulein Bürstner, you are completely mistaken, I know her very well, all you have said is quite untrue. But perhaps I'm going too far, I don't wish to stop you, tell her what you like. Good night.' 'Herr K.,' Frau Grubach implored him, and hurried after K. as far as his door, which he had already opened, 'I don't want to speak to the young lady yet, of course I want to keep an eye on her a little longer before I do, you're the only one I've told what I know. After all, it must be in every lodger's interest if I try to keep the boarding-house respectable, and that is all I'm trying to do.' 'Respectable!' cried K. through the partly closed door, 'if you want to keep these lodgings respectable, you'll have to give me notice first.' Then he slammed the door shut, and paid no further attention to a faint knocking on the other side.

Nevertheless, since he had no wish to sleep, he decided to stay up and take this opportunity to find out when Fräulein Bürstner would get back. It would perhaps even be possible, however unsuitable it might be, to have a few words with her. As he lay by the window and closed his weary eyes, he even thought for a moment of punishing Frau Grubach by persuading Fräulein Bürstner to give in her notice at the same time as he did. But this immediately struck him as a gross over-reaction, and he even suspected himself of wishing to move out of his apartment because of the events of that morning. Nothing would have been more senseless, above all nothing would have been more pointless and contemptible.

When he had tired of looking out at the empty street, he lay down on the sofa, having first opened the door to the hallway a little so that he could see anyone who entered the apartment. Until about eleven o'clock he lay quietly on the sofa, smoking a cigar. But then he felt he could not lie there any longer, and went a little way out into the hall, as if by doing so he could hasten Fräulein Bürstner's return. He had no particular desire for her, he could not even remember exactly what she looked like; but he did want to speak to her, and it irritated him that by coming back so late she had brought disruption and disorder to the end of that day too. It was also her fault that he had not eaten that evening, and that he had put off his planned visit to Elsa. To be sure, he could still make up for that by going to the wine bar where Elsa worked; he would do this later after his talk with Fräulein Bürstner.

It was gone half-past eleven when he heard someone on the stairs. K., who was pacing up and down in the hallway lost in thought as if he were in his own room, quickly retreated behind his door. Fräulein Bürstner had arrived. Shivering, she drew a silk shawl around her narrow shoulders as she locked the door. In a moment she would go into her room, which K. certainly could not enter at midnight, so he had to speak to her now. Unfortunately he had not switched on the light in his room, and if he emerged from the unlit room she might think she was being attacked; at the very least it would give her a great shock. Feeling helpless, and because there was no time to lose, he whispered through the door: 'Fräulein Bürstner.' It sounded more like a plea than a summons. 'Is someone there?' asked Fräulein Bürstner, looking round anxiously. 'It's only me,' said K. as he stepped forward. 'Oh, Herr K.!' said Fräulein Bürstner with a smile. 'Good evening.' She held out her hand. 'I wanted to have a few words with you just now, would you mind?' 'Now?' asked Fräulein Bürstner. 'Does it have to be now? Isn't that a little odd?' 'I have been waiting for you since nine o'clock.' 'Well, I was at the theatre. I had no idea you were waiting.' 'The reason I wanted to talk to you is something that only happened today.' 'I see; well, I have no real objection, except that I'm so tired I'm ready to drop. Come into my room for a few minutes, then. We can't possibly talk out here, we would wake everyone up, and that would be even worse for us than for them. Wait here until I've switched the light on in my room, and then turn this one off.'

K. did so, but then waited until Fräulein Bürstner from her own room quietly asked him once again to come in. 'Do sit down,' she said, pointing to the ottoman. She remained standing by the bedpost, in spite of the fatigue she had mentioned; she did not even remove her hat, which, though small, was decorated with a mass of flowers. 'Well, what is it? I'm really curious to know.' She crossed her legs casually. 'Perhaps you will say,' began K., 'that the matter is not so urgent that it must be discussed now, but . . . ' 'I never pay any attention to preambles,' said Fräulein Bürstner. 'That makes my task easier,' said K. 'In a sense, it was my fault that this morning your room was thrown into some disorder, it was done by strangers and against my will, but as I say, through my fault; I wanted to apologise for it.' 'My room?' asked Fräulein

Bürstner, looking enquiringly at K., not at the room. 'Yes,' said K., and now for the first time they looked into each other's eyes. 'Just how it happened is not worth discussing.' 'But surely that is the whole point,' said Fräulein Bürstner. 'No,' said K. 'Well,' said Fräulein Bürstner, 'I don't wish to pry into secrets; if you insist that it's unimportant, I have no objection. I gladly accept your apology, especially since I can see no sign of disorder.'

With her hands laid flat on her hips, she made a tour of the room. She stopped at the screen with the photographs. 'Yes, look!' she cried, 'my photographs are all mixed up. But that's horrible. So someone has been in my room, someone who has no right to be here.' K. nodded, and silently cursed the clerk Kaminer, who could never control his silly, pointless fidgeting. 'It's strange,' said Fräulein Bürstner, 'that I have to forbid you to do something you should not have permitted yourself to do, namely, to enter my room in my absence.' 'But I have explained, Fräulein Bürstner,' said K., also going over to the photographs, 'that I didn't interfere with your photographs; since you don't believe me, I must tell you that the investigating commission brought the bank clerks with them, one of whom probably handled the photographs. I shall have him dismissed from the bank at the earliest opportunity. Yes, there was an investigating commission here,' added K., for the young lady was looking at him quizzically. 'To investigate you?' she asked. 'Yes,' replied K. 'No!' she cried, and laughed. 'Oh yes,' said K., 'do you think I'm innocent, then?' 'Well, innocent . . . ' she said, 'I don't want to make a snap judgement on what might be a serious matter, and I don't know you; but it must be a serious crime if they sent an investigating commission after you. But since you are clearly at liberty – and I assume, since you are so calm, that you haven't escaped from prison – you cannot have committed such a crime.' 'Yes,' said K., 'but the commission might have realised that I am innocent, or at least not as guilty as they had assumed.' 'That's certainly possible,' said Fräulein Bürstner, paying close attention. 'You see,' said K., 'you don't have much experience in legal matters.' 'No, I don't,' said Fräulein Bürstner, 'and I've often regretted it, for I would like to know about everything, and I'm particularly interested in legal matters. The law has a peculiar attraction, doesn't it? But I shall certainly be able to learn a great deal about it, because next month I am joining the staff of a legal firm.' 'That's very good,' said K., 'then you will be able to give me some help with my case.' 'Perhaps I will,' said Fräulein Bürstner, 'why not? I like to make good use of my knowledge.' 'I mean it seriously,' said K., 'or at least half-seriously, as you do. The matter is too trivial to engage a lawyer, but I could do with an adviser.' 'Yes, but if I am to advise you, I ought to know what it is about,' said Fräulein Bürstner. 'That's just the snag,' said K., 'I don't know what it is myself.' 'Then you have been making fun of me,' said Fräulein Bürstner, extremely disappointed, 'it was quite unnecessary to come and tell me so late at night.' And she moved away from the photographs where they had been standing together for so long. 'But Fräulein Bürstner,' said K., 'I wasn't joking. I do wish you would believe me. I have already told you what I know about it, in fact more than I know; it was not an investigating commission, that's what I said because I didn't know what else to call it. There was no investigation. I was simply arrested, but I was arrested by a commission.'

Fräulein Bürstner sat down on the ottoman and laughed again. 'What was it like, then?' she asked. 'Dreadful,' said K.; but now he was not thinking about that at all. Instead, he was wholly engrossed in the figure of Fräulein Bürstner, who was lying with one hand under her chin, her elbow resting on the cushion of the ottoman, while her other hand slowly caressed her hip. 'That's too vague,' she said. 'What is too vague?' asked K. Then he recovered himself and asked: 'Shall I show you what happened?' He wanted to move, but he did not want to leave. 'I'm so tired,' said Fräulein Bürstner. 'You came back so late,' said K. 'So now I'm getting the blame, and that's quite right, because I shouldn't have asked you in; and there was no need to, as it turns out.' 'Oh, yes, there was, you'll see,' said K. 'May I move the bedside table away from your bed?' 'What are you thinking of?' said Fräulein Bürstner, 'of course you may not!' 'Then I can't show you what happened,' said K. with agitation, as if this caused him profound distress. 'All right, go on, move the table then, if you need to in order to show me what happened,' said Fräulein Bürstner; and after a pause she added wearily: 'I am so tired that I'm letting you do more than I ought to.' K. placed the table in the middle of the room and sat behind it. 'You must imagine just where people were in the room, it's most important. I am the supervisor, the two guards are sitting on the chest there, three young people are standing by the photographs. Oh, and by the way, a white blouse is hanging on the window-latch. Now I can begin. But I was forgetting: the most important person, that is myself, is standing here in front of the table. The supervisor is sitting very comfortably, his legs crossed, his arm draped over the back of the chair here, a slovenly oaf. Now we can begin. The supervisor shouts as if he wants to wake me up, he really yells at me. I'm afraid I shall have to shout too, to show you just how it was; but it's only my name that he yells like that.' Fräulein Bürstner, who was listening and laughing, put a finger to her lips to stop K. shouting, but it was too late. K. was too involved in the part he was playing, and called slowly: 'Josef K.!' – not as loudly as he had threatened, but still in such a way that the sudden burst of sound only seemed to spread gradually through the room.

Then there was a knocking on the door of the next room, a short series of loud, regular knocks. Fräulein Bürstner went pale and put her hand on her heart. K. was particularly startled, because for a while he was quite incapable of thinking of anything other than the events of that morning and of the young woman to whom he was demonstrating them. No sooner had he pulled himself together than he rushed over to Fräulein Bürstner and took her by the hand. 'Don't be afraid,' he whispered, 'I'll see to everything. But who can it be? Next door there's only the sitting-room, and no one sleeps there.' 'Oh yes,' whispered Fräulein Bürstner into K.'s ear, 'since yesterday Frau Grubach's nephew, a captain, has been sleeping there. There's no other room at the moment. I forgot about it. Why did you have to shout like that? It really upset me.' 'There's no need for that,' said K., and as she sank back onto the cushion, he kissed her on the forehead. 'No, no,' she said, getting hurriedly to her feet, 'go away, go away, what are you thinking of, he's listening at the door, he can hear everything. Stop tormenting me!' 'I'm not going,' said K., 'until you have calmed down a little. Come over to the far corner of the room, he can't hear us there.' She let him lead her there. 'You don't realise,' he said, 'although this is embarrassing for you, you are not in any trouble. You know how Frau Grubach worships me and believes implicitly everything I say; she has the last word in this matter, especially as the captain is her nephew. Besides, she is under an obligation to me because she borrowed a large sum of money from me. I will support anything you suggest that might help to explain why we are here together, and I guarantee that I will persuade Frau Grubach to believe it, and not just for the sake of appearances, but truly and sincerely. You must have no consideration for me. If you wish to make it known that I have assaulted you, then Frau Grubach will be informed of it, and she will believe it without losing any of her faith in me, she is so devoted to me.'

Fräulein Bürstner, drained and motionless, hung her head. 'Why should Frau Grubach not believe I have assaulted you?' continued K. He looked at her hair, her auburn hair, parted, gathered at the back and firmly fastened. He thought she would turn to look at him, but she remained as she was and said: 'I'm sorry, I was so startled by that sudden knocking, not so much by the presence of the captain or what that might lead to. It was so quiet after you had called out, and then there was the knocking; that's why I was so startled, I was sitting near the door, it was very close to me. I'm grateful for your suggestions, but I won't accept them. I can take responsibility for everything that happens in my room, I can answer to anyone. I am surprised that you don't realise what a slur your suggestions cast on me, though of course I recognise that they are well meant. But now go, leave me alone, I need to be alone now even more than I did earlier. The few minutes you asked for have turned into half an hour or more.' K. grasped her by the hand, and then by the wrist. 'You are not angry with me, though?' he said. She removed his hand and replied: 'No, no, I never get angry with anyone.' He took her by the wrist again; this time she let him take it and so led him to the door. He was firmly resolved to leave. But as they reached the door, he hesitated as if he had not expected to find a door there, and Fräulein Bürstner took advantage of this moment to free herself, open the door, and slip out into the hallway. From there she spoke quietly to K.: 'Now, come, please. Look,' – she pointed to the captain's door, under which a strip of light could be seen – 'he has put his light on and is laughing at us.' 'I'm coming,' said K., quickly following her. He put his arms round her and kissed her on the mouth, then all over her face, like a thirsty animal greedily lapping the water of a pool it has at last discovered. Finally he kissed her throat, letting his lips linger there. A noise from the captain's room made him look up. 'Now I am going,' he said. He wanted to call Fräulein Bürstner by her first name, but he did not know it. She nodded wearily, and offered him her hand to kiss, already half turning away as if she were unaware of it, and with her head bowed went back into her room. Soon afterwards K. lay in his own bed. He fell asleep quickly, but before he did he thought for a while about his behaviour. He was satisfied with it, but surprised that he was not even more satisfied; because of the captain he was seriously concerned for Fräulein Bürstner's sake.

CHAPTER TWO

First Investigation

K. had been informed by telephone that a brief investigation into his case would be held the following Sunday. He was told that these investigations would take place regularly; not every week, perhaps, but at frequent intervals. On the one hand it was in everyone's interest to finish the case quickly, but on the other hand the investigations had to be thorough in every respect; yet because of the strain involved they must not be allowed to last too long. For this reason the authorities had resorted to this series of short but frequent interviews. Sunday had been chosen in order not to interfere with K.'s work. It was assumed that he agreed to this; but if he should prefer a different time, they would try to meet his wishes as far as possible. It would, for example, be possible to hold the interviews at night; but no doubt K. would then be too tired. And so, provided he had no objection, they would settle on Sunday. It was understood that he must appear without fail – they were sure he did not need to be reminded of this. He was given the number of the house to which he should report; it was a house in the remote suburbs, in a street K. had never been to before.

When he had heard this message, K. hung up the receiver without replying. He had made up his mind at once to go there that Sunday, he must certainly do that, his case was getting under

way and he had to fight it; this first interview was also going to be
the last. He was still standing by the telephone deep in thought,
when behind him he heard the voice of the deputy manager who
was wanting to use the telephone, but found K. in his way. 'Bad
news?' asked the deputy manager casually, not because he wanted
to know, but in order to get K. away from the telephone. 'No,
no,' said K., who moved to one side but did not go away. The
deputy manager took the phone, and while he was waiting to be
put through lowered the receiver and said: 'Just one question,
Herr K. Would you give me the pleasure of joining a group of us
on my yacht on Sunday morning? It will be quite a large party, and
there are sure to be some people you know among them. The
State Attorney Hasterer, among others. Won't you come along?
Please do!' K. tried to pay attention to what the deputy manager
was saying. It was not unimportant to him, for this invitation from
the deputy manager, with whom he had never got on very well,
signified an attempt at reconciliation on his part; it showed how
important K. had become in the bank and how much its second
most senior official valued his friendship, or at least his neutrality.
It was also chastening for the deputy manager to issue this invitation, even if it had been made casually while he was waiting for
an answer on the telephone. But K. had to chasten him even
further. 'Thank you, but no,' he said. 'I'm afraid I have no time
on Sunday. I already have an engagement.' 'A pity,' said the
deputy manager, and having just been put through, turned to
speak into the telephone. It was a brief conversation, but K.,
preoccupied, stood by the instrument all the while. Only when
the deputy manager rang off, he started, and by way of excuse for
his unnecessary presence, said: 'I have just been told by telephone
to report somewhere, but they forget to tell me what time I should
be there.' 'Why don't you ring back and ask?' said the deputy
manager. 'It's not that important,' said K., although this weakened
his earlier excuse, which had already been unconvincing enough.
Before he left, the deputy manager talked of other things. K.
forced himself to answer, but above all else he was thinking that it
would be best to get there at nine o'clock on Sunday morning,
since all the courts began work at this time on weekdays.

The weather on Sunday was dull. K. was very tired. There
had been a celebration at his regular table at the inn; he had stayed

late into the night, and almost overslept. Hurriedly, having no time to collect his thoughts or to think over the various plans he had devised in the course of the week, he dressed and without taking any breakfast rushed off to the designated suburb. Strangely, although he had little time to look around, he came across the three clerks involved in his case, Rabensteiner, Kullick, and Kaminer. The first two were in a tram that crossed K.'s path; Kaminer was sitting on a café terrace, and just as K. went by he leaned with some curiosity over the balcony. No doubt they all stared after him, surprised to see their senior colleague rushing along. A certain sense of defiance had prevented K. taking any form of transport. He hated the idea of having the slightest help from anyone else in his case; he did not wish to call on anyone and thus make them even remotely privy to his affairs; and finally, he did not have the slightest wish to demean himself before the investigating commission by being too punctual. Even so, he was now hurrying in order to get there at nine o'clock, although he had not even been given a specific time.

He had thought he would recognise the house long before he reached it by some sign that he had not clearly imagined or some sort of activity around the entrance. He paused for a moment at the end of the Juliusstrasse, where he was to be interviewed; but on both sides stood almost uniform tall grey tenements where poor people lived. This Sunday morning most of the windows were occupied, men leaned out in their shirtsleeves, some smoking, others holding small children cautiously and tenderly on the window ledges. In other windows bed-linen was piled high for airing, above which the tousled head of a woman would appear momentarily. They were calling to each other across the way, and one such shout provoked a great burst of laughter just above K.'s head. At regular intervals along the street were small shops, a few steps below street level, selling various kinds of food. Women were going in and out or chatting on the steps. A fruit-seller who was hawking his wares to the windows above, and paying as little attention to where he was going as K. was, almost knocked him over with his barrow. Just then a gramophone that had done long service in a better area of the town began to play with a murderous noise.

K. ventured further down the narrow street, slowly, as if he now had time to spare, or as if the examining magistrate could see him

out of one of the windows and so knew that K. had arrived. It was
shortly after nine. The house was some distance away, it was more
extensive that the rest; in particular, the main entrance was high
and wide. It was obviously designed for the waggons belonging to
the various warehouses, now closed, that surrounded the broad
courtyard and displayed the names of firms, some of which K.
knew from his work at the bank. Taking in all these external
features more closely that he would normally do, he stood for a
while at the entrance to the yard. Nearby a man sat barefoot on a
crate reading a newspaper. Two boys were playing seesaw on a
handcart. A frail young girl was standing at a pump in her nightgown, staring at K. while the water poured into her bucket. In the
corner of the yard a line was stretched between two windows, on
which laundry was already being hung out to dry. A man was
standing underneath directing the work with occasional shouts.

K. turned towards the staircase to get to the interview room, but
then stopped, for as well as these stairs he could see three other
staircases in the yard, and at the far end a narrow passage also
seemed to lead to a second courtyard. He felt annoyed that he had
not been given the location of the room more accurately; he really
was being treated in a most casual and offhand way, a point he
intended to make loud and clear. In the end he climbed the first set
of stairs, reflecting on the words of the guard Willem that the court
was drawn towards guilt, from which it followed that the interview room must be on the staircase that K. happened to choose.

As he climbed the stairs he disturbed a large group of children
playing there, who scowled at him as he brushed past them. 'If I
have to come here again,' he said to himself, 'I must bring some
sweets with me to make friends with them, or else a stick to beat
them with.' Just before he reached the first floor he even had
to wait a while until a marble had stopped rolling. Two small
boys with villainous adult faces held on to his trousers; he could
have hurt them if he had shaken them off, and he was afraid they
might scream.

On the first floor his search began in earnest. He could scarcely
ask where to find the investigating commission, so he invented a
joiner called Lanz – the name occurred to him because that was
the name of Frau Grubach's nephew, the captain – and he intended to ask at all the apartments whether Lanz the joiner lived

there, so that he would have an opportunity to look into all the rooms. But it turned out that he could do this anyway, for nearly all the doors stood open, and children were running in and out. By and large they were small rooms with a single window, in which meals were being cooked. Some of the women held babies on one arm and worked at the stove with their free hand. Teenage girls, apparently dressed only in an apron, were busiest of all, rushing to and fro. In all the rooms the beds were still occupied by invalids or people sleeping or lying there fully dressed. K. knocked at the apartments whose doors were closed and asked whether a joiner called Lanz lived there. Usually it was a woman who opened the door, listened to his question and turned to someone who was getting out of bed. 'The gentleman wants to know whether Lanz the joiner lives here.' 'Lanz the joiner?' asked the man from the bed. 'Yes,' said K., although it was clear the investigating commission was not here, so he had no more business there. Many people thought it must be very important for K. to find Lanz the joiner; they thought it over for some time, mentioned a joiner, but not one called Lanz, or a name that sounded vaguely like Lanz, or they asked their neighbours, or led K. to a door some way away, where they thought such a person might be living as a lodger, or where someone lived who might be able to give him better information than they could. In the end K. hardly needed to repeat his question; in this way he was dragged through every floor. He regretted the plan that had seemed so practical to him at first. Before he reached the fifth floor he decided to give up the search, said goodbye to a friendly young workman who wanted to take him further up, and went down the stairs. But then he felt annoyed again at the pointlessness of the whole business; he went back and knocked on the first door of the fifth floor. The first thing he saw in the small room was a large wall-clock that already pointed to ten. 'Does Lanz the joiner live here?' he asked. 'Please come in,' said a young woman with bright dark eyes, who was washing children's clothes in a tub, pointing with a wet hand towards the open door of the next room.

To K. it was as if he had entered a large gathering. A crowd of all kinds of people – no one took any notice of the newcomer – crammed into a medium-sized room with two windows, around which ran a gallery just below the ceiling which was also packed with people who could not stand upright and crouched with their heads and backs pressed against the ceiling. K. found the air too stuffy; he went back out and said to the young woman, who seemed to have misunderstood him: 'I was looking for a joiner, a man called Lanz.' 'Yes,' said the woman, 'please go in.' K. would perhaps not have done as she said if she had not gone up to him, taken hold of the door handle and said: 'I must lock the door after you; no one else may go in.' 'Very sensible,' said K., 'it's far too full already.' But then he went in again after all.

Between two men who were talking just by the door – the one was holding his hands out in front of him as if he were counting out money, while the other looked him closely in the eye – a hand reached out to K. It was a small rosy-cheeked boy. 'Come on, come on,' he said. K. let the boy lead him; it turned out that there was after all a narrow way through the teeming crush of people, possibly marking the dividing line between two factions – an impression that was confirmed by the fact that in the first rows on either side K. scarcely saw a single face turned towards him, but only the backs of people who addressed their words and gestures to those on their side. Most were dressed in black, in old, long tail-coats that hung loosely on them. These clothes were the only thing that confused K.; but for them he would have taken the whole assembly for a local political meeting.

At the other end of the hall, towards which K. was being led, a small table was set at an angle across a very low, also overcrowded platform. Behind the table near the edge of the platform sat a small, stout man who wheezed as he talked amid much laughter to a man standing behind him, who had crossed his legs and was leaning against the back of the chair. Now and again he threw his arm into the air as if he were mimicking someone. The boy who was leading K. had some difficulty in delivering his message; twice already, standing on tiptoe, he had tried to say something, without being noticed by the man above. Only when one of the people on the platform drew his attention to the boy did the man turn to him and bend down to hear as he whispered to him. Then he drew out his watch and glanced quickly at K. 'You should have appeared an hour and five minutes ago,' he said. K. was about to answer; but he had no time, for the man had scarcely finished speaking when a general murmur of disapproval rose from the right-hand side of the hall. 'You should have appeared an hour and five minutes ago,' the man repeated, raising his voice and glancing down quickly into the hall. Immediately the muttering grew louder, but as the man said nothing further, it died down gradually. It was now much quieter in the hall than when K. had come in. Only the people in the gallery continued to make comments. As far as it was possible to make out anything in the hazy, dusty half-light up there, they seemed to be more poorly dressed than those below. Some had brought cushions with them to put between their heads and the ceiling to protect them from injury.

K. had made up his mind to observe things rather than to speak, so he made no excuses for his alleged lateness and simply said: 'I may have arrived late, but I am here now.' A burst of applause, again from the right-hand side of the hall, greeted these words. These people are easily swayed, thought K.; he was put out only by the silence from the left-hand side directly behind him, from which only sporadic clapping could be heard. He thought about what he could say to win them all over at the same time, or, if that was not possible, to win over the others for the time being at least.

'Yes,' said the man, 'but I am no longer obliged to examine you now' – again the muttering started, but this time its meaning was unclear, for the man waved it aside and continued: 'Exceptionally, however, I will do so today. But such unpunctuality must not occur again. Now, step forward!' Someone jumped down from the platform to make room for K., who climbed up to take his place. He stood pressed up against the table; the crush behind him was so great that he had to resist it to avoid pushing the examining magistrate's table, and even the magistrate himself, off the platform.

The magistrate, however, was unconcerned; he sat quite comfortably in his chair, and after exchanging a final word with the man behind him, picked up a small notebook, which was the only object on his table. It was like an old school exercise-book, worn out of shape from constant thumbing. 'So,' said the magistrate. He leafed through the notebook and addressed K., as if establishing a fact: 'You are a house-painter.' 'No,' said K., 'I am a senior official in a large bank.' This answer was greeted by such hearty laughter from the right-hand section below that K. could not resist joining in. People doubled up with their hands on their knees, shaking as if from a severe fit of coughing. Even one or two in the gallery

laughed. The examining magistrate, who probably had no authority over the people in the hall below, instead turned in fury to
the gallery; he jumped to his feet, and as he threatened those in the
gallery his eyebrows, inconspicuous until now, bristled dark and
menacing above his eyes.

The left-hand side of the hall, however, was still quiet; the
people there stood in rows, they had turned to face the platform
and were listening to the exchanges above them just as calmly as
they had to the noise from the other section. They even allowed
some from their own ranks to mingle here and there with the
other side. Those on the left, who were less numerous, might well
in fact have been just as insignificant as the faction on the right,
but their composure made them seem more important. As K.
now began to speak, he was convinced that what he said reflected
their views.

'You asked, Sir, whether I was a house-painter – or rather, you
did not ask me at all, but told me so to my face; this is typical of the
whole way this investigation is being conducted. You may object
that it is not an investigation at all; you are quite right, for it is only
an investigation if I recognise it as such. So for the time being I do
recognise it, on sufferance as it were. If one is going to take it at all
seriously, one can only take it on sufferance. I am not saying these
proceedings are slovenly; but I would put it to you in these terms
for your own consideration.'

K. paused and looked down into the hall. He had spoken
sharply, more so than he had intended; but he was right. He might
have deserved some applause, but all was quiet; they were clearly
waiting expectantly for what was to follow, perhaps out of that
silence a great burst of applause would put an end to everything
once and for all. But then came a distraction; the door at the back
of the hall opened, and the young washerwoman, who had no
doubt finished her work, came in and in spite of her caution
attracted several glances. Only the examining magistrate's reaction
gave K. unqualified satisfaction, for the words seemed to have an
immediate effect on him. Until then he had been listening while
standing up, for K.'s speech had taken him unawares as he stood up
to address the gallery. Now, during the pause, he sat down slowly,
as if he wanted no one to notice. No doubt in order to compose
himself, he again picked up the notebook.

'There is no more to be said,' K. continued. 'Your own note-book, Sir, bears me out.' K. heard his own calm words in this un-familiar assembly with satisfaction; he even dared without further ado to take the notebook from the magistrate and hold it up fastidiously between his fingertips by one of the middle pages, so that the closely-written, stained, yellowing pages hung down on either side. 'These are the examining magistrate's records,' he said, dropping the notebook on the table. 'Just carry on reading them, Sir; I assure you I am not afraid of these records, although they are inaccessible to me since I can only pick them up between two fingers and would never handle them.' It could only be a sign of deep humiliation, or at least it could only be perceived as such, that the magistrate picked up the book as it lay there on the table where it had fallen, tried to put it into some kind of order, and began to read it again.

The faces of the people in the front row were fixed on K. so expectantly that he gazed down at them for a while. They were all elderly men, some with white beards. Were they perhaps the ones who made decisions and could influence the whole assembly, which could not be roused from the apathy into which it had sunk since K's speech, even by the humiliation of the examining magistrate?

'What has happened to me,' K. continued, rather more quietly than before, all the while scrutinising the faces in the front row, which made his words sound somewhat distracted, 'what has happened to me is only an individual case, and as such not very important because I do not let it affect me; but it is typical of the proceedings taken against many people. It is these I represent here, not myself.'

He had raised his voice without realising it. In the hall someone clapped, his hands held above his head, and shouted: 'Bravo! Why not? Bravo! And bravo again!' Those in the front row tugged at their beards, but none of them turned round at this outburst. Nor did K. attach any importance to it, though it did encourage him. He no longer thought it necessary that everyone should applaud; it was enough for him if the majority began to think about his case, and if just an occasional one was won over by persuasion.

'I do not seek success as an orator,' said K., following this train of thought. 'That may be beyond my abilities. The examining

magistrate no doubt speaks much better than I do, that is his
profession after all. All I ask for is the public discussion of a public
outrage. Hear what I have to say. About ten days ago I was
arrested; I find that fact itself risible, but that is neither here nor
there. I was seized in bed early in the morning. Perhaps the order
had been given – it is quite possible, given what the examining
magistrate said – to arrest some house-painter who is just as
innocent as I am; but they chose me. The next room was
occupied by two boorish guards. If I were a dangerous criminal
they could not have taken better precautions. These guards,
moreover, were unprincipled riff-raff; they talked all kind of
nonsense, they solicited bribes, they tried to take my clothes and
linen by false pretences, they asked for money, supposedly to bring
me some breakfast after they had shamelessly eaten my own
breakfast in front of my eyes. And that was not all. I was taken into
a third room to appear before their supervisor. The room belongs
to a lady for whom I have the greatest respect, and I had to look on
as this room, through no fault of mine and yet on my account, was
as it were polluted by the presence of the guards and their
supervisor. It was not easy for me to remain calm. I managed to
do so, however, and asked the supervisor perfectly calmly – if he
were here, he would have to agree – why I was under arrest. And
what did this supervisor reply? – I can still see him sitting there in
front of me, in that lady's chair, the very image of ignorant
arrogance. Essentially, gentlemen, he did not answer me at all.
Perhaps he really knew nothing; he had arrested me and was
content with that. As if that were not enough, he had brought
three minor officials from my bank to that lady's room, who
spent their time handling photographs, which were that lady's
property, and disarranging them. The presence of these employees, of course, had a further purpose; they were, like my landlady
and her maid, to spread the news of my arrest, to damage my
public reputation and, quite particularly, to jeopardise my position
at the bank. Now, they have not succeeded, not in the slightest, in
any of these things; even my landlady, who is quite an ordinary
person – I mention her name here with all due respect, she is called
Frau Grubach – even Frau Grubach was intelligent enough to see
that such an arrest had no more significance than being attacked in
the street by some unruly youths. I repeat: the whole affair merely

caused me some embarrassment and annoyance for a while, but could it not also have had more serious consequences?'

Here K. broke off and looked over at the silent magistrate; as he did so, he thought he saw him glance at someone in the crowd, as if giving a signal. K. smiled and said: 'I see the examining magistrate here has just given one of you a secret sign. So there are some among you who take instructions from above. I do not know whether this sign was meant to provoke disapproval or applause; by exposing this ruse in good time, I quite deliberately forgo the opportunity of knowing what it might mean. I could not care less about it, and I publicly authorise the magistrate to give his instructions to his hirelings down there out loud instead of by secret signals, by telling them either "Hiss now!", or else "Clap now!"'

Whether with embarrassment or impatience, the magistrate shifted about on his chair. The man behind him, to whom he had spoken earlier, bent over him again, perhaps to give him some specific piece of advice or simply to encourage him. Down below the audience talked in hushed but animated voices. The two factions, who had earlier seemed to have such opposing views, mingled with each other; some individuals pointed at K., others at the magistrate. The thick haze in the hall was most oppressive; it even made it impossible to make out the people at the back. It must have been particularly annoying for those in the gallery, who were forced, albeit with nervous and furtive glances at the magistrate, to whisper questions to members of the assembly in order to find out what was going on. The answers were given just as quietly behind raised hands.

'I have almost finished,' said K., and since there was no bell available, he banged his fist on the table. Startled, the magistrate and his adviser immediately looked up from their huddle. 'I am quite detached from the whole matter, so I can judge it calmly; and if you attach any importance at all to this so-called court, you would do well to listen to me. I beg you to put off discussing my submission among yourselves until later, for I am short of time and I am going to leave soon.'

Such was K.'s hold over the audience that there was immediate silence. People no longer shouted across each other as at the beginning, they did not even applaud any more; they seemed already convinced, or very nearly so.

'There can be no doubt,' said K. very quietly, for he was pleased
with the expectant attention of the whole assembly; in that silence
arose a murmur that was more stimulating than the wildest applause.
'There can be no doubt that all the activities of this court, and
therefore my own arrest and today's investigation, are backed by a
large organisation. An organisation that not only employs corrupt
guards, foolish supervisors, and examining magistrates who are
at best minor officials, but which also supports a high-ranking
judiciary with its inevitable vast retinue of attendants, clerks,
police, and other auxiliaries, perhaps even – I am not afraid to
use the word – executioners. And what is the purpose of this
organisation, gentlemen? It is to arrest innocent individuals and to
institute meaningless and for the most part – as in my case –
fruitless proceedings against them. If the whole system is as senseless as this, how could the whole body of officials avoid being
grossly corrupt? It would not be possible, even the highest judge
could not preserve his own integrity. That is why the guards
attempt to steal the clothing off the backs of those they arrest, that
is why supervisors break into other people's homes, that is why
innocent people, instead of being interrogated, are humiliated in
front of large assemblies. The guards talked of depots where the
property of those under arrest is kept; I would like to see these
depots in which their hard-earned possessions are left to rot, if they
are not stolen by thieving officials.'

K. was interrupted by shrieks from the back of the hall. He
shielded his eyes to see what was going on, for the dim daylight
made the hazy atmosphere white and dazzling. It was the washerwoman who, as K. had noticed, had caused a considerable
disturbance when she had come in. It was not possible to tell
whether this time she was to blame or not; he only saw how a
man had pulled her into a corner by the door, and was hugging
her closely. But it was not the woman who was shrieking; it was
the man. His mouth was wide open and he was looking up at the
ceiling. A small circle had gathered round them; the people in the
gallery nearby seemed delighted that the solemn note K. had
introduced into the proceedings had been interrupted in this way.
K.'s first impulse was to rush over to them. He thought it would
be in everyone's interest that order should be restored and that the
pair of them should, at the very least, be expelled from the hall; but

the nearest rows in front of him stayed put, no one moved, and no one let K. through. On the contrary, they obstructed him, old men held out their arms, and someone's hand – he did not have time to turn round – held him from behind by the collar.

K. was no longer thinking about the couple; it seemed to him that his freedom was being restricted, as if he were really under arrest, and throwing caution to the winds he leapt down from the platform. Now he was face to face with the crowd. Had he judged these people correctly? Had he overestimated the effect of his speech? Had they concealed their reactions while he was speaking, and had they had enough of this pretence once he had concluded his argument? What faces surrounded him! Their small dark eyes darted to and fro, their cheeks drooped like those of drunkards, their long thin beards stiffened, and when they pulled at them, it was as if they were clawing at them rather than stroking them. But underneath the beards – and this was a real revelation to K. – badges of various sizes and colours gleamed on their lapels. As far as he could see, they all wore these badges. These factions, apparently divided into right and left, all belonged together; and when he suddenly looked round, he saw the same badges on the lapel of the examining magistrate, who was looking on calmly with his hands folded in his lap. 'Ah, I see!' cried K., throwing up his hands to emphasise his sudden discovery, 'you are all officials, you are the corrupt gang my speech was aimed at, you have packed this hall as spectators and eavesdroppers, you pretended to form factions, and one of them applauded to test me, you wanted learn how to lead innocent people astray! Well, I hope you haven't wasted your time here. Either you have derived some amusement from listening to someone who expected you to defend innocence, or – leave me alone, or I'll hit you!' K. shouted at a trembling old man who had come particularly close to him – 'or else you really have learnt something. And so I wish you good luck in your trade.'

He grabbed his hat, which was lying on the corner of the table, and amid general silence, or at any rate amid the silence of stunned surprise, pushed his way towards the exit. But the examining magistrate appeared to have moved even more quickly than K., for he was waiting for him at the door. 'One moment,' he said. K. was not looking at the magistrate, but at the door; his hand was already on the handle. 'I simply wanted to let you know,' said the magistrate, 'that, although you may not have realised it, you have deprived yourself of the advantage that an examination invariably gives to someone who is under arrest.' Still turning towards the door, K. laughed. 'You scoundrels,' he cried, 'you can keep all your examinations!' He opened the door and hurried down the stairs. Behind him rose the hubbub of the assembly, which had come to life again and was probably starting to discuss the morning's events like a class of students.

Chapter Three
In the Empty Hall – the Student – the Court Chambers

During the next week K. waited daily for a further communic-ation; he could not believe that his refusal to be questioned had been taken literally, and when the expected notification had not arrived by Saturday evening, he assumed that he was tacitly summoned to the same house at the same time. And so on the Sunday he again made his way there, this time going straight up stairs and along passages; some people, who remembered him, greeted him from their doorways, but he did not need to ask the way and soon arrived at the right door. He knocked, and it was opened at once; without bothering to turn to the same woman as the week before, who was standing by the door, he made straight for the next room. 'There is no meeting today,' said the woman. 'Why is there no meeting?' asked K., who could not believe her. But the woman convinced him by opening the door into the next room. It was indeed empty, and its emptiness made it look even more dismal than the previous Sunday. On the table, which stood on the platform as before, lay a few books. 'Can I take a look at these books?' asked K., not because he was particularly curious, but because he did not wish his visit to be completely wasted. 'No,' said the woman, shutting the door again, 'that is not allowed. The books belong to the examining magistrate.' 'I see,' said K., nodding. 'I suppose these books are legal texts, and it is in the nature of this legal system to condemn people who are not only innocent but also ignorant of the charges against them.' 'That will be it,' said the woman, who had not understood him properly. 'Well then, I shall be off,' said K. 'Shall I give the examining magistrate a message?' said the woman. 'Do you know him?' asked K. 'Of course,' said the woman, 'my husband is a court attendant.'

Only then did K. notice that the room, which the previous week had contained nothing but a wash-tub, was now a fully-furnished living-room. The woman noticed his surprise and said: 'Yes, we live here rent-free, but we must clear out the room on days when there is a sitting. My husband's position has some disadvantages.' 'I'm not so surprised by the room,' said K., giving her a stern look, 'but rather that you are married.' 'Perhaps you are referring to what happened at the last meeting, when I interrupted your speech,' said the woman. 'Of course,' said K. 'That's all in the past now and I had almost forgotten about it, but at the time I was really furious. And now you tell me you are a married woman.' 'It was in your own interests that your speech was interrupted,' said the woman. 'They judged you very unfavourably afterwards.' 'That may be so,' said K. dismissively, 'but it doesn't excuse your behaviour.' 'Everyone who knows me will excuse it,' said the woman. 'The man who threw his arms around me has been pursuing me for a long time. I may not be attractive to everybody, but I am to him. No one can protect me, and my husband has come to terms with it; he has to put up with it if he wants to keep his job, for that man is a student and is expected to reach a position of some power. He is always after me; he left just now before you came.' 'It fits in with everything else,' said K., 'it doesn't surprise me.' 'I suppose you want to improve some things here?' asked the woman slowly, watching K. as if she were saying something dangerous both to herself and to him. 'I gathered that from your speech, which personally I liked very much. Of course, I only heard part of it; I missed the beginning, and for the end of it I was lying on the floor with the student.'

After a pause she took K.'s hand and said: 'Oh, it's so dreadful here. Do you think you will be able to improve things?' K. smiled, rubbing her soft hands lightly with his fingers. 'It's not really my place,' he said, 'to improve things here, as you put it, and if you said that to the examining magistrate, for instance, you would be laughed at or punished. It's true that I would never have interfered with things here of my own accord, and I would never have lost any sleep over the need to improve this judicial system. But because I was allegedly arrested – you see, I am under arrest – I have been forced to intervene here strictly in my own interests. However, if I can also help you in any way while I am about it, I shall be very glad to do so – not simply out of human kindness, but also because you can help me too.' 'But how could I do that?' asked the woman. 'By showing me those books on the table, for example.' 'Of course', cried the woman, dragging him quickly after her. They were old, tattered books; one of the covers was almost split down the middle, held together only by threads. 'How dirty everything is here,' said K., shaking his head, and before he could reach out for the books the woman wiped off at least some of the dust with her apron.

K. opened the first book and found an indecent picture. A man and a woman were sitting naked on a sofa; the lewd intention of the illustrator was quite clear, but it was done so clumsily that all that could be seen was a man and a woman who stood out all too boldly in the flesh, sitting stiffly upright. Because of the poor perspective, they seemed to have some difficulty turning towards each other. K. did not peruse the book further, but simply opened the second book at the title page. It was a novel entitled 'The Sufferings of Grete at the Hands of her Husband Hans'. 'So these are the law books they study here,' said K. 'I am to be judged by people like this.' 'I will help you,' said the woman. 'Do you want me to?' 'Could you really do that without putting yourself at risk? Didn't you tell me just now that your husband was entirely dependent on his superiors?' 'I want to help you all the same,' said the woman, 'come with me, we must talk it over. Don't say any more about the risks to me, I'm only afraid of risks if I want to be. Come over here.'

She pointed to the platform and invited him to sit on one of the steps with her. 'You have lovely dark eyes,' she said, sitting down and looking into K.'s face. 'They tell me I have beautiful eyes too, but yours are much nicer. I noticed them as soon as you came in here the first time. That was why I came into the hall later, something I normally never do, in fact in a sense I am not allowed to.' So that's it, thought K. – she's offering herself to me, she's corrupt like all of them round here, she's had enough of the court officials, which is understandable, so she welcomes every stranger who comes along with a compliment about his eyes. He stood up without a word, as if he had spoken his thoughts out loud and had thus made his attitude clear to the woman. 'I don't think you can help me,' he said. 'To give me any real help, you would have to be in touch with senior officials. But I'm sure you only know the minor officials who swarm around here. I dare say you know them very well, and no doubt they could do quite a lot for you; but even the best they could do would not have the slightest effect on the outcome of my case, and in the process you would only lose some of your friends. I don't want that. Just continue your relationship with these people, because it seems important to you. I say this with some regret, for if I may return your compliment, I find you very attractive, especially when you look at me so sadly like that, although you have no reason at all to do so. You belong to the organisation I have to fight against, and you are quite comfortable with it; you even have the student – or, if you don't love him, then at least you prefer him to your husband. That was easy to tell from what you said.' 'No!' she cried. She would not get up, and seized K.'s hand, which he did not withdraw quickly enough. 'You can't go now, you can't go away with a false impression of me. Could you really bring yourself to leave now? Am I really so worthless that you won't even do me the favour of staying here for just a little while?'

'Don't misunderstand me,' said K., sitting down. 'If it really means so much to you, I'll be glad to stay here, after all I have plenty of time; I came here expecting that a hearing would be held today. What I said just now was only to ask you not to do anything to help me with my case. But there's no need to be offended, because the outcome of the case is of no concern to me at all, and I should only laugh if I were convicted. If, that is, the case ever comes to a proper conclusion, which I very much doubt. I think it more likely that the proceedings have already been suspended, or very soon will be, because of laziness, forget-fulness, or perhaps even fear on the part of the officials. Of course, it's also possible that they will pretend to continue with the case in the hope of some fat bribe; but I can tell them now it's a waste of time, because I never give bribes. Still, you could do me a good turn by informing the examining magistrate, or anyone who likes spreading important news, that I shall never be induced to pay a bribe, not by any of the tricks I'm sure these gentlemen have up their sleeves. It would be quite pointless to try, you can tell them straight. Besides, they may already have noticed this themselves, and even if they haven't, it doesn't bother me if they are told now. It would only save these gentlemen trouble, and indeed it would save me some unpleasantness – though I'd be glad to cope with that as long as I know I'm striking a blow for others at the same time. And I'll make sure that is what I shall be doing. By the way: do you know the examining magistrate?'

'Of course,' said the woman, 'he was the first one I thought of when I offered to help you. I didn't know he was only a minor official, but if you say so, it's probably true. Even so, I think the reports he submits to the authorities still have some influence. And he writes so many reports. You say the officials are lazy, but I'm sure not all of them are, especially not the examining magistrate, he writes a lot. Last Sunday, for instance, the session went on into the evening. They all left, but the magistrate stayed in the hall, I had to bring him a lamp. I only had a small kitchen lamp, but he was quite happy with that and started writing straight away. My husband, who happened to have that Sunday off, arrived in the meantime; we fetched our furniture and arranged the room, and then some neighbours came round. We talked by candlelight, forgot about the magistrate and went to bed. Suddenly – it must have been the middle of the night – I woke up and found the magistrate standing by the bed, shielding the lamp with his hand so that the light didn't fall on my husband; it was an unnecessary precaution, my husband sleeps so soundly that even the light wouldn't have wakened him. I was so startled I almost screamed, but the magistrate was very friendly and told me not to stir. In a whisper he told me that he had been writing until now, that he was returning the lamp, and that he would never forget the sight when he found me asleep. I'm only telling you all this to show that the examining magistrate really does write a lot of reports, especially about you, because your interrogation was definitely one of the main items in Sunday's session. And I'm sure these long reports can't be completely insignificant. Besides, you can see from this incident that the examining magistrate has taken a fancy to me, and at this early stage – he can't have noticed me until then – I can have a lot of influence with him. Since then, too, there have been other signs that I mean a lot to him. Yesterday he sent me silk stockings as a present, delivered by the student who works with him and is trusted by him; they were supposedly in return for tidying the assembly hall, but that is only a pretext, that's my job after all, and my husband is paid for it. They're beautiful stockings, look' – she stretched out her legs, drew her skirt up to her knees and looked at the stockings herself – 'they're beautiful stockings, but they're really too good for me.'

Suddenly she broke off, put her hand on K.'s as if to calm him, and whispered: 'Hush, Berthold is watching us.' K. looked up slowly. In the door of the hall stood a young man; he was small, his legs were not quite straight, and he sought to lend himself some dignity by means of a short, sparse, reddish beard which he fingered constantly. K. looked at him with interest, for this was the first time he had met personally, as it were, a student of this alien legal system, a man who would very probably rise to a high official position one day. For his part, the student appeared to ignore K. completely; he simply beckoned to the woman with a finger, which he removed from his beard for a moment, and went to the window. The woman leaned over to K. and whispered: 'Don't be angry with me, please, don't think badly of me. I must go with him now, with this dreadful person – just look at his bandy legs. But I'll be back right away, and then I'll go with you, if you will take me with you. I'll go wherever you want, you can do what you like with me, I'll be happy to get away from here for as long as possible, preferably for ever, in fact.'

She fondled K.'s hand once more, then jumped up and ran to the window. Automatically, K. reached out for her hand, but she was gone. He was strongly attracted to the woman, and despite all his reservations could find no good reason why he should not give in to this temptation. He quickly dismissed the momentary suspicion that she might be working for the court and leading him into a trap. How could she entrap him? Was he not still free enough that he could, at least as far as his case was concerned, destroy the whole court in a moment? Surely he had enough confidence in himself? Her plea for help sounded honest; it might perhaps be of some value to him – and there was probably no better way of taking revenge on the examining magistrate and his hangers-on than to take this woman from them and have her for himself. It might even happen some time that the magistrate, after slaving over his lying reports on K., would come to her bed late at night and find it empty. Empty because she belonged to K., because this woman at the window, this voluptuous, lithe, warm body clothed in a dark dress made of coarse, heavy material, belonged to him alone.

After ridding himself of his suspicions about the woman in this way, he began to feel that the whispered conversation at the window had lasted long enough; he rapped his knuckles on the platform, then banged it with his fist. The student glanced briefly over the woman's shoulder in K.'s direction, but carried on undisturbed, in fact he moved closer to the woman and embraced her. She bent down towards him as if she were listening attent-ively, and as she bent down he gave her a loud kiss on her neck without any great interruption to what he was saying. K. saw this as a confirmation of the tyranny which, according to the woman's complaints, the student exercised over her. He stood up and walked around the room, glancing sideways at the student from time to time, deliberating how to get rid of him as soon as possible. So he was glad when the student, clearly annoyed by K.'s walking up and down, which by now had developed into a steady tramp, remarked: 'If you are so impatient, you can go. You could have left earlier, no one would have missed you. In fact, you ought to have left as soon as I arrived, and you should have been quick about it too.' While this outburst might have been one of intense fury, it also had all the arrogance of a future court official addressing a defendant he disliked. K. went to stand very close to him and said with a smile: 'I am impatient, that's true, but the easiest way to cure it is for you to leave us. If you have perhaps come here to study – I have heard you are a student – I will gladly make room for you and leave with this woman. What's more, you have a lot of studying to do before you become a magistrate. Although I don't know your legal system very well, I assume it requires a great deal more than just making offensive remarks – which you certainly seem able to do shamelessly well already.'

'They shouldn't have let him run around so freely,' said the student, as if trying to explain K.'s insulting remarks. 'It was a mistake. I said so to the examining magistrate. They should at least

have kept him in his room between interrogations. Sometimes I
don't understand the examining magistrate.' 'All this talk is pointless,' said K., holding out his hand to the woman, 'come with me.'
'I see,' said the student, 'no, no, you're not having her.' And with
a strength one would not have thought him capable of, he lifted
her with one arm and, bent under her weight, ran to the door,
gazing tenderly up at her. He could not disguise a certain fear of
K., but he still dared to provoke him by fondling and squeezing
the woman's arm with his free hand. K. ran a few paces alongside
him, prepared to get hold of him and, if necessary, to throttle him,
but the woman said: 'It's no use, the examining magistrate has sent
for me, I can't go with you; this little horror' – as she said this, she
stroked the student's face with her hand – 'this little horror won't
let me.' 'And you don't want to be rescued!' cried K., grasping the
student by the shoulder. The student snapped at K.'s hand with his
teeth. 'No!' cried the woman, pushing K. away with both hands,
'no, you mustn't do that, what do you think you're doing? That
would ruin me. Leave him alone, please leave him. He is only
carrying out the examining magistrate's orders and taking me to
him.' 'Let him go then, and as for you, I never want to see you
again,' said K., furious with disappointment, and gave the student
a push in the back which made him stumble for a moment; but
then, so pleased was he not to have fallen, he hoisted his burden
even higher. K. walked slowly after them; he realised that this was
the first unmistakable defeat he had suffered at the hands of these
people. Of course, that was no cause for concern; he had been
defeated only because he had set out to fight them. If he stayed at
home and carried on with his normal life he would be infinitely
superior to every one of them, and could kick any of them out of
his way. And he imagined to himself the most ridiculous scene if
this wretched student, for example, this arrogant child, this bandy-
legged bearded creature, were to kneel by Elsa's bed, clasp his
hands together and beg for mercy. K. was so pleased with this idea
that he decided, should the opportunity ever arise, to take the
student to meet Elsa.

  Out of curiosity, K. hurried to the door to see where the woman
was being taken; the student would scarcely carry her through the
streets in his arms. Just across from the flat was a narrow wooden
staircase, probably leading to a garret; it had a bend in it, so it was

not possible to see where it ended. The student carried the woman up this staircase; by now he was climbing very slowly and gasping for breath, for his previous exertions had exhausted him. The woman looked down and waved to K. in an attempt to suggest that she was not to blame for her abduction; but the gesture did not convey very much regret. K. watched her blankly as if she were a stranger; he did not wish to show his disappointment, but neither did he wish to suggest that he could easily get over it.

The two soon disappeared, but K. still stood in the doorway. He was forced to conclude that the woman had not only betrayed him, but had also lied to him when she had told him she was being taken to the examining magistrate. The magistrate would surely not sit and wait in a garret. The wooden staircase gave him no clue, however long he looked at it. Then K. saw a small notice at the foot of the stairs. He went over to it and read it. In an immature childish hand was written: 'Entrance to the Court Chambers'. So the court chambers were here, in the attic of this tenement? It was not an establishment to inspire much respect, and it was reassuring for a defendant to think how impoverished this court must be if its chambers were housed in a part of the building where the tenants, who were themselves from the poorest classes, threw their useless junk. Of course, it was not impossible that the court had enough money, and that the officials seized it before it could be used for legal purposes. To judge from K.'s previous experiences, this was indeed very probable; and yet, although such a corrupt court might seem to demean the defendant, it was still more reassuring than an impoverished court would be. K. now understood why at the first hearing they had been ashamed to summon the accused to their attic, and why they preferred to plague him in his apartment. What a superior position he was in compared to the magistrate, who sat in a garret, while at the bank he had a large office with a waiting-room and a view of the busy main square through a huge window! Of course, he could not supplement his income with bribes or embezzlement, nor could he have a woman brought to his office in the arms of a servant; but he was willing to forgo all that, in this life at least.

K. was still standing in front of the notice when a man came up the stairs, looked through the open door into the living-room, from which the courtroom could also be seen, and finally asked K.

whether he had seen a woman here just now. 'You are the court attendant, aren't you?' asked K. 'Yes,' said the man. 'Ah, you're the defendant K. Now I recognise you. Welcome.' And to K.'s surprise he held out his hand. 'But the court is not sitting today,' continued the attendant when K. did not reply. 'I know,' said K., examining the attendant's everyday jacket; the only indication of his official position was the two gilt buttons which stood out from the other ordinary buttons, and which seemed to have been taken from an old officer's uniform. 'I was speaking to your wife a while ago. She is no longer here; the student has carried her up to the examining magistrate.' 'You see,' said the attendant, 'they're always taking her from me. It's Sunday today, and I'm not on duty, but just to get me out of the way they send me off with a quite unnecessary message. They don't send me far, either, so that if I really hurry I can hope to get back in good time. So I run as fast as I can, and shout my message through the half-open door of the office I've been sent to, but I'm so out of breath they won't have understood half of it. Then I run back, but the student is even quicker; of course, he doesn't have so far to go as I did, he only has to run down the stairs from the attic. If I weren't so dependent on them I would have smashed the student against this wall long ago. Just here, by this notice; I dream about it all the time. Here, a little bit off the floor, he's squashed tight, his arms spread out, his fingers splayed, his bandy legs bent into a circle, and splashes of blood all round. But so far it's only a dream.'

'Is there no other way?' asked K., smiling. 'Not that I know of,' said the attendant. 'And it's getting worse, until now he's only taken her for himself, now he takes her to the magistrate as well. But then, I've been expecting that for a long time.' 'But don't you blame your wife for all this?' asked K. He had to control himself as he said it, for even now he felt fiercely jealous. 'Of course,' said the attendant, 'she's to blame most of all. She's thrown herself at him. As for him, he chases all the women. In this block alone he's been thrown out of five apartments he's sneaked into. The fact is, my wife is the best-looking woman in the whole place, and I'm the only one who can't fight back.' 'If that's the way it is, then I'm sure nothing can be done,' said K. 'Why ever not?' asked the attendant. 'That student is a coward. Somebody ought to give him such a thrashing when he tries to touch my wife that he'll never dare to do it again. But I can't do it, and no one else will do it for me because they're all afraid of the power he has. Only a man like you could do it.' 'But why could I do it?' asked K., astonished. 'Because you're a defendant,' said the man. 'Yes,' said K., 'but that means I have all the more reason to fear that, even if he might not be able to influence the outcome of my trial, he could probably have some influence on the preliminary hearings.' 'Yes, certainly,' said the attendant, as if K.'s view were just as valid as his own. 'But as a rule the trials here are not hopeless cases.' 'I don't agree with you,' said K., 'but that won't stop me teaching the student a lesson some time.' 'I would be most grateful to you,' said the attendant somewhat formally; he did not seem to believe his fondest wish could be granted.

'Perhaps,' continued K., 'some of your other officials, perhaps even all of them, deserve the same.' 'Yes indeed,' said the attendant, as if there were no question about it. Then he gave K. a confiding glance, which for all his friendliness he had not done before, and added: 'There's always something to protest about.' But the conversation seemed to have made him uneasy, for he broke off, saying: 'Now I must report to the chambers. Do you want to come with me?' 'There's nothing for me to do there,' said K. 'You can have a look at the chambers. No one will bother about you.' 'Is there anything worth seeing?' asked K. uncertainly, though he very much wanted to go with him. 'Well,' said the attendant, 'I thought you would be interested.' 'All right,' said K. finally, 'I'll come with you.' And he ran up the stairs faster than the attendant.

As he went in he almost fell, for there was another step behind the door. 'They don't have much consideration for the public,' he said. 'They don't have any at all,' said the attendant, 'just look at the waiting-room.' It was a long corridor with a series of crudely constructed doors, each leading to a compartment in the attic. Although there was no direct light source, it was not completely dark, for some of the compartments were boarded off from the corridor not by solid walls, but by wooden grilles, and though the grilles reached to the ceiling some light shone through them. Behind them individual officials could be seen writing at their desks or standing at the grilles and watching the people in the corridor through the gaps. Probably because it was Sunday, there were few people in the corridor; they made a very modest impression, sitting at almost regular intervals on two rows of long wooden benches either side of the corridor. They were all shabbily dressed, though most of them, to judge by their expression, their bearing, the cut of their beards, and many other scarcely definable small details, belonged to the better classes. Since there were no hat-stands, they had placed their hats under the benches – no doubt following each other's example.

When those sitting nearest to the door caught sight of K. and the attendant, they stood up by way of greeting; when the others saw this they felt they ought to do the same, so that everyone stood as the two went by. None of them stood fully upright; their backs and knees were bent, and they stood like street beggars. K. waited for the attendant, who was walking just behind him, and said: 'How humiliated they must be.' 'Yes,' said the attendant, 'they are all defendants, all these people here are defendants.' 'Really?' said K. 'Then they are my colleagues.' And he turned to the nearest one, a tall, slim man with almost completely grey hair. 'What are you waiting here for?' asked K. politely. But the man became confused at being addressed so unexpectedly, and looked all the more embarrassed because he was clearly a man of the world who in any other situation would surely know how to keep his self-control, and would be reluctant to give up the superiority he enjoyed over many others. Here, however, he did not know how to answer such a simple question, and looked at the others as if they were duty bound to help him, and as if he could not be expected to answer unless such help were forthcoming. Then the attendant went up to him and said, by way of reassurance and encouragement: 'This gentleman is only asking what you are waiting for. Why don't you answer him?' The no doubt familiar voice of the attendant had a better effect: 'I'm waiting . . . ' he began, then hesitated. He had obviously chosen to begin like this in order to answer the question with complete accuracy, but now he did not know how to continue. Some of the people waiting had approached and gathered round; the attendant told them: 'Get back, get back, keep the corridor free.' They moved back a little, but did not return to their places.

Meanwhile the man who had been questioned had composed himself and even smiled faintly as he replied: 'A month ago I submitted some evidence in my case, and I am waiting for the result.' 'You seem to be going to a lot of trouble,' said K. 'Yes,' said the man, 'it's to do with my case, after all.' 'Not everyone thinks as you do,' said K., 'I, for instance, have also been accused, but I give you my solemn word that I have not submitted any evidence or anything of the kind. Do you think it is necessary, then?' 'I don't know exactly,' said the man, once again totally uncertain of himself. He clearly thought K. was joking, and he would probably have preferred, for fear of making another mistake, to repeat his earlier answer all over again; but seeing K.'s impatient expression he said only: 'For my part, I have submitted my evidence.' 'I suppose you don't believe I've been accused?' said K. 'Oh yes, of course,' said the man, moving aside; but his answer suggested not belief, but fear. 'So you don't believe me?' asked K. Unconsciously provoked by the man's servile demeanour, he seized him by the arm as if he were trying to force him to believe him. He had no wish to hurt him, and had only taken hold of him quite lightly, but in spite of this the man shrieked as if K. had grasped him not with two fingers, but with red-hot pincers. This ridiculous screaming made K. lose patience with him. If this man did not believe he was a defendant, so much the better; perhaps he even thought he was a magistrate. And before he moved on, he gripped the man even tighter and pushed him back onto the bench. 'Most of the defendants are so sensitive,' said the attendant. Behind them nearly all those who were waiting gathered round the man, who had stopped screaming by now, and seemed to be questioning him closely about the incident. A man now approached whom K. took to be a guard, mainly because he wore a sabre in a sheath which, to judge by its colour, was made of aluminium. This surprised K., and he even put out his hand to touch it. The guard, who had come to see what the screaming was about, asked what had happened. The attendant spoke a few words to reassure him, but the guard insisted he must look into it himself. He saluted and walked on with rapid but very short steps, probably the result of gout.

K. did not concern himself for very long with the guard or the people gathered in the corridor, especially since he saw that on the right about half-way along the corridor he could turn off through an opening that had no door. He asked the attendant whether this was the right way to go; the attendant nodded, and K. turned off to the right. It annoyed him that he always had to walk a step or two ahead of the attendant, because it might appear, at least in this place, that he was being escorted under arrest. So he often stopped to wait for the attendant, but the man immediately held back. Finally, to put an end to his unease, K. said: 'Now I've seen what it's like here, I'm going to leave.' 'But you haven't seen everything yet,' said the attendant artlessly. 'I don't want to see everything,' said K., who now felt really tired, 'I want to leave. Where is the way out?' 'Surely you haven't lost your way?' asked the attendant in surprise. 'You go to the corner here, and then turn right down the corridor straight to the door.' 'Come with me,' said K., 'and show me. I won't be able to find it, there are so many ways here.' 'It's the only way,' said the attendant, who was beginning to lose patience, 'I can't go back with you, I have to deliver my message, and I'm already very late because of you.' 'Come with me!' repeated K. more sharply, as if he had finally caught the attendant trying to deceive him. 'Don't shout so loud,' whispered the attendant, 'there are chambers everywhere here. If you don't want to go back alone, you can come along with me for a while or wait here until I've delivered my message, then I'll be glad to go back with you.' 'No, no,' said K., 'I won't wait, and you must come with me now.'

So far K. had not so much as glanced at his surroundings, and only now, when one of the many wooden doors opened, did he look up. A young woman, no doubt in response to K.'s shouting, appeared and asked: 'Can I help you, Sir?' Some way behind her in the gloom a man was also approaching. K. looked at the attendant; he had told K. that no one would bother about him, and now there were already two people here; before long every official would be alerted and would want him to explain why he was there. The only convincing and acceptable explanation was that he was a defendant who wanted to know the date of the next examination; but he was particularly reluctant to offer that explanation because it was not the truth, for he had only come here out of curiosity or — and this was even more impossible as an explanation — because he wanted to find out whether this legal organisation was just as repugnant from the inside as it was from the outside. And since it seemed that he was correct in this assumption, he had no wish to go any further into it; what he had already seen of it was quite depressing enough, and just now he was in no state of mind to deal with a senior official who might emerge from any of these doors. He wanted to leave, whether with the court attendant or, if needs be, on his own.

But he must have drawn attention to himself by standing there mutely, because the young woman and the attendant looked at him as if at any moment they expected him to undergo some great transformation which they did not want to miss. And in the doorway stood the man K. had noticed earlier some distance away; he was holding on to the lintel of the low door and standing on tiptoe like an eager spectator. But the young woman was the first to realise that K. was not feeling very well. She brought a chair and asked: 'Won't you sit down?' K. sat down at once and rested his elbows on the arms of the chair to support himself. 'You're feeling a bit dizzy, aren't you?' she asked him. Her face was now close up to him; it wore the severe look that many women have in the most beautiful phase of their youth. 'Don't worry about it,' she said, 'it's nothing out of the ordinary here, nearly everyone is affected like that the first time they come here. Is this your first time? Well then, it's quite normal. The sun heats up the rafters, and the warm wood makes the air close and heavy. That's why this place is not very suitable as office space, though it has many other advantages. When it's very busy here – that's nearly every day – the air is hardly fit to breathe. And when you think of all the washing the tenants hang out to dry – they can't ban it completely – then you can't be surprised if you don't feel very well. But in the end you get quite used to the atmosphere; the second or third time you come, you'll hardly notice how oppressive it is. Are you feeling better now?'

K. did not answer; he was too put out that his sudden faintness had put him at the mercy of these people. Besides, now that the cause of his nausea had been explained to him he felt no better, but rather worse. The young woman noticed this at once; in order to give K. some fresh air, she took a pole with a hook that was propped against the wall and pushed open a small skylight just above K.'s head to let in some air. But so much soot fell in that she had to shut the skylight at once and use her handkerchief to clean the soot off K.'s hands, for he was too tired to do this for himself. He would have been happy to sit there quietly until he felt strong enough to leave; the less they bothered him, the sooner he would recover. But now the young woman went on: 'You can't stay here, we are in the way.' K. looked at her enquiringly, as if to ask what sort of obstruction he could be causing. 'If you wish, I'll take you to the sick-room. Help me, please,' she said to the man in the doorway, who came at once. But K. did not want to go to the sick-room, indeed he wanted to avoid being taken any further; the further he went, the more difficult it would become. So he said: 'I can walk now.' But because he had got used to sitting, he trembled as he stood up. Then he found he could not stand upright. 'I just can't manage,' he said, shaking his head, and with a sigh he sat down again. He thought of the court attendant, who could easily show him the way out in spite of everything, but it seemed that he had gone some time ago; K. looked between the young woman and the man, who were standing in front of him, but he could not see the attendant.

'I believe,' said the man, who was smartly dressed, with a particularly striking grey waistcoat which ended in two sharp points, 'that this gentleman's faintness is due to the atmosphere in here, so it would be best not to take him to the sick-room, but to get him out of the chambers altogether. I'm sure that's what he would prefer.' 'That's it,' cried K., almost interrupting the man in his delight, 'I shall feel better at once, and I'm not so weak at all, just some support under my arms is all I need, I won't give you much trouble. It's not very far, just take me to the door, then I'll sit on the steps for a while and soon get over it. I don't usually have these attacks, it's taken me by surprise. I'm an official too, you see; I'm used to an office atmosphere, but here it just seems too much for me, as you say. So if you would be so kind as to give me some help, because I feel dizzy and sick if I stand up by myself.' And he raised his shoulders so that the two of them could take him under the arms.

But the man did not do as he was asked; he calmly kept his hands in his pockets and laughed out loud. 'You see,' he said to the young woman, 'I was right. It's only in here the gentleman feels unwell, not elsewhere.' The woman smiled too, but struck the man lightly on the arm with her fingertips, as if he had gone too far in his amusement at K.'s expense. 'What is that supposed to mean?' said the man, still laughing, 'I really am going to show the gentleman the way out.' 'Very well then,' said the woman, nodding her dainty head briefly. 'Don't take his laughter too seriously,' she said to K., who was gazing dejectedly into space and did not appear to need an explanation, 'this gentleman – may I introduce you?' – the man made a gesture of assent – 'this gentleman is the information officer. He gives our waiting clients all the information they need, and since the public knows very little about our legal organisation, a great deal of information is asked for. He can answer any questions, if you wish you can try him out. But that is not his only quality; the other is his elegant clothing. We, that is the officials, decided that the information officer, who is always dealing with clients and is the first person they meet, should be smartly dressed in order to make a good first impression. I'm afraid the rest of us, as you can see from me, are very badly dressed in old-fashioned clothes; there is not much point in spending anything on our clothes, because we are nearly always in chambers, in fact we even sleep here. But as I say, we thought the information officer really ought to be well dressed. But we couldn't get any smart clothes out of our administration (they are rather odd in that respect), so we made a collection – even the clients contributed to it – and bought him this good suit, and other things as well. So we did everything to make a good impression, but then he spoils it by laughing, which alarms people.'

'That's how it is,' said the man sardonically. 'But I don't under-stand, Miss, why you are telling this gentleman all our secrets, indeed why you force them on him when he isn't in the least interested. Just look at him, he's sitting there obviously preocc-upied with his own affairs.' K. did not even feel like contradicting him; the young woman might have meant well, perhaps she wanted to divert his attention or let him gather his thoughts; but she had not gone the right way about it. 'I had to explain to him why you were laughing,' she said, 'because it was rude.' 'I think he would excuse far worse rudeness if I were to show him the way out.' K. said nothing, he did not even look up; he let the two of them argue over him as if he were some inanimate object, in fact he preferred it. But suddenly he felt the information officer's hand on one arm and the young woman's on the other. 'Up you get then, you poor weak man,' said the information officer. 'Thank you both very much,' said K., surprised and delighted; he stood up slowly and guided the strangers' hands to where he most needed their support. 'It may look,' whispered the young woman in K.'s ear as they approached the corridor, 'as if I were particularly keen to show the information officer in a good light; but believe me, I'm just telling you the truth. He is not callous — he's not duty bound to show clients who have been taken ill the way out, but as you can see, he does it all the same. Perhaps none of us are callous, perhaps we all want to help, but as court officials we can easily appear callous and unhelpful. I feel really bad about it.'

'Wouldn't you like to sit down here for a while?' asked the information officer. By now they had reached the corridor and were standing in front of the defendant K. had spoken to earlier. K. felt almost ashamed in his presence; then he had been standing so straight when he spoke to him, now he needed two to support him. The information officer was balancing K.'s hat on his outstretched fingers, his hair was untidy and hung down over his forehead, which was drenched in sweat. But the defendant seemed to notice nothing of all this; he stood humbly in front of the information officer, who ignored him, and attempted only to excuse his presence there. 'I know,' he said, 'that my submissions cannot be dealt with today, but I came all the same. I thought I could wait here — it's Sunday after all, and I'm not bothering anyone.' 'There's no need to apologise,' said the information officer, 'your conscientiousness is very commendable. You may be taking up space here unnecessarily, but as long as you don't get in my way I haven't the slightest wish to interfere with your close attention to the progress of your case. When one has seen people who shamelessly neglect their duties, one learns to have patience with people like you. Please sit down.' 'Doesn't he know how to talk to clients?' whispered the young woman. K. nodded, but then started when the information officer again asked him: 'Won't you sit down here?' 'No,' said K., 'I don't need a rest.' He said this as decisively as he possibly could, though in fact it would have done him a lot of good to sit down. It was as if he were seasick, as if he were on a ship in heavy seas, as if the waves were crashing against the wooden walls, as if from the far end of the corridor he could hear the roaring of surf, as if the corridor were rolling from side to side and the waiting clients were rising and falling on either side.

All the more baffling, then, was the calmness of the young woman and the man beside him. He was at their mercy; if they let go of him, he would surely fall like a wooden post. They darted keen glances from their small eyes, K. could feel their steady gait, but could not keep pace with them; he was practically being carried step by step. Finally, he realised that they were talking to him, but he could not understand them; he heard only a noise that filled the whole place, through which a constant high-pitched note wailed like a siren. 'Louder,' he whispered, his head hanging; he felt embarrassed, because he knew that they had been speaking loud enough, though he had not been able to understand. Then at last, as if the wall in front of him had been torn down, a draught of fresh air came to meet him, and he heard someone beside him say: 'First he wants to leave, and then you can tell him a hundred times that this is the way out, and he doesn't move.'

K. noticed that he was standing in front of the outside door, which the young woman had opened. He felt as if he had suddenly recovered all his strength; in order to get a foretaste of freedom, he at once stepped out onto the stairs and from there took leave of his companions, who bent down over him. 'Many thanks,' he repeated, shook them both again and again by the hand, and only desisted when he thought he noticed that they, accustomed as they were to the atmosphere of the chambers, could not tolerate the relatively fresh air on the staircase. They could scarcely answer him, and the young woman might well have collapsed had K. not immediately closed the door. He then stood there for a moment, tidied his hair with the help of a pocket-mirror, picked up his hat, which was lying on the step below – the information officer must have thrown it down there – and then ran down the stairs so smartly and with such long strides that he almost felt alarmed by this sudden change in himself. His otherwise perfectly healthy constitution had never before given him such a shock. Was his body trying to rebel and present him with a new challenge because he had managed so effortlessly before now? He did not entirely reject the idea of seeing a doctor at the next opportunity; but at any rate – and in this matter he could take his own advice – he would spend all his future Sunday mornings more profitably than this one.

Chapter Four
Fräulein Bürstner's Friend

Over the following days it proved impossible for K. to exchange even a few words with Fräulein Bürstner. He tried to approach her in all manner of ways, but she always managed to avoid him. He came home straight after work, stayed in his room and sat on the sofa without switching on the light, and did nothing but watch the entrance hall. If the maid went by and closed the door of the apparently empty room, after a while he would get up and open it again. In the mornings he got up an hour earlier than usual in the hope that he might catch Fräulein Bürstner on her own as she went to work; but none of these attempts succeeded. Then he wrote her a letter, sending one copy to her office and one to her apartment, in which he again sought to justify his behaviour, offered to make amends in every way, promised to respect any restrictions she might impose on him, and asked only for one chance to speak to her, especially since he could not approach Frau Grubach until he had consulted her first. Finally, he informed her that for the whole of the following Sunday he would wait in his room for a sign from her that she might be prepared to grant his request, or at least that she would be willing to explain why she could not do so – though he had admittedly promised to defer to her in every way. The letters were not returned, but they were not answered either. On Sunday, however, there was a sign that was quite clear enough. Very early K., looking through the key-hole, noticed an unusual degree of activity in the hallway, which was soon explained. A French teacher, a German woman called Montag, a frail, pallid young woman with a slight limp who had until then occupied a room of her own, was moving into Fräulein Bürstner's room. For hours he saw her shuffling along the hall-way; there was always a piece of linen or a tablecloth or a book that had been forgotten, that had to be fetched separately and taken to the new room.

When Frau Grubach brought K.'s breakfast – since K. had been so angry with her she did not leave even the most trifling task to the maid – K. could not avoid speaking to her for the first time in five days. 'Why is there so much noise in the hallway today?' he asked as he poured his coffee. 'Can nothing be done about it? Must the house be cleaned on a Sunday?' Although K. did not look up at Frau Grubach, he still noticed that she breathed a deep sigh of relief. She took even K.'s abrupt questions as a sign of forgiveness, or as the beginning of a reconciliation. 'It's not being cleaned, Herr K.,' she said. 'Fräulein Montag is just moving into Fräulein Bürstner's room and taking her things in there.' She said no more, but waited to see how K. would react and whether he would let her continue. But K. did not help her; he stirred his coffee thoughtfully and said nothing. Then he looked up at her and said: 'Have you given up your suspicions about Fräulein Bürstner?' 'Herr K.,' cried Frau Grubach, who had only been waiting for this question. She clasped her hands and held them out to him. 'Recently you took a casual remark of mine so seriously. I never had the slightest thought of offending you or anyone else. You've known me long enough, Herr K., to be sure of that. You have no idea how I've suffered these last few days! That I should slander my lodgers! And you, Herr K., believed that! You said I should give you notice! Give you notice!' This last cry was stifled by her tears; she lifted her apron to her face and sobbed aloud.

'Please don't cry, Frau Grubach,' said K., looking out of the window; he was thinking only of Fräulein Bürstner, and how she had taken a stranger into her room. 'Please don't cry,' he repeated as he turned back into the room to see that Frau Grubach was still crying. 'I didn't really mean to upset you the other day; it was just a misunderstanding. That happens sometimes, even among old friends.' Frau Grubach removed her apron from her eyes in order to see whether K. really meant it. 'That's all it was,' said K. And since he gathered from Frau Grubach's attitude that the captain had not told her anything, he ventured to add: 'Do you really think I would fall out with you over a young woman I don't know?' 'That's just it, Herr K.,' said Frau Grubach – it was an unfortunate failing of hers that as soon as she felt less anxious, she immediately said something tactless – 'I kept asking myself: why should Herr K. be so concerned about Fräulein Bürstner? Why should he fall out with me over her, when he knows I lose sleep over every cross word from him? After all, I didn't say anything about the young lady that I hadn't seen with my own eyes.' K. said nothing; if he had, his first impulse would have been to drive her out of the room, and he did not want to do that. He contented himself with drinking his coffee and letting Frau Grubach feel she was not wanted.

Outside they heard Fräulein Montag again as she shuffled the length of the hallway. 'Can you hear it?' asked K., pointing to the door. 'Yes,' said Frau Grubach with a sigh. 'I wanted to help her, I wanted the maid to help too, but she is stubborn, she wanted to move everything herself. I'm surprised at Fräulein Bürstner. I often regret having Fräulein Montag as a lodger, but now Fräulein Bürstner has taken her into her own room.' 'You mustn't let that bother you,' said K., crushing the remains of the sugar in his cup. 'But will it cause you any loss of income?' 'No,' said Frau Grubach, 'actually it's quite welcome, it gives me a free room, and I can put up my nephew the captain there. I've been afraid for some time that he might have disturbed you over the last few days while I had to let him live in the sitting-room next door. He is not very considerate.' 'What are you thinking!' said K., standing up. 'Nothing of the sort. You seem to think I'm over-sensitive because I can't stand Fräulein Montag's comings and goings – there she is again.' Frau Grubach felt quite helpless. 'Herr K., shall I tell her to put off the rest of her move? If you wish, I'll do it at once.' 'But she has to move in with Fräulein Bürstner!' said K. 'Yes,' said Frau Grubach; she did not fully understand what K. meant. 'Well then,' said K., 'she's got to move her things in there.' Frau Grubach simply nodded. This dumb helplessness, which outwardly just looked like defiance, irritated K. even more. He began to walk up and down between the window and the door, and thus prevented Frau Grubach from leaving, which otherwise she probably would have done.

Just as K. reached the door again, there was a knock. It was the maid, who said Fräulein Montag would like a few words with Herr K., and that she had asked him to come into the dining-room, where she was waiting for him. K. listened carefully to the maid, then he turned and glanced almost scornfully at Frau Grubach, who looked startled. This glance seemed to suggest that K.

had long since expected Fräulein Montag's invitation, and that it was all part and parcel of the harassment he had to put up with from Frau Grubach's tenants that morning. He sent the maid back with the reply that he would come straight away, then he went to the wardrobe to change his coat; he had nothing to say to Frau Grubach, who was muttering under her breath about this tiresome person, except to ask her to clear the breakfast table. 'But you've hardly touched anything!' said Frau Grubach. 'Oh, just take it away!' cried K.; he felt that Fräulein Montag was somehow involved in everything and was making things difficult for him.

As he went through the hallway he glanced at the door to Fräulein Bürstner's room, which was closed. But he was not invited in there, so he flung the door of the dining-room open without even knocking. It was a very long narrow room with one window. There was just enough space for two cupboards to be placed at an angle on either side of the door, while the rest of the room was fully occupied by the long dining-table that stretched from near the door right up to the large window, which as a result was almost inaccessible. The table was already laid with places for several people, for on Sundays almost all the lodgers took their midday meal here.

As K. entered, Fräulein Montag moved away from the window and came towards him along one side of the table. They greeted each other silently. Then Fräulein Montag, who as always held her head unusually high, said: 'I don't know whether you know me.' K. frowned at her. 'Of course,' he said, 'after all, you have been staying with Frau Grubach for a long time.' 'But I rather think you don't take much notice of things in the boarding house.' 'No,' said K. 'Won't you sit down?' said Fräulein Montag. Without a word, they each pulled out a chair at the far end of the table and sat down opposite one another. But Fräulein Montag immediately stood up again, for she had left her handbag on the window-sill and went to fetch it, shuffling the whole length of the room. When she returned, swinging the handbag gently, she said: 'I would just like to say a few words to you on behalf of my friend. She would have come herself, but she feels rather unwell today. She asks you to excuse her and listen to me instead. She would have had no more to say to you than what I shall say. On the contrary, I even think I can say more than she can because I am relatively uninvolved. Don't you agree?'

'What is there to be said, then?' replied K., who was growing tired of seeing Fräulein Montag's eyes constantly fixed on his lips; it was an attempt on her part to control what he had to say before he said it. 'Fräulein Bürstner is clearly unwilling to speak to me personally, as I asked her to.' 'That is so,' said Fräulein Montag, 'or rather, that is not the case at all; you express yourself in a strangely forthright way. After all, it is not usual to require consent to talk to someone, nor to refuse it. But it can be thought unnecessary to talk to someone, and that is exactly the case here. Now, after your remarks I can speak frankly. You have asked my friend to communicate with you, in writing or by word of mouth. But my friend knows – at least, this is what I must assume – what you wish to discuss with her, and she is convinced, for reasons unknown to me, that such a discussion would benefit no one. Besides, she only mentioned it to me yesterday, quite incidentally, and said you cannot attach much importance to it anyway, because the idea had only occurred to you by chance, and that you would, even without any specific explanation, very quickly realise how pointless the whole thing was – if not now, then before very long. I replied that she might well be right, but that I thought it would help to clear the whole matter up if she were to give you a definite answer. I offered to do this myself, and after some hesitation my friend agreed. But I hope I have also acted in your interests; for even the slightest uncertainty in the most trivial matter is always cause for concern, and when it can easily be cleared up, as it can in this case, then the sooner it is done the better.'

'Thank you,' said K. at once. He stood up slowly, looked at Fräulein Montag, then across the table out of the window – the house opposite lay in sunshine – and went to the door. Fräulein Montag followed a few steps behind him, as if she did not quite trust him. But at the door both of them had to step back, for the door opened and Captain Lanz came in. It was the first time K. had seen him close at hand. He was a tall man of about forty with a plump tanned face. He made a slight bow, which also included K., then he went up to Fräulein Montag and respectfully kissed her hand. He was very poised in his movements. His courtesy towards Fräulein Montag was in striking contrast to the manner in which K. had treated her. In spite of this, Fräulein Montag did not seem angry with K., for she was actually about to introduce him to the captain, or so K. imagined. But K. did not want to be introduced, he would not have been capable of being at all civil to either the captain or Fräulein Montag; that gesture of kissing her hand, he felt, had made them party to a plan that was designed, under the guise of the utmost innocence and consideration, to keep him away from Fräulein Bürstner. But that was not all K. suspected. He also realised that Fräulein Montag had chosen a clever, if two-edged stratagem; she was exaggerating the significance of his relationship with Fräulein Bürstner, and especially the significance of the interview he had requested, and at the same time she was trying to convey the impression that it was K. who was exaggerating everything. Let her fool herself; K. did not wish to exaggerate anything, he knew that Fräulein Bürstner was just a little typist who could not resist him for long. In this he deliberately ignored what Frau Grubach had told him about Fräulein Bürstner.

He was thinking about all this as he left the room with scarcely a gesture of farewell. He intended to go straight to his room; but when he heard Fräulein Montag's quiet laugh from the dining-room behind him, it occurred to him that he could surprise them both, the captain and Fräulein Montag. He looked round and listened in case there might be any interruption from one of the surrounding rooms, but all was quiet; he could hear only the conversation in the dining-room and, from the corridor leading to the kitchen, the voice of Frau Grubach. It seemed an opportune moment; K. went to Fräulein Bürstner's door and knocked softly. There was not a sound, so he knocked again; still no reply. Was she asleep? Was she really unwell? Or was she pretending not to be there because she knew that only K. would knock so softly? K. assumed that she was pretending and knocked louder; finally, since there was no response to his knocking, he opened the door carefully, not without feeling that he was doing something wrong and indeed futile. There was no one in the room; moreover, it was now scarcely recognisable as the room K. had known. Now there were two beds placed one behind the other against the wall, three chairs near the door were piled high with clothes and linen, and a wardrobe stood open. Fräulein Bürstner had probably left while Fräulein Montag was holding forth to K. in the dining-room. K. was not too dismayed by this; by now he hardly expected to meet

Fräulein Bürstner so easily – he had made this attempt almost entirely to defy Fräulein Montag. Even so, he was all the more embarrassed when, as he shut the door behind him, he saw Fräulein Montag and the captain talking to each other at the open door of the dining-room. Perhaps they had been standing there since K. had opened the door. They avoided any impression that they might have been watching K.; they talked quietly and only followed his movements with the casual look of those who glance round during a conversation. But these glances weighed heavily on him; keeping close to the wall, he hurried along the hallway to his room.

CHAPTER FIVE
The Flogging

On one of the following evenings, as K. was passing along the corridor that led from his office to the main staircase – today he was almost the last to leave, only two bank messengers in the post room were still working by the sparse light of a single lamp – he heard groans coming from behind a door to what he had always assumed was a lumber-room, although he had never seen it himself. Astonished, he stopped and listened again to make sure he was not mistaken; for a while it was quiet, but then he heard the groans again. His first thought was to call one of the messengers in case a witness was needed; but then he was gripped by such overwhelming curiosity that he just wrenched the door open. It was, as he had correctly suspected, a lumber-room. Inside, useless out-of-date printed documents and empty earthenware inkwells lay scattered about behind the door. But in the room itself stood three men, stooping in the confined space. A candle, stuck on a shelf, provided some light. 'What's going on here?' demanded K., who could barely control his agitation, though he kept his voice down. One of the men, who was evidently in control of the other two, caught K.'s attention first; he was dressed in some sort of dark leather costume that left his neck open to his chest and his arms bare. He did not reply, but the other two cried: 'Sir! We're going to be flogged because you complained to the examining magistrate about us.'

It was only then that K. realised that they were in fact the guards Franz and Willem, and that the third man was holding a cane to beat them with. 'Why,' said K., staring at them, 'I did not complain; I only said what had happened in my room. And after all, your behaviour left something to be desired.' 'Sir,' said Willem, while behind him Franz was obviously trying to shield himself from the third man, 'if you knew how badly we were paid, you would not judge us so harshly. I have a family to feed, and Franz here was going to get married. You try to make some money as best you can, but you can't do it just by working, however hard you work. I was tempted by your fine linen; of course guards are forbidden to behave like that, it wasn't right, but it's traditional that the clothes belong to the guards, it's always been like that, believe me. It's understandable, too – what's the importance of such things to anyone who's unfortunate enough to be arrested? But then, if he mentions it publicly, punishment is bound to follow.'

'I knew nothing of all this, and I did not once demand that you should be punished; for me it was a matter of principle.' 'Franz,' said Willem to the other guard, 'didn't I tell you the gentleman didn't ask for us to be punished? He's telling us he didn't even know we were going to be punished.' 'Don't be swayed by that kind of talk,' said the third man to K., 'the punishment is as just as it is inevitable.' 'Don't listen to him,' said Willem, breaking off only to lift his hand to his mouth when it was caught by a slash of the cane, 'we are only being punished because you complained about us. Otherwise nothing would have happened to us even if they had found out what we had done. Do you call that justice? Both of us, especially me, had done good service as guards for a long time – you must admit yourself that from the authorities' point of view, we guarded you well. We had good promotion prospects, and would certainly have been made floggers like this man, who happened to be lucky enough not to be accused by anyone, for complaints like that are really very rare. And now, Sir, we've lost everything, our careers are finished, we shall have to do much more menial work than being guards, and on top of that we are now getting these dreadfully painful floggings.'

'Can the cane be so painful, then?' asked K., examining the cane which the flogger was swishing in front of him. 'We shall have to strip naked,' said Willem. 'I see,' said K., looking at the flogger; he was sunburnt like a sailor, with a fierce, healthy face. 'Is there no way these two can be spared their flogging?' he asked him. 'No,' said the flogger, smiling and shaking his head. 'Take off your clothes!' he ordered the guards. To K. he said: 'You mustn't believe all they say, they're already a bit witless because they're afraid of the flogging. What this one told you about his possible career' – he pointed to Willem – 'is just ridiculous. Look how fat he is; the first strokes will be lost in his fat. Do you know how he got so fat? He has a habit of eating the breakfast of anyone he arrests. Didn't he eat your breakfast? There you are, I told you. But a man with a belly like that can never become a flogger, it's quite out of the question.' 'There are floggers like that,' Willem insisted as he unfastened his belt. 'No,' said the flogger, striking him such a blow on the shoulder that he winced. 'Don't listen to us, just get undressed.'

'I'd pay you well if you let them go,' said K., and without looking at the flogger – these transactions are best conducted with eyes averted by both parties – he took out his wallet. 'And then I suppose you'll report me as well,' said the flogger, 'and get me flogged too. Oh no.' 'Do be reasonable,' said K., 'if I had wanted these two to be punished, I wouldn't be trying to get them off now; I could just shut this door behind me, refuse to see or hear anything further and go home. But I'm not doing that, on the contrary I'm seriously interested in freeing them; if I had had any idea they were going to be punished, or even that they could be punished, I would never have mentioned their names. Because I don't hold them guilty at all, it's the system and the higher officials that are guilty.' 'That's right!' cried the guards, who were immediately given a stroke of the cane across their bare backs. 'If you were about to flog one of the senior judges,' said K., holding down the cane just as it was about to be raised again, 'I promise you I wouldn't stop you; far from it, I would even pay you to do it more vigorously.' 'What you say sounds plausible,' said the flogger, 'but I'm not going to be bribed. I am employed to do the flogging, so that's what I do.'

The guard Franz who, perhaps hoping that K.'s intervention might work out in their favour, had so far been quite reticent, now went to the door, dressed only in his trousers, knelt down, hanging on K.'s arm, and whispered: 'If you can't manage to get a reprieve for both of us, then at least try to get me off. Willem is older than me, he's far less sensitive, and he has had a light flogging before, a few years ago. But I have never been disgraced before, and I was only led astray by Willem, who is my teacher for better or worse. Downstairs outside the bank my poor fiancée is waiting to see what happens. I'm so miserably ashamed.' He dried his face, which was streaming with tears, on K.'s coat. 'I'm not waiting any longer,' said the flogger. He seized the cane with both hands and lashed out at Franz, while Willem cowered in a corner and watched furtively without daring to turn his head. Franz uttered a scream that seemed not to be that of a human being, but to come from an ill-treated instrument. It rose in a single unwavering note and filled the whole corridor; it must have been heard through the whole building. 'Don't scream,' cried K., unable to contain himself. On tenter-hooks, he looked in the direction from which the messengers must surely appear, and bumped into Franz, not violently, but hard enough to knock the dazed man to the ground, where he clawed the floor feverishly with his hands. But he could not escape the blows, and the cane reached him even as he lay on the floor; as he writhed under it, the tip swished up and down in regular strokes.

And now, some way off, a messenger did appear, with another a few paces behind him. K. had quickly slammed the door, gone over to one of the windows overlooking the courtyard and opened it. The screams had stopped completely. To prevent the messengers coming any closer, K. called: 'It's me!' 'Good evening, Sir,' came the reply. 'Is anything the matter?' 'No, no,' replied K., 'it's only a dog howling in the courtyard.' When the messengers still did not move away, he added: 'You can go back to your work.' In order to avoid having to speak to them, he leaned out of the window. After a while he looked back down the corridor again, and they had gone. But K. stayed at the window; he did not dare to go back into the lumber-room, and he did not want to go home either. He was looking down into a small square courtyard with offices all round; all the windows were now dark, only the upper ones caught the reflection of the moon.

K. strained his eyes to see into a dark corner of the courtyard where some handcarts had been stacked together. It distressed him that he had not been able to stop the flogging, but it was not his fault that he had not succeeded; if Franz had not screamed – of course, it must have hurt very much, but at crucial moments one has to control oneself – if he had not screamed, then K., in all probability at least, would have found some way of dissuading the flogger. If all the lower officials were menials, why should the flogger, who held the most inhumane post, be an exception? K. had noticed how his eyes had lit up at the sight of the banknote; clearly he had only carried on with the flogging in earnest because he wanted to increase the amount of the bribe. And K. would have increased it – he really had wanted to free the guards; since he had already embarked on a battle against this corrupt legal system, it went without saying that he should have intervened at this point. But of course that became impossible the moment Franz had started to scream. K. could not let the messengers and perhaps all kinds of other people come and interrupt him in his dealings with those creatures in the lumber-room; no one could really expect that of him. If that was what he had intended, it would almost have been easier to take his own clothes off and offer himself to the flogger in place of the guards. But in any case, the flogger would certainly not have agreed to this substitution, because he would have seriously violated his duty without any advantage to himself, and would probably have made things far worse because surely no court employee could lay a hand on K. as long as he was under investigation – though of course, special conditions might apply here too. At all events, K. had had no alternative but to slam the door, though this had by no means put him out of danger. It was regrettable that he had bumped into Franz; only his agitation could excuse that.

In the distance he heard the messengers' footsteps; he did not want them to see him, so he shut the window and went towards the main staircase. At the door of the lumber-room he stopped and listened; it was all quiet. The man could have flogged the guards to death, they were completely at his mercy. K. had already put out his hand towards the door-handle, but then withdrew it. He could not help anyone now, and the messengers might appear at any moment; but he vowed that he would bring the matter up and, as far as it lay in his power, would see that the truly guilty parties, the senior officials, not one of whom had dared to show his face, were suitably punished. As he went down the steps outside the bank he carefully observed all the passers-by, but even in the wider vicinity there was no sign of a young woman who might be waiting for someone. Franz's claim that his fiancée was waiting for him turned out to be a lie, albeit an excusable one, which was only designed to arouse greater sympathy.

The next day K. could still not get the guards out of his mind; he could not concentrate on his work, and in order to get it done he had to stay in the office rather later than the previous day. As he left, he once again passed the lumber-room, and opened the door as if by habit. He had expected nothing but darkness; but what he saw unsettled him completely. Everything was exactly as he had found it when he had opened the door the evening before: the papers and inkwells just behind the door, the flogger with his cane, the still quite naked guards, the candle on the shelf – and the guards started to lament, shouting 'Sir!' K. immediately slammed the door, and then banged it with his fist as if that would shut it more firmly. Almost in tears, he rushed to where the messengers were working quietly at their duplicating machines; they stopped, astonished. 'It's high time the lumber-room was cleared out!' he shouted. 'We're up to our ears in filth!' The messengers were willing to do it the next day. K. nodded; he had intended to tell them to do it there and then, but he could not force them to – it was too late in the evening. He sat down for a moment to keep them company for a while, and shuffled through some papers as if he were checking them, then, seeing that the messengers would not dare to leave at the same time as himself, he went home exhausted, his mind quite blank.

CHAPTER SIX
The Uncle - Leni

One afternoon, when K. was working hard to catch the post, his uncle Karl, a small landowner from the country, pushed his way into the room past two messengers who were bringing papers for him. K. was not too alarmed to see him; for some time he had been dreading the thought of a visit from his uncle. He was bound to come – K. had been quite certain of that for a month. He had already imagined how he would arrive, slightly stooped, his Panama hat crushed in his left hand, his right hand extended long before he rushed over and held it out across the desk with ill-considered haste, knocking over everything in his way. His uncle was always in a hurry, for he was haunted by the unhappy notion that every time he visited the capital – and he only ever came for the day – he had to complete all the business he had set himself. On top of this, he could not miss any opportunity of a chance conversation, a business transaction, or any form of entertainment. In all this K. was under a particular obligation to his uncle, who had been his guardian; he had to help him in every possible way, and in addition he was expected to put him up for the night. He called him 'the Spectre from the Country'.

As soon as they had exchanged greetings – K. invited him to sit in an easy chair, but he had no time for that – he asked K. if he could speak to him privately for a moment. 'It is essential,' he said, gulping painfully, 'it is essential for my peace of mind.' K. at once sent the messengers out of the room with instructions to let no one in. 'What is this I hear, Josef?' cried his uncle when they were alone; he sat down on the desk, and to make himself more comfortable stuffed a sheaf of papers under him without looking at them. K. said nothing; he knew what was coming, but, suddenly released from the strain of his work, he surrendered for the moment to a pleasant weariness and looked out of the window to the far side of the street. From where he was sitting he could see only a small triangular section, a stretch of blank house wall between two shop windows. 'You're gazing out of the window!' cried his uncle, throwing up his arms, 'for heaven's sake, Josef, answer me! Is it true, can it be true?' 'Dear Uncle,' said K., shaking himself out of his reverie, 'I have no idea what you're driving at.' 'Josef,' said his uncle reprovingly, 'you have always told the truth, as far as I know. Should I take what you've just said as a bad sign?' 'I can imagine what you mean,' said K. obediently, 'you must have heard about my trial.' ' That's right,' replied his uncle, nodding slowly, 'I have heard about your trial.' 'Who told you, then?' asked K. 'Erna wrote to me,' said his uncle. 'She has not seen you – I'm sorry to say you don't have very much to do with her – but still she got to know about it. I had her letter today, and of course I came here right away. For no other reason, but that seems reason enough to me. I can read out what she says about you.'

He took the letter from his wallet. 'Here it is. She writes: "I have not seen Josef for a long time. Last week I went to the bank, but Josef was too busy to see me. I waited for nearly an hour, but then I had to go home because I had a piano lesson. I would have liked to talk to him, perhaps I shall have an opportunity before long. He sent me a big box of chocolates for my birthday, which was very kind and thoughtful of him. I had forgotten to write to you about it, I only just remembered when you asked. You see, chocolates disappear very quickly in the boarding school, you hardly know you've been given them before they're gone. But about Josef – there's something else I wanted to tell you. As I said, I was not allowed to see him at the bank because he was in a meeting with a gentleman. After I had waited quietly for a while, I asked one of the attendants whether the meeting would last very long. He said it might well, because it probably concerned the case being brought against Herr K. I asked him what sort of case it was, he must be mistaken; but he said he was not mistaken. Proceedings were under way, and they were serious, but he did not know any more about it. For his part, he would like to help Herr K., for he was a good and fair man; but he did not know how to go about it, and he wished that some influential people would take up his case. This, he said, would surely happen, and it would all turn out well; but for the time being things were not going well – he could tell that from Herr K.'s mood. Of course, I did not attach much importance to what he said, and tried to reassure the man; I told him not to talk to anyone else about it, and that I thought it was all just gossip. All the same, perhaps it would be as well, dear Father, if you were to look into the matter on your next visit, it will be easy for you to find out more details and, if it should be really necessary, to intervene with the help of some of your important and influential acquaintances. However, should it not be necessary, which is the most likely outcome, it will at least give your daughter the opportunity to embrace you before long, which would give her great pleasure".'

'She's a good child,' said K.'s uncle when he had finished reading, and wiped the tears from his eyes. K. nodded; because of the various upsets of the last few days he had completely forgotten about Erna. He had even forgotten her birthday, and the story about the chocolates was clearly only invented to put him in a good light with his aunt and uncle. It was very touching, and the theatre tickets he intended to send her regularly from now on would certainly not be reward enough; but at the moment he did not feel up to visiting her in her boarding school and holding conversations with a little eighteen-year-old schoolgirl. 'And what do you say to that?' asked his uncle. The letter had made him forget all his haste and agitation, and he seemed to be reading it all over again. 'Yes, Uncle,' said K., 'it is true.' 'True?' cried his uncle. 'What is true? How can it be true? What sort of a case is it? Surely not a criminal case?' 'It is a criminal case,' replied K. 'And you sit here calmly with a criminal case hanging over you?' cried his uncle, whose voice was getting louder. 'The calmer I am, the better it is for the outcome,' said K. wearily, 'there's nothing to fear.'

'That's no comfort!' cried his uncle, 'Josef, my dear Josef, think of yourself, think of your relatives, think of our good name! Until now you have been a credit to us, you cannot disgrace us.' He looked at K. reproachfully from under his eyebrows. 'I don't like your attitude. An innocent man in his right mind who has been accused of a crime doesn't behave like that. Quick, tell me about it so that I can help you. It's a bank matter, I suppose?' 'No,' said K., standing up. 'But you are speaking too loud, dear Uncle, the attendant is probably standing by the door listening to us, and that makes me uncomfortable. We'd better go somewhere else, then I will answer all your questions as far as I can. I know very well that I owe the family an explanation.' 'That's right!' shouted his uncle. 'Quite right, but hurry up, Josef, hurry up!' 'I still have to give some instructions,' said K., and summoned his assistant on the telephone, who appeared a few moments later. In his agitation, his uncle gestured to indicate that K. had called for him, though this was perfectly clear. Standing in front of his desk, K. referred to various documents and explained to him in a low voice what needed to be done in his absence. The young man listened impassively but attentively. At first K.'s uncle stood there glaring and biting his lip nervously; though he was not listening, he gave the impression that he was, which was distracting enough. But then he walked up and down the room and paused every now and then by the window or in front of a picture. Each time he stopped he made some exclamation such as: 'I find it quite incomprehensible!' or: 'Just tell me what's to become of this!' The young man listened calmly to all K.'s instructions as if he did not hear any of this, noted down a few things and left after bowing to K. and his uncle just as the latter turned away to look out of the window and stretched out his arms to clutch at the curtains.

He had scarcely shut the door when the uncle cried: 'At last that clown has gone, now we can go too. At last!' Unfortunately, they reached the entrance hall of the bank, where some officials and attendants were standing around, just as the deputy manager was crossing the hall, and K. could not stop his uncle asking questions about the case. 'So, Josef,' he began, acknowledging the bows of those around him with a casual nod, 'now tell me frankly what sort of a case this is.' K. made a few vague remarks, laughing from time to time; only when they reached the steps outside did he explain to his uncle that he had not wanted to speak openly in front of these people. 'Very well,' said his uncle, 'but talk now.' He listened with his head bowed, taking short, quick puffs at a cigar. 'The main point, Uncle,' said K., 'is that this is not a case that is being tried before an ordinary court.' 'That's bad,' said his uncle. 'Pardon?' said K., looking at him. 'I say that's bad,' repeated his uncle. They were standing on the steps leading down to the street; since the porter seemed to be listening, K. led his uncle away, and they were swallowed up in the busy traffic.

K.'s uncle, who had taken his arm, stopped asking such urgent questions about the case, and for a while they walked on in silence. Finally he asked: 'But how did it happen?' He stopped so suddenly that the people behind him, startled, had to swerve to avoid him. 'Things like that don't happen out of the blue, they take a long time to develop. There must have been some indications; why didn't you write to me? You know I'll do anything for you, in a way I'm still your guardian, and until today I was proud to be. Of course I'll still help you, but now that the trial is under way, that's very difficult. At all events, the best thing for now would be for you to take some leave and come and stay with us in the country. You've lost some weight, I can see that now. In the country you'll get your strength back, that will do you good, because you're going to have a hard time, that's for sure. Besides, that way you will be out of the court's reach to a certain extent. Here they have all sorts of powers they can use against you, which they have to do as a matter of course; but out in the country they have to delegate these powers to others, or get at you by letter or telegraph or telephone. That, of course, is less effective; it may not set you free, but it will give you a breathing space.' 'They might forbid me to leave,' said K., who was beginning to follow his uncle's train of thought. 'I don't think they will do that,' said his uncle thoughtfully, 'they wouldn't lose very much authority if you were to go away.' 'I thought,' said K., taking his uncle's arm to prevent him standing still, 'that you would attach even less importance to the whole thing than I do, and now you are taking it so seriously.' 'Josef,' cried his uncle. He tried to shake him off in order to stop, but K. would not let go. 'You have changed. You always had such a clear mind, why can't you see? Do you want to lose your case? Do you know what that means? It means you will simply be ostracised. It means the whole family will be disgraced, or at least deeply humiliated. Josef, pull yourself together. Your nonchalance is driving me out of my mind. When I look at you, I can almost believe the adage: "With a case like that, it's as good as lost".'

'Dear Uncle,' said K., 'there's no point in either of us getting worked up about it. You don't win a case that way. Give me some credit for my practical experience, just as I have always given you credit for yours, and still do, even when it surprises me. Since you tell me the family would also be made to suffer from this case – for my part, I can't possibly imagine why, but that's by the by – I shall be glad to follow your advice in everything. It's just that I think your plan for going to the country, even for the reasons you give, would be inadvisable, because it would suggest I was running away and suffered from a sense of guilt. What's more, although while I am here I can be followed more closely, I can also give the matter more of my attention.' 'That's true,' said his uncle in a voice that suggested they were at last coming to see each other's point of view, 'I only suggested it because I thought your lack of commitment would jeopardise your case if you stayed here, and I thought it would be better if I acted for you instead. But if you are willing to put all your effort into it, of course that is much better.' 'Then we are agreed,' said K. 'And now have you any suggestion as to what my first step should be?' 'Of course, I shall have to give the matter more thought,' said his uncle, 'you must remember that I've been living in the country almost continuously now for twenty years, and that blunts one's instincts in such things. Over the years I have lost touch with several important people who know more about such matters. You know quite well that I'm rather isolated in the country, but one only realises it at times like this. Your case rather took me by surprise, although strangely enough I guessed it was something of the sort after reading Erna's letter, and when I saw you today I was almost certain. But that is beside the point; the important thing now is not to lose any time.'

Even as he was speaking, he had been standing on tiptoe to hail a cab, and now, as he shouted an address to the driver, he pulled K. after him into the taxi. 'We're going to see Huld, the advocate,' he said, 'he was at school with me. You must have heard of him. No? That's astonishing. He has a huge reputation as a defence lawyer and as an advocate for the poor. But I have particular confidence in him as a person.' 'I'm quite willing to do anything you suggest,' said K., although he felt uneasy at the hasty and urgent way his uncle was treating the matter, and as a defendant he was not very happy to be taken to a poor man's lawyer. 'I didn't know,' he said, 'that one could engage an advocate in a case like this.' 'But of course,' said his uncle, 'that goes without saying. Why not? And now tell me everything that has happened so far, so that I know all about the case.' K. began to tell him. He did not withhold anything; complete candour was the only protest he could make against his uncle's view that his trial was a great disgrace. He only mentioned Fräulein Bürstner's name once quite casually; but that did not detract from his candour, because she had no connection with his case.

As he told his story, he looked out of the window and saw that they were approaching the suburb where the court chambers were situated; he drew his uncle's attention to this, but he did not find the coincidence particularly striking. The cab stopped in front of a darkened house; his uncle rang the bell at the first door on the ground floor. While they were waiting, he bared his big teeth in a smile and whispered: 'Eight o'clock − an unusual time for a client to call, but Huld won't mind.' Through a hatch in the door two large dark eyes appeared, examined the visitors for a while, and disappeared, but the door did not open. K. and his uncle agreed that they had seen the two eyes. 'A new parlour-maid who is afraid of strangers,' said his uncle, and knocked again. Again the eyes appeared; one could almost imagine they looked sad, but perhaps this was only an impression caused by the naked gas flame which burned with a loud hiss just above their heads, but shed little light. 'Open the door!' cried the uncle, banging it with his fist, 'we are friends of the advocate.' 'The advocate is ill,' whispered a voice behind them. In a doorway at the other end of the short passage stood a man in his nightgown who conveyed this information in an extremely quiet voice. The uncle, by now furious because they had had to wait so long, turned round abruptly and cried: 'Ill? He's ill, you say?' He went up to him almost threateningly, as if the man himself were the illness. 'They've opened the door now,' said the man, pointing to the advocate's door. He pulled his nightgown around him and disappeared.

And indeed, the door had been opened; a young woman − K. recognised her dark, slightly protruding eyes − stood in the hall-way in a long white apron, a candle in her hand. 'Open it a bit sooner next time!' said the uncle by way of greeting to the maid, who bobbed a small curtsey. 'Come along, Josef,' he said to K., who pushed slowly past the maid. 'Herr Huld is ill,' she said as the uncle made straight for a door. K. was still staring at the maid, who had turned to lock the front door. She had a round doll's face; not just her pale cheeks and chin, but also her temples and forehead were rounded. 'Josef,' his uncle called again, and asked the maid:

'It's his heart, isn't it?' 'I think so,' said the maid, who had had time
to light their way to the door and open it. In a corner of the room
where the candle shed no light, a face with a long beard rose from
the pillows of a bed. 'Who is it, Leni?' asked the advocate, who
was dazzled by the candlelight and did not recognise his visitors.
'It's your old friend Albert,' said K.'s uncle. 'Oh, Albert,' said the
advocate, and fell back onto the pillows as if he needed to make no
effort for these visitors. 'Are you really in such a bad way?' asked
the uncle, sitting down on the edge of the bed. 'I don't think you
are. It's a recurrence of your heart trouble, and it will pass as it has
before.' 'Perhaps,' said the advocate quietly, 'but it's worse than
ever. I find it hard to breathe, I can't get any sleep, and I'm getting
weaker by the day.' 'I see,' said the uncle, squashing his Panama on
his knee with his large hand. 'That's bad news. Are you getting the
right treatment, though? It's so dark and gloomy here. It's a long
time since I was here last, but it seemed more cheerful to me then.
And your little Missie here doesn't seem very cheerful either, at
least she doesn't look it.'

The maid was still standing by the door with the candle, looking
at them vaguely; she seemed to be looking at K. rather than at his
uncle, even while he was talking about her. K. leaned against a
chair that he had pushed up close to her. 'When you are as ill as I
am,' said the advocate, 'you need peace and quiet. I don't feel
gloomy.' After a pause he added: 'And Leni looks after me well,
she's a good girl.' But the uncle was not convinced. He clearly did
not think the maid capable of caring for the patient; he made no
reply, and followed her with severe looks as she went over to the
bed, placed the candle on the bedside table, bent over the sick man
and whispered to him as she rearranged his pillows. He almost
forgot any consideration for the patient; he stood up and followed
her to and fro, and K. would not have been surprised if he had
seized her from behind by her skirt and dragged her away from the
bed. K. himself watched it all calmly, indeed the advocate's illness
was not entirely unwelcome to him; he had been unable to restrain
his uncle's zeal in pursuing his case, and he was now glad to see this
zeal diverted without any intervention on his part. Then, perhaps
only to annoy the maid, his uncle said: 'Fräulein, please leave us
alone for a while, I have a personal matter to discuss with my
friend.' The maid, who was bending right over the patient to

smooth the bedclothes by the wall, simply turned her head and in a very calm voice, in striking contrast to the uncle who spluttered and ranted in his rage, said: 'You can see, my master is too ill to discuss any matters.'

She had probably only repeated the uncle's words unthinkingly, but even an impartial observer might have taken it as mockery; the uncle of course jumped as if he had been stung. 'Damn you!' he spluttered, somewhat indistinctly in his initial fit of rage. K. was alarmed, although he had expected something of the sort; he rushed over to his uncle with the firm intention of putting his hands over his mouth to silence him. But fortunately the invalid sat up behind the maid, the uncle grimaced as if he had swallowed something disgusting, and then said more calmly: 'Of course, we haven't taken leave of our senses yet. I'm not asking the impossible, otherwise I wouldn't ask. Now leave us, please!' The maid stood at the bed and turned to face the uncle; with one hand, K. fancied, she was stroking the advocate's hand. 'You can say anything in front of Leni,' said the patient with an urgent plea in his voice. 'It's not about me,' said the uncle, 'it's not my secret.' And he turned as if he did not intend to discuss the matter further, but was giving the other time to think it over. 'What is it about, then?' asked the advocate in a frail voice, sinking back into the pillows. 'My nephew,' said the uncle. 'I've brought him with me.' He introduced him: 'Josef K., assistant bank manager.' 'Ah,' said the invalid with more animation, holding out his hand to K., 'forgive me, I didn't notice you. Leave us, Leni,' he said to the maid, who did not protest at all; he gave her his hand as if they were parting for a long time.

'So,' he said at last to the uncle, who, now mollified, had moved closer to him, 'you haven't come to see me because I am ill, you're here on business.' The advocate looked so robust now; it was as if the idea of a visit to his sickbed had enfeebled him earlier. He supported himself all the while on his elbow, which must have been quite a strain, and kept tugging at a strand of hair from the middle of his beard. 'You look better already,' said the uncle, 'now that witch has gone.' He broke off, whispered, 'I'll bet she's listening!' and sprang to the door. But there was no one behind the door, and he returned, not disappointed (for he seemed to think that not listening was an even greater piece of villainy on her part), but certainly annoyed. 'You misjudge her,' said the advocate; but he did not say any more in her defence. Perhaps he wished to suggest that there was no need to defend her. But he continued in a much more sympathetic tone: 'Concerning this affair of your nephew's, I would be only too happy if I had enough strength for this extremely difficult task; I am afraid I may not, but I shall make every effort. If I cannot do it, we could bring in someone else. To be honest with you, I find this case too interesting to be able to resist taking some part in it. If my heart is not up to it, then at least this is a worthy cause in which it can fail completely.'

K. could not understand a word he was saying; he looked at his uncle for an explanation, but he was sitting holding the candle on the bedside table, from which a bottle of medicine had already fallen onto the floor. His uncle nodded at everything the advocate said, agreed with everything, and every now and then looked at K., inviting his agreement too. Had his uncle perhaps already told the advocate about his case? But that was impossible; everything that had happened suggested otherwise. So he said: 'I don't understand . . . ' 'Have I perhaps misunderstood you, then?' asked the advocate, just as astonished and embarrassed as K. was. 'Perhaps I was too hasty. What did you want to talk to me about? I thought it was about your case.' 'Of course,' said the uncle, and asked K.: 'Isn't that what you want?' 'Yes, but how can you know anything about me or my case?' asked K. 'Ah,' said the advocate, smiling, 'you see, I am a lawyer, I move in legal circles, where various cases are discussed. And one remembers the more striking ones, especially when they involve the nephew of a friend. Surely there's nothing remarkable about that.' 'What is it you want, then?' K.'s uncle asked him again. 'You're so agitated.' 'So you move in these legal circles?' asked K. 'Yes,' said the advocate. 'You're asking questions like a child,' said his uncle. 'Who should I associate with, if not with my professional colleagues?' added the advocate. It sounded so undeniable that K. did not reply. 'But surely you work at the High Court, not that one in the attic,' was what he wanted to say, but he could not bring himself to say it. 'You must understand,' continued the advocate in a manner that suggested he was explaining, quite unnecessarily and incidentally, something that was perfectly obvious, 'you must understand that I gain considerable advantages for my clients in all sorts of ways from such contacts, though one must be discreet about all that. Of course, just now I am rather hindered by my illness; but I still have visits from good friends at the court and get to hear quite a lot. Perhaps I learn more than many of those who are in the best of health and spend all day at the court. For example, at this very moment I have a visit from a dear friend.'

He pointed to a dark corner of the room. 'Where?' asked K., almost brusquely in his surprise. He looked round him uncertainly; the light shed by the small candle did not reach anywhere near the far wall. Then something did begin to stir over in the corner. By the light of the candle, which K.'s uncle was now holding up, an elderly gentleman could be seen sitting at a small table. He could scarcely have been breathing to have remained unnoticed for so long. Now he reluctantly stood up, clearly unhappy to have their attention drawn to him. It was as if, by flapping his hands like short wings, he wished to fend off all greetings and introductions, as if he had no wish whatever to disturb the others by his presence, and was begging them to allow him to return to the darkness and forget all about him. But this was no longer possible. 'You took us by surprise, you see,' said the advocate by way of explanation, beckoning him to come nearer, which he did slowly, looking around hesitantly, yet with a certain dignity. 'This is the Head of Chambers – oh, forgive me, I have not introduced you. This is my friend Albert K., and this is his nephew Josef K., assistant bank manager – our Head of Chambers, who was kind enough to pay me a visit. The value of such a visit can only be really appreciated by those in the know, who are aware that the Head of Chambers is inundated with work. Well, he came in spite of that, and we were having a quiet talk as far as my weak condition allowed. We had not forbidden Leni to let in any visitors, for we did not expect any, but we both thought we should be left alone. Then you started banging on the door, Albert, so the Head of Chambers moved into a corner with a table and chair; but now it turns out that we might have a matter of mutual interest to discuss – that is, if it is your wish – so we would do well to sit down together.'

'Sir,' he said to the Head of Chambers, inclining his head with an obsequious smile, indicating an armchair by the bed. 'I am afraid I can only stay a few minutes.' said the Head of Chambers affably, settling himself in the armchair and looking at his watch.

'Business calls; all the same, I don't want to miss the opportunity to get to know the friend of a friend.' He gave a slight nod to K.'s uncle, who seemed very pleased with this new acquaintance, but who was by nature unable to express any feelings of obligation and responded to the Head of Chambers' words with a burst of embarrassed but loud laughter. A hideous sight! K. was able to watch all this calmly, for no one had paid any attention to him. Now that he had been given due prominence, the Head of Chambers took the lead in the conversation, as he was evidently used to doing. The advocate, whose initial weakness had perhaps only been designed to get rid of his most recent visitors, listened attentively, his hand cupped to his ear; the uncle, who was holding the candle – he was balancing it on his thigh, and the advocate made frequent anxious glances in his direction – soon got over his shyness and was simply delighted both by the Head of Chambers' conversation and by the delicate flowing gestures that accompanied his words. K., who was leaning on the bed-post, was completely ignored by the Head of Chambers, perhaps deliberately, and served only as an audience for the old gentlemen. In any case, he hardly knew what they were talking about; he was either thinking about the maid and how badly she had been treated by his uncle, or else wondering whether he had seen the Head of Chambers before, perhaps even at the meeting during his first examination. Even if he was mistaken, he would have fitted perfectly into the front row of the assembly, among the elderly gentlemen with straggling beards.

Just then a noise from the hall, as of breaking crockery, made them all stop and listen. 'I'll go and see what it is,' said K., and left the room slowly, as if he were giving the others the chance to stop him. He had scarcely reached the hall and was still holding the door handle, trying to find his bearings in the dark, when he felt a much smaller hand on his own, and the door was gently closed. It was the maid, who had been waiting there for him. 'There's nothing wrong,' she whispered, 'I only threw a plate at the wall to get you out here.' K. said shyly: 'I was thinking about you too.' 'I'm glad,' said the maid, 'come on.' In a few steps they reached a door with frosted glass, which the maid opened for K. 'Do go in,' she said. It was apparently the advocate's study; as far as he could see in the moonlight, which only shed a small patch of light on the floor, it was fitted with heavy, old-fashioned pieces of furniture.

'Over here,' said the maid, pointing to a dark brown bench with a carved wooden back. K. sat down and continued to look round the room. It was a large, high room; the advocate's poorer clients must have felt lost in it. K. imagined them shuffling up to the massive desk with short, timid steps. But then he forgot about them and had eyes only for the maid, who sat close next to him, almost pushing him against the arm of the bench.

'I thought,' said the maid, 'I wouldn't have to call you out here; I thought you would come of your own accord. It was strange; when you first came in you stared at me all the time, and then you made me wait. Call me Leni, by the way,' she added quickly and abruptly, as if she had no time to lose. 'Certainly,' said K., 'but I can easily explain why I acted so oddly. Firstly, I had to listen to those two old men chattering, and I couldn't walk out of the room for no reason; and secondly, I'm not a forward person, in fact, I'm shy, and you, Leni, didn't look as if you were to be had just like that.' 'That's not it,' said Leni, draping her arm over the back of the bench and looking at K., 'you didn't like me, and you probably still don't like me.' 'It wouldn't mean much if I only liked you,' said K. evasively. 'Oh?' she said, smiling. K.'s remark and her brief reply seemed to give her the upper hand, so K. said nothing for a while. By now he had grown used to the darkness in the room, and he could make out various details of the furnishings. He noticed in particular a large picture hanging to the right of the door, and leaned forward to see it better. It was a portrait of a man in a judge's gown, who sat enthroned on a raised gilded chair; the gold shone out of the canvas. What was unusual about the portrait was that this judge was not sitting there in a calm and dignified posture, but was pressing his left arm firmly against the back and side of the chair, while his right arm was quite free; but that hand grasped the arm of the chair, as if at any moment he would jump up with a violent and perhaps furious gesture to make some decisive judgement or even to pronounce sentence. One could picture the accused standing at the foot of the steps of which the topmost, covered with a yellow carpet, could be seen in the picture.

'Perhaps that is my judge,' said K., pointing at the picture. 'I know him,' said Leni, also looking at the portrait, 'he often comes here. It was painted when he was young, but he can never have looked anything like his portrait, because he's a tiny little man. He had himself painted very tall, he's insanely vain like all of them here. But I'm vain, too, and I'm very unhappy you don't like me.' K. did not reply to this last remark, but simply put his arm around Leni and drew her close to him. She said nothing, and laid her head on his shoulder. Returning to the previous subject, he said: 'What sort of position does he hold?' 'He's an examining magistrate,' she said; she took K.'s hand, which was round her waist, and played with his fingers. 'Just another examining magistrate,' said K. in disappointment, 'the senior officials stay out of sight. But he's sitting on a high court bench.' 'That's all for show,' said Leni, bending her face over K.'s hand, 'actually he is sitting on a kitchen chair covered with an old horse-blanket. But must you always be thinking about your trial?' she added slowly. 'No, not at all,' said K., 'I probably don't think about it enough.' 'That's not the mistake you're making,' said Leni, 'you're too stubborn, or so I've heard.' 'Who told you that?' asked K. He could feel her body against him, and looked down at her thick, tightly-plaited dark hair. 'I'd be giving too much away if I told you that,' she answered. 'Please don't ask me for names, but do try to correct your mistake. Don't be so stubborn, you can't defend yourself against this court, you have to admit your guilt. Take the first opportunity to admit it. Until you do, you'll have no chance of being cleared, none at all. But even that is not possible without help from someone else, but you mustn't worry about that, because I'll help you.'

'You know a lot about this court and the tricks you have to use,' said K. She was pressing against him too heavily, so he lifted her onto his knee. 'That's better,' she said, settling onto his knee while she smoothed her skirt and adjusted her blouse. Then she clasped both hands about his neck, leaned back and gave him a long look. 'And if I don't make an admission – can you help me then?' he asked tentatively. I'm taking on female helpers, he thought in amazement; first Fräulein Bürstner, then the court attendant's wife, and now this little sick-nurse who seems to have taken a fancy to me. She's sitting on my knee as if that were the only proper place for her! 'No,' replied Leni, 'then I couldn't help you. But you don't want my help at all, you're not interested, you are stubborn and won't be persuaded.' After a while she asked: 'Do you have a girlfriend?' 'No,' said K. 'Go on,' she said. 'Actually, yes,' said K. 'Just think — I told you I didn't, and yet I'm actually carrying her photograph on me.' At Leni's request he showed her a picture of Elsa and, crouching on his knee, she examined it. It was a snapshot which had been taken just as Elsa had finished whirling round in a dance as she often did in the wine bar; the folds of her skirt were still flying round her as she pirouetted, she had put her hands on her broad hips, and with her head thrown back was smiling as she looked to one side. It was not possible to tell from the photograph who she was smiling at.

'She's very tightly corseted,' said Leni, pointing to where she thought this was visible. I don't like her, she's clumsy and coarse. But perhaps she's gentle and kind to you, I can see that from the picture. Big hefty girls like that are often kind and gentle, they can't be anything else. But would she make sacrifices for you? ' 'No,' said K., 'she isn't kind and gentle, and she wouldn't make sacrifices for me either. In fact, I haven't even examined her picture as closely as you have.' 'So she doesn't mean very much to you at all,' said Leni. 'She isn't your girlfriend, then.' 'Yes, she is,' said K., 'I'm not going back on what I said.' 'Well, even if she is your girlfriend at the moment,' said Leni, 'you wouldn't miss her very much if you lost her, or changed her for someone else like me, for example.' 'Certainly,' said K. with a smile, 'that's possible, but she has one great advantage over you; she knows nothing about my trial, and even if she did, she wouldn't give it a thought. She wouldn't try to persuade me to give in.'

'That's no advantage,' said Leni. 'If that's the only advantage she has over me, I shan't be discouraged. Does she have a physical defect?' 'A physical defect?' asked K. 'Yes,' said Leni, 'you see, I've got a small defect, look.' She splayed the ring finger and middle finger of her right hand; the skin between them almost reached the top joint of her short fingers. In the darkness K. did not at first notice what she was trying to show him, so she guided his hand to let him feel it. 'What a freak of nature!' said K. After he had examined her hand all over, he added: 'What a pretty little claw!' Leni watched with something like pride as K. opened and closed her two fingers over and over again in amazement, until finally he kissed them lightly and let them go. 'Oh!' she cried at once, 'you kissed me!' Her mouth wide open, she clambered up quickly and kneeled in his lap. K. looked up at her, almost dismayed. Now that she was close to him she gave off a bitter, enticing smell like pepper; she drew his head towards her, bent over him, bit and kissed his neck, and even took his hair between her teeth. 'You've swapped her for me!' she cried from time to time. 'See, I've taken her place now!' Her knee slipped, and with a small cry she almost fell onto the carpet. K. held her tight to stop her falling, and was pulled down towards her. 'Now you belong to me!' she said.

'Here is the house key, come whenever you like,' were her last words, and a misdirected kiss landed on the back of his neck as he left. A light drizzle was falling when he emerged from the front door; he was about to step out into the middle of the street to see whether he could catch a glimpse of Leni at the window, when his uncle jumped out of a car waiting outside the house, which K. in his distraction had not noticed. He seized K. by the arms and pushed him against the front door as if he wanted to nail him to it. 'Wretched boy!' he cried. 'How could you do that? Your case was going well, and now you've done it terrible harm. You crawl into a corner with that dirty little creature, who in any case is obviously the advocate's mistress, and you're away for hours. You don't even look for an excuse, you don't try to hide anything; no, you're quite open about it, you run after her and spend your time with her. And meanwhile we're sitting there together, your uncle who is doing his best to help you, the advocate whose support you need, and above all the Head of Chambers, that distinguished man who is actually in charge of your case at this stage. We're trying to discuss how best to help you; I have to handle the advocate carefully, he has to do the same with the Head of Chambers, and you have every reason to support me, at least. Instead of which you stay away. In the end there was no hiding it. Well, these are polite, clever men; they don't mention it, they spare my feelings, but in the end even they can't keep up the pretence, and since they can't talk about it, they say nothing. We sit there in silence for several minutes, and listen to see whether you are finally going to come back; but no. In the end the Head of Chambers, who had stayed for longer than he had intended, stands up and takes his leave. It's clear he feels sorry for me, but can't do anything to help me; then he shows extraordinary kindness by waiting for a while at the door, then he goes. Of course I was glad he had gone; I could hardly breathe. And all this affected the advocate far more, ill as he is; the good man could hardly speak when I left. You have probably contributed to his total collapse and hastened the death of a man you depend on. And then you leave me, your uncle, frantic with worry, waiting here for hours in the rain. Just feel my coat, I'm wet through!'

CHAPTER SEVEN

The Advocate – the Manufacturer – the Painter

One winter morning – outside in the gloom snow was falling – K. was sitting in his office. Although it was still early, he was extremely tired. In order not to be disturbed, by the junior clerks at least, he had instructed his attendant to let none of them in as he was busy with important work. But instead of working he twisted and turned in his chair, slowly rearranged a few objects on his desk, then, without realising it, let his whole arm rest on the desk-top and sat motionless, his head bowed.

The thought of his trial never left him now. He had often considered whether it would be best if he were to write out a plea in his defence and submit it to the court. He would include a short account of his life; for every event of any importance he would explain why he had acted as he did, he would state whether in his present opinion that course of action was commendable or reprehensible, and would put forward reasons for his judgement. The advantages of submitting such a plea, rather than simply being defended by an advocate who was in any case not above criticism, could not be doubted. K. had no idea what the advocate was doing; not very much at any rate, because he had not sent for K. for a whole month now, and at none of his earlier interviews had K. been under the impression that this man could achieve very much for him. Especially since he had hardly asked him any questions – and there were so many questions to ask. Asking questions was the whole point. K. felt that he himself could ask all the necessary questions; the advocate, however, instead of putting questions, either talked himself or sat in silence opposite him, bending forward slightly over his desk, presumably because he was hard of hearing, pulling at a hair from the depths of his beard, and gazing at the carpet – perhaps at the very spot where K. had lain with Leni. Now and then he cautioned K. with empty words of warning, like those one gives to children, useless and tedious words for which K. resolved not to pay a penny in the final account.

When the advocate thought he had humiliated K. sufficiently, he would usually begin to encourage him a little; he would tell him that he had won, or partially won, many similar cases. Cases which, even if they were not actually as difficult as this one, had on the face of it been even more hopeless. He had a list of these cases here in a drawer – he tapped at one of the drawers of his desk – but unfortunately he could not show them to him, they were official files, and confidential. Even so, K. would of course benefit from the great experience he had accumulated from all these cases. Naturally, he had started work at once, and the first submission was almost ready; this was most important, because the first impression made by the defence often determined the whole course of the proceedings. Unfortunately, it sometimes happened – it was his duty to remind K. – that the first submissions were not read in court at all. They were simply filed away, which showed that in the first instance, questioning and observing the accused was more important than any written evidence. If the defendant insists, before the final judgement is made, and after all the evidence has been assembled, they will additionally examine all the files in their proper order, including of course the first submission. Unfortunately, however, even this was not always the case; usually the first submission would be mislaid or completely lost, and even if it was preserved until the end of the trial, it was hardly ever read, or so the advocate had heard it rumoured, at least.

This was all regrettable, but not wholly unjustified. K. should also bear in mind that the proceedings were not public; if the court thinks it necessary, they can be made public, but the law did not stipulate that they should. It followed from this that all court documents, and above all the indictment, were not available to the accused or to his defence, and so there was no means of knowing in general, or at least in particular, how the first submission should address the charges, since only by accident could it contain material bearing on the case. Only later could effective and pertinent submissions of evidence be prepared, once the separate charges, and the grounds for these charges, emerged more clearly, or could be inferred, during the examination of the defendant. Under these conditions the defence is of course in a difficult and most unfavourable position. But that, too, is intentional; for the defence is not actually sanctioned by the law, only tolerated, and there is some controversy as to whether the relevant passage in the statutes can be interpreted even as tolerating it.

So strictly speaking, there are no advocates who are recognised by the court; all those who appear before this court are basically only hole-in-the-corner advocates. This, of course, casts the whole profession in a very disreputable light, and when K. next went to the court chambers, he could visit the advocates' room to see for himself. He would probably be horrified at the people who gathered there. The low, cramped room allocated to them would be enough to show the contempt in which the court held these people. The only light comes from a small skylight, which is so high up that anyone who wants to look out of it has to find a colleague who will let him climb onto his back; he also has to put up with the smoke from a nearby chimney that gets up his nose and blackens his face. Just as another example of the conditions here, for more than a year there has been a hole in the floor of this room, not big enough to fall into, but big enough to put one's leg through. The advocates' room is in the upper attic; if anyone does put his leg through the hole, it goes through the ceiling of the corridor below, just where the clients are waiting.

The advocates call these conditions disgraceful, and that is no exaggeration. Complaints to the administration have not the slightest effect; but the advocates are strictly forbidden to make any changes to the room at their own expense. And yet there is a reason why the advocates are treated like this: to exclude the defence as far as possible − everything should be left to the defendant. Not a bad point of view in principle; but it would be quite wrong to conclude that in this court the defendant does not need an advocate. On the contrary, in no other court is an advocate as essential as in this one; the proceedings are not only kept secret from the public, but also from the defendant – only as far as this is possible, of course, but it is possible to a very great extent. For the defendant has no access to the court documents, and it is very difficult to infer from the hearings what they might contain, especially for the defendant, who is inhibited and has all sorts of worries to distract him.

This, explained the advocate, was where the defence comes in. Defence counsel are not generally allowed to attend the hearings, and so immediately after each one, if possible at the door of the courtroom, they must question the defendant closely about the hearing and extract any information helpful to the defence from these often very confused reports. But this is not the most important thing, for there is not much to be learned from this, though of course here, as everywhere else, a competent person can learn more than others. The most important thing is still the advocate's personal connections, these are the most valuable factors in the defence. Now, as K. had no doubt gathered from his own experiences, the very lowest echelons of the court are not quite perfect; corrupt officials who neglected their duties could be said to subvert the proper functioning of the court.

This was where the majority of advocates seized their chance; at this level bribery and gossip flourished, indeed, there were even cases when documents had been stolen, at least in earlier times. It could not be denied that these methods achieved, at least for a while, surprisingly good results for the defendant, and these minor advocates boasted about their success and attracted more clients; but this had no effect on the progress of the trial, and even jeopardised it. Only reputable personal connections had any real value – that is, connections with higher officials, which means, of course, with higher officials of the lower ranks. Only in this way could the progress of the trial be influenced, at first perhaps imperceptibly, but later more and more decisively. Of course, only a few advocates could do this, and in this respect K. had made a fortunate choice. Perhaps only one or two advocates could boast such good connections as Dr Huld, and they paid no attention to that crowd in the advocate's room, in fact they had nothing to do with them. But their relations with the court officials were all the closer. Dr Huld did not even have to go to court and hang about in the magistrates' waiting-rooms on the chance that they might appear and, depending on their mood, gain some no doubt illusory advantage, or perhaps not even that. No – K. had seen it for himself – the officials, some of them quite senior, came to see him themselves and willingly gave him information, either openly or at least easily inferred; they discussed the next stages of the case, indeed they were even open to persuasion in individual cases and glad to adopt someone else's view.

And yet in this respect especially they could not be trusted too far, however firmly they expressed their new judgement in favour of the defence, because they might go straight back to their chambers and draw up a court ruling for the next day which affirmed just the opposite, and which might be even more severe on the defendant than the original judgement they claimed to have abandoned completely. Of course, nothing could be done about that, for what they had said in private was only said in private and could not be used in public, even if the defence were not in any case obliged to make every effort to retain the favour of these gentlemen. On the other hand it was also true that these gentlemen did not communicate with the defence (and they communicated, of course, only with expert defence counsel) simply out of friendship or kind-heartedness, but rather because in a certain sense they were also dependent on the defence. It was this that showed up the drawbacks of a legal system that had established the secrecy of the courts from the very beginning. The officials have no contact with the public at large; they are well equipped to deal with ordinary run-of-the-mill cases, which run along well-worn lines and only require small adjustments now and again. But confronted with very simple cases as well as particularly difficult ones, they are often at a loss. Because they are forever bound up in their laws, day and night, they do not have a proper understanding of human relationships, and in such cases that is quite essential.

Then they come to an advocate for advice, with an attendant behind them carrying the files that are otherwise so secret. At this very window one could have seen many of these men, among them those one might least expect, gazing despondently out into the street while he, the advocate, studied the documents on his desk in order to give them some sound advice. It was on occasions such as these, moreover, that one could tell how uncommonly seriously these gentlemen took their profession, and how they fell into deep despair when they came across obstacles which by their very nature they could not cope with. Their position was in no way an easy one; one would do them an injustice to think it was. The ranks of the court hierarchy were endless, and even an initiate could not grasp it in its entirety. Generally, court proceedings were kept secret from minor officials, so they could hardly ever wholly follow the cases they were dealing with as they progressed; court matters came to their notice without their knowing where they came from, and continued without their knowing how or where. So any knowledge that might be gained from studying the separate stages of a trial, the final verdict and the reasons for it, was all lost to these officials. They were allowed only to deal with the particular stage of a trial that is designated for them by the law, and in most cases they know less about its further progress, that is about the results of their own work, than the defence, which as a rule stays in touch with the accused almost until the end of the case. So in this area, too, the officials can glean valuable information from the defence.

Bearing all this in mind, said the advocate, could K. be surprised that the officials were so irritable and – as everyone had experienced – sometimes treated the clients insolently? All officials were in a state of agitation, even when they appeared calm. Of course, the lesser advocates in particular had to put up with this. For example, the following story had the ring of truth: an elderly official, a kind, quiet man, had worked continuously day and night on a difficult case that had been made particularly complicated by the submissions of an advocate – these officials really are hard-working, more than anyone else. Well, towards morning, after twenty-four hours of probably not very profitable work, he went to his front door, hid behind it, and threw every advocate who tried to come in down the stairs. The advocates gathered at the foot of the staircase and discussed what they should do. On the one hand they had no actual right to be admitted, and so they could scarcely take legal action against him – as I have already mentioned, they must be careful not to antagonise the officials; on the other hand, however, every day not spent in court is a day lost for them, and it was most important that they should be let in. In the end they agreed to tire the old gentleman out. Again and again an advocate was sent running up the stairs and, while putting up all possible, albeit passive, resistance, was thrown back down again. This went on for about an hour, when the old gentleman, who was in any case already tired out by working through the night, became exhausted and went back into his chambers. Those below could not believe it at first, and sent someone up to look behind the door to see that there was really no one there. Only then did they go in, and probably did not even dare to complain.

You see, the advocates — and even the most junior ones have at least some insight into court matters — have not the slightest wish to introduce or implement any improvements, whereas it is notable that almost every defendant, even quite simple people, will start thinking up suggestions for improvements as soon as their case gets under way, and thus often waste time and energy that could have been better expended on other things. The only proper thing to do is to come to terms with things as they are. Even if it were possible to improve some details — but that is an absurd notion — then at best one would achieve something that might affect future cases; but one would do immeasurable harm to one's own case by attracting the attention of officials who are always ready for revenge. Just don't draw attention to yourself! Keep quiet, however much it goes against the grain! Try to understand that this huge legal body is, as it were, forever in a state of balance; by making changes to one's own situation, it is possible to lose one's footing and come to grief, whereas the whole system can easily compensate for such a minor disturbance by making an adjustment elsewhere and so remain unchanged, for everything is interrelated. Indeed, it is more likely that as a result the system will become more impenetrable, more vigilant, even more severe, even more cruel. So one should leave things to the advocates and not interfere.

Recriminations, the advocate went on, were not much use, especially when one could not fully explain the reasons for them; but it had to be said that K.'s behaviour towards the Head of Chambers had greatly jeopardised his case. This influential man might as well be removed from the list of those who could help K.; it was clear he was deliberately ignoring even the most casual references to K.'s case. In some matters the officials were just like children; often they could be so offended by trivialities (though unfortunately K.'s behaviour could not be classed as such) that

they would stop speaking even to old friends, would turn away
when they met them, and would do everything they could to
obstruct them. But then, unexpectedly and for no particular
reason, some small joke that one made because everything seemed
hopeless would make them laugh, and they would be reconciled.
It was at one and the same time difficult and easy to handle them;
there were scarcely any basic principles for dealing with them,
and sometimes one could not imagine that an average lifetime's
experience would be enough to learn how to achieve anything.

Indeed, there were gloomy times, such as everyone experiences,
when one thought nothing whatever had been achieved, when it
seemed that the only successful cases were those that were destined
to succeed from the start, as they would have done without any
assistance, while all the others were lost in spite of all one's running
about, all one's efforts, and all the apparent minor triumphs that
one was so pleased with. At such times nothing seemed certain any
more, and one had to admit that some cases that were in themselves going quite well were actually thrown off course by one's
own intervention. Even that could give one some sense of achievement – but that was all one was left with. Advocates were
especially prone to such moods – and they were of course just
moods, nothing more – when a case they had been conducting
satisfactorily for some time was suddenly taken out of their hands.
That was probably the worst thing that could happen to an
advocate. He would not be removed from the case by the accused,
that would never happen; a defendant who had instructed a certain
advocate was obliged to stay with him, come what may. How
could a defendant who had accepted counsel possibly manage on
his own? That did not happen; but sometimes it could be that the
case took a turn in a direction beyond the scope of the advocate.
The case, the defendant, and everything else was simply with-
drawn from the advocate, and then even his best contacts with
officials were of no help, because they knew nothing themselves.
The case had simply reached a stage where no more help might be
given, it was being dealt with by inaccessible courts, where even
the advocate could not reach the defendant. Then one could come
home one day and find on one's desk all the submissions one had
made in the case with such labour and such high hopes; they had
all been returned because they could not be transferred to the stage

the case had now reached, they had become worthless scraps of paper. But the case was not necessarily lost for all that, not by any means, or at least there was no compelling reason for this assumption; it was simply that one knew nothing further about the case, nor would one be able to find out any more about it.

Fortunately however, the advocate assured him, such cases were exceptional, and even if K.'s case were one of them, it was for the time being far from reaching that stage. There was still plenty of scope for the help of an advocate, and K. could rest assured that it would be used to his advantage. As he had said, the plea had not yet been submitted, but there was time enough for that; the preliminary discussions with the relevant officials were much more important, and they had already taken place. With varying degrees of success, he had to admit quite frankly. It was much better not to reveal any details for the time being, for these could have an undesirable effect on K.; his hopes might be raised unduly, or he might become over-anxious. The advocate could only say this much: some had spoken very favourably and had expressed great willingness to help, while others had been less favourable, though they had by no means refused their support. So the result was on the whole very gratifying; but one should not draw any particular conclusions from this, since all preliminary discussions began in a similar fashion and it was during the course of further developments, and only then, that the value of these early discussions would emerge. At all events, nothing had been lost, and if in spite of everything the Head of Chambers could be won over — various steps had already been taken to achieve this — then the whole affair, as surgeons say, would be 'a clean wound', and one could await further developments with confidence.

The advocate had an inexhaustible fund of such pronounce-ments, which were repeated at every visit. There was always some progress, but the exact nature of this progress could never be divulged. Work continued on the first submission, but it was always unfinished; this usually turned out at the next visit to be a great advantage, because these last few days would have been a most unfavourable time to hand it in — something that could not have been foreseen. If K., drained by all this talk, occasionally remarked that even taking account of all the problems, things were progressing very slowly, the answer was that they were not going at all slowly, though certainly they would have progressed much more quickly if K. had approached the advocate at the right time. Unfortunately, however, he had not; and this omission would entail other disadvantages than simply a loss of time.

The only salutary diversion during these visits was provided by Leni, who always contrived to bring the advocate his tea while K. was there. Then she would stand behind K., pretending to watch the advocate as he poured out his tea and drank it, bending greedily over the cup, and let K. surreptitiously hold her hand. This was done in complete silence; the advocate drank, K. squeezed Leni's hand, and Leni sometimes ventured to stroke K.'s hair gently. 'Are you still there?' the advocate would ask her when he had finished. 'I was going to take the cups away,' she would say, giving K.'s hand a last squeeze; the advocate would wipe his mouth and begin to harangue K. with renewed energy.

What was the advocate trying to achieve: to reassure him, or drive him to despair? K. did not know, but he was convinced that his defence was not in good hands. All the advocate told him might well be true, even if it was clear that he was keen to present himself as a leading player as far as he could, and that he had probably never conducted a case as important as K. believed his own to be. What he found dubious was the constant emphasis on personal contacts with the officials. Were these necessarily being used to K.'s advantage? The advocate never failed to mention that they were only very minor officials in very dependent positions, whose careers would probably be furthered by steering the case in certain directions. Were they perhaps using the advocate to steer it in directions that would always be unfavourable to the defendant? Perhaps they did not do this in every case, surely that was improbable; then again, there must be cases in which they granted the advocate certain favours for his services, for they too must have an interest in preserving his good reputation. But if it was really like that, how would they intervene in K.'s case which, as the advocate had explained, was a very difficult and therefore very important one that had aroused great interest in the court from the very beginning? There could be little doubt as to what they would do; one could already read the signs. The first plea had still not been submitted, although the case had been going on for months; everything was still in the early stages, according to the advocate.

All this was of course designed to dupe the defendant and keep him helpless until he was suddenly taken unawares by the verdict, or at least by the announcement that the commission of investigation had not ruled in his favour and had referred his case to the higher authorities.

It was absolutely vital for K. himself to intervene. It was especially when he was exhausted, as he was on this winter's morning when all these thoughts raced through his mind, that this conviction was overwhelming. The earlier contempt with which he had treated the case was no longer appropriate. If he had been alone in the world, he could easily have ignored it – though for sure it would then not have been brought at all. But now that his uncle had taken him to the advocate, the family had to be considered. He was no longer wholly independent of the course of his trial; he himself had been careless enough to mention it, with a certain inexplicable sense of satisfaction, to his acquaintances. Others had got to know about it, he did not know how, and his relations with Fräulein Bürstner seemed as unpredictable as his case – in short, he hardly had the choice any more whether to accept or reject his trial, he was in the middle of it and had to defend himself. It would not help him if he was so tired.

Nevertheless, for the time being there was no reason to be unduly worried. At the bank he had managed to work his way up to his present senior position in a relatively short time and to prove himself worthy of it, as everyone recognised; now he only had to apply to his case some of the abilities that had made that possible, and there could be no doubt that it would end well. Above all, in order to achieve anything, it was essential to resist from the start any notion that he might be guilty. There was no guilt. The trial was no more than an important business deal such as he had often made to the benefit of the bank, a deal in which, as was usually the case, lurked various dangers that had to be guarded against. To handle it successfully, one could not entertain notions of some kind of guilt, but do everything to concentrate on one's own interests. In this respect it was necessary to take the case out of the advocate's hands very soon, preferably that very evening. According to everything the advocate had told him, this was an outrageous thing to do, and probably a great insult; but K. could not allow his efforts in the case to be hindered by obstacles that his own advocate might put in his way. Once he had got rid of the advocate, his plea must be submitted at once, and if possible every day must be used to ensure that the court took notice of it. Of course this could not be achieved if K. were simply to sit in the corridor like the others and put his hat under the bench. He himself, or the women, or anyone else he might send must pester the officials day after day and force them to sit down at their desks and study K.'s submission, instead of peering through the grille into the corridor. These efforts must be unremitting, everything must be organised and controlled; the court would finally come across a defendant who knew how to defend his rights.

However, though K. was confident he could manage all this, the difficulties involved in drawing up his plea were overwhelming. Earlier, until about a week ago, he had felt only shame at the very thought that he might have to write such a plea himself; it had not occurred to him that it might also be difficult to write it. He remembered how one morning, just when he was inundated with work, he had suddenly pushed everything to one side and taken a notepad to sketch out the broad lines of a submission which he could hand on to his ponderous advocate. At that very moment the door to the manager's office opened and the deputy manager came in, laughing heartily. It had been very awkward for K., although the deputy manager had not, of course, been laughing at his submission, of which he knew nothing, but at a funny story he had just heard from the stock exchange. A sketch was needed to explain the joke, so the deputy manager leaned over K.'s desk, took the pencil out of his hand, and drew on the notepad intended for the plea.

Today K. no longer felt ashamed; the submission had to be written. It was most unlikely that he would have time for it in the office, so he would have to do it during the night at home. If the nights were not enough, he would have to take leave. He must not get stuck halfway – that was the most stupid thing to do, not only in business, but as a general rule. To be sure, the submission would involve an almost endless amount of work. Though he was not a worrier by nature, he could very easily come to believe that it would never be finished, not out of laziness or deviousness, which were all that prevented the advocate from completing it, but because he did not know either what he was accused of or any further charges that might arise; as a result, he would have to recall the most trivial events and actions of a whole lifetime, record them and examine them from every angle. What a dismal task! In retirement, say, it might serve to occupy a senile mind and help to fill out the long days. But now, when K. needed to concentrate on his work, when he was making his way professionally and even posing a threat to the deputy manager, when every hour passed so quickly and he wanted to enjoy the short evenings and nights as a young man should – now he was supposed to write this submission!

Once again his thoughts had turned into self-pity. Almost automatically, just to put an end to all this, he felt for the button of the electric bell that rang in the anteroom. As he pressed it, he looked at the clock. It was eleven o'clock; he had wasted two hours daydreaming, two long precious hours, and was of course feeling more listless than before. However, the time had not been wasted; he had made decisions that could prove valuable. The messengers brought in various letters and two business cards from gentlemen who had been waiting to see K. for some time. They happened to be very important customers of the bank; on no account should they have been kept waiting. Why did they come at such an inconvenient time? And why – so the gentlemen behind the closed door seemed to ask in turn – was K., a hard-working employee, using prime business hours for his private affairs? Weary from all that had gone before, and wearily awaiting what was to come, K. stood up to receive the first customer.

He was a small, cheerful man, a manufacturer K. knew well. He apologised for interrupting K. in important work, and K. for his part apologised for keeping the manufacturer waiting so long. But he expressed his apologies in such a mechanical way, almost stumbling over his words, that the manufacturer would surely have noticed it if he had not been wholly absorbed in his business. Instead, he took tables and calculations out of every pocket, spread them out in front of K., explained various points, corrected a small error in the figures that he had noticed at a glance, reminded K. of a similar agreement he had made with him about a year before, mentioned casually that this time another bank was prepared to offer the very best terms to secure his custom, and finally paused to hear K.'s opinion. At first K. had indeed followed what the manufacturer was saying, and had also been interested in this important piece of business, but unfortunately not for long; he soon stopped listening, then for a while he nodded at the manufacturer's louder remarks, but finally he even gave up even that and confined himself to gazing at the bald head bent over the papers and wondering when the manufacturer would finally realise that everything he was saying was fruitless.

When the manufacturer finally stopped talking, K. at first actually thought he had done so to give him the chance to admit that he was not capable of paying attention; but he was disappointed to see from the man's expectant look that he was obviously prepared to answer any objections, and that the business discussion would have to be continued. So he nodded as if obeying an order and began to move his pencil slowly across the papers, stopping now and again to examine a figure. The manufacturer assumed K. had reservations; perhaps the figures were not really final, he conceded, perhaps they were not the deciding factor; at any rate, he covered the papers with his hand, pulled his chair very close to K., and embarked on a general presentation of his proposal. 'It's difficult,' said K.; he pursed his lips, and since the only thing he could hold on to – the papers – were covered up, he slumped limply against the arm of his chair.

He hardly had the strength to look up as the door to the manager's office opened and he saw the deputy manager appear, indistinctly, as if through a gauze veil. K. did not give this any further thought; he only noticed the immediate consequence, which came as a great relief to him. For the manufacturer jumped up from his chair and rushed over to the deputy manager – though K. could have wished he were ten times more agile, for he feared the deputy manager might disappear again. But there was no need; the two gentlemen met, shook hands, and came over to K.'s desk. The manufacturer complained that the bank had shown so little enthusiasm for his proposal, pointing at K., who under the deputy manager's eye had bent over the papers again. As the two of them leaned over the desk, the manufacturer began to try to win over the deputy manager; K. felt as if the two men, whom he imagined to be far taller than they were, were haggling over him above his head. Slowly and cautiously, he turned his eyes upwards to see what was going on, and without looking picked up one of the papers from the desk, laid it on the palm of his hand, stood up slowly and presented it to the two men. He was not thinking of anything in particular as he did so; he simply felt that this was what he ought to do when he had finally completed the great sub-mission that was to free him from his burden once and for all.

The deputy manager, who was wholly engrossed in convers-ation, glanced briefly at he document without reading a word of it – for what was important to K. was of no importance to him – and took it, saying: 'Thank you, I know all about it,' then put it calmly back on the desk. K. looked at him resentfully, but the deputy manager either did not notice or, if he did, was only amused; he frequently burst out laughing, at one point clearly embarrassed the manufacturer with a sharp riposte, then immed-iately made up for it, and finally invited him into his office where they could conclude their business. 'It is a very important matter,' he said to the manufacturer, 'I can see that quite clearly. And I am sure Herr K.' – even as he said this, he was speaking only to the manufacturer – 'will be only too glad if we relieve him of it. It needs to be thought out calmly, and he seems to be overworked today; besides, there are some people outside who have been waiting to see him for hours.' K. had just enough self-control to turn away from the deputy manager and give the manufacturer a friendly but forced smile. Otherwise he said nothing; leaning forward, he supported himself with both hands on his desk like a junior clerk and watched as the two men continued their con-versation, took the papers from the desk and disappeared into the manager's office. At the door the manufacturer turned to say that he would not say goodbye to Herr K. just yet, as he would of course report to him the result of the discussion; moreover, he had a further small matter to speak to him about.

At last K. was alone. He had no intention of admitting any other clients, and he realised vaguely how glad he was that the people outside believed he was still in discussion with the manufacturer, and so no one, not even the bank messenger, could come in. He went to the window, sat on the sill, holding on to the latch with one hand, and looked out into the courtyard. It was still snowing, and the light had not improved.

He sat there for a long time, not really knowing what was worrying him; but every now and then, startled, he looked back over his shoulder at the door to the anteroom, where he mistakenly thought he had heard a noise. But when no one appeared he became calmer, went over to the wash-stand, washed his face in cold water and returned to his seat at the window with a clearer head. His decision to take his case into his own hands seemed to him more momentous that he had originally assumed. As long as he had left his defence to the advocate, the case had not greatly affected him. He had observed it distantly, it had scarcely encroached directly on his life, he had been able to find out how things stood when he wanted to; but he had also been able to draw back from it whenever he wished. But now that he was going to conduct the case himself, he would be at the mercy of the court, at least for the time being; the end result would be his final and unconditional acquittal, but to achieve this he would in the meantime be exposed to far greater danger than he had been so far. If he doubted this at all, today's encounter with the deputy manager and the manufacturer would have convinced him; he had simply sat there, bewildered by his decision to conduct his own defence. What would it be like when he did? What lay in store for him? Would he find his way through all this to a successful outcome? If he were to conduct a considered defence – and anything other than that would be pointless – did that not mean he would virtually have to abandon all other activities? Was he capable of doing that? And how could he do it while he was at the bank? There was not just the matter of his plea – a spell of leave might have been sufficient for that, though to ask for leave just now would be most ill-advised; there was his whole trial to consider, and there was no saying how long it would last. What an obstacle had suddenly been put in the way of his career!

And how was he supposed to do his job at the bank? He looked at his desk. Was he supposed to see clients and discuss things with them? While his case was proceeding, while up there in the attic court officials sat examining the documents in his case, was he supposed to do the bank's business? Was this not some kind of torture sanctioned by the court that was all to do with his trial? Perhaps it was part of it? And would they make allowances at the bank for his particular situation when they assessed his work? No one would ever do that. They were not entirely unaware of his trial, even if it was not yet clear who knew about it and how much was known. He hoped the news had not reached the deputy manager; if it had, it would surely have been quite obvious, because he would have used it against K. with no regard for human feelings or consideration for him as a colleague. And the manager? He certainly thought well of K., and as soon as he heard of the case would probably have done what he could to lighten his duties; but he would surely not have been able to, because K.'s position had become weaker and he could no longer counter the influence of the deputy manager, who also took advantage of the manager's ill-health in order to bolster his own power. So what could K. hope for? Perhaps he was weakening his resistance by indulging in such thoughts; but it was also essential not to delude himself and to view everything as clearly as he possibly could at present.

For no particular reason, just to avoid having to go back to his desk, he opened the window. He had some difficulty doing this, and had to use both hands to turn the latch. Then a great cloud of smoke and fog poured through the window, and a faint smell of burning filled the room. A few snowflakes drifted in too. 'A terrible autumn,' said the voice of the manufacturer behind K.; he had entered the room from the deputy manager's office unnoticed. K. nodded and looked uneasily at the manufacturer's briefcase, expecting him to pull out his papers and tell him the result of his discussions with the deputy manager. But the manufacturer caught K.'s glance, tapped his briefcase and, without opening it, said: 'You'll want to know how it turned out; the whole thing is practically settled − it's in here. A charming man, your deputy manager; but you've got to watch your step with him.' He laughed and shook K.'s hand, trying to make him join in the laughter. But now it struck K. as suspicious that the manufacturer did not want to show him the papers, and he found nothing to laugh about in the manufacturer's words.

'Herr K.,' said the manufacturer, 'the weather must be affecting you, you look so depressed today.' 'Yes,' said K., putting his hand to his temples, 'headaches, family problems.' 'Yes indeed,' said the manufacturer, who was an impatient man, unable to listen to anyone, 'we all have our cross to bear.' Automatically, K. had made towards the door to see the manufacturer out; but he said: 'I have something else to tell you, Herr K. I'm afraid today may not be the best time to bother you with it, but I've been to see you twice recently, and each time I forgot about it. But if I put it off any longer, there will probably be no point in telling you. That would be a pity, for what I have to say may not be entirely worthless.' Before K. had time to answer, the manufacturer stepped up close to him, tapped his knuckles lightly on his chest and said quietly: 'You are on trial, aren't you?' K. stepped back and cried: 'The deputy manager told you that!' 'Oh no,' said the manufacturer, 'how could the deputy manager know?' 'And how did you find out?' asked K., more composed now. 'I hear things now and again from the court,' said the manufacturer, 'that's just what I was going to tell you.' 'So many people are in touch with the court!' said K., hanging his head. He led the manufacturer to his desk, they sat down as before, and the manufacturer said: 'I'm afraid I can't tell you very much; but in such matters one should not overlook the slightest detail. Besides, I'm keen to help you, however modest my contribution may be. We have been good business friends, have we not? Well, then.'

K. wanted to apologise for his conduct at their earlier meeting, but the manufacturer would not be interrupted. He tucked his briefcase firmly under his arm to show he was keen to leave, and continued: 'I know about your case from a man called Titorelli. He is a painter, Titorelli is his *nom d'artiste*, I've no idea what his real name is. For years he has been coming to my office now and again; he brings some small pictures for which I give him a sort of handout – he's almost a beggar. Besides, his paintings are quite pretty, moorland landscapes, that sort of thing. These purchases – we had both got into the habit – went quite smoothly. But then he started coming too frequently, and I objected; we fell into conversation, because I was interested to know how he could support himself just by painting, and to my astonishment he told me his main source of income was portrait painting. He worked for the court, he said. "For which court?" I asked. And then he told me about the court. I'm sure you can well imagine how astonished I was at this information. Since then I hear bits of news from the court every time he comes, and so I gradually get some idea of what goes on. Certainly, Titorelli is a chatterbox, and I often have to stop him, not just because I'm sure he is a liar, but above all because a businessman like myself, with my back almost breaking under my own troubles, can't bother much about other things.

But that is by the way. Then I thought: perhaps Titorelli can be of some help to you; he knows many of the judges, and even if he may not have much influence himself, he can still give you some tips on how to approach various influential people. And even if his tips are not so vital in themselves, I still think it very important that you should have them. You are almost an advocate. I always say: Herr K. is almost an advocate. Oh, I have no worries about your case. Would you like to see Titorelli, then? He is sure to do everything he can on my recommendation. I really think you ought to go and see him; it needn't be today — some time, any time. But let me add that of course you are not obliged to go and see him just because I advise you to, not in the slightest. No — if you think you can do without Titorelli, it would certainly be better to do without him. Perhaps you already have a definite plan, and Titorelli could upset it; then of course you must not think of seeing him! It certainly goes against the grain to take advice from a fellow like that. Well, just as you wish. Here is my letter of introduction, and this is the address.'

Disheartened, K. took the letter and put it in his pocket. Even at best, the benefits this introduction might bring were far outweighed by the fact that the manufacturer knew about his case and that the painter was spreading news of it. He could hardly bring himself to murmur a few words of thanks to the manufacturer, who was already making for the door. 'I will go and see him,' he said as he saw the manufacturer out, 'or else write and ask him to come and see me at the office; I'm very busy at the moment.' 'Of course I knew you would find the best solution. Though I thought you might prefer to avoid inviting someone like Titorelli to the bank to discuss your case. It isn't always advisable for letters to get into the hands of people like him. But I'm sure you have thought it all over and know what you should do.' K. nodded and accompanied the manufacturer through the anteroom. But though he was outwardly calm, he was very disturbed at what he had said. He had actually only told the manufacturer that he would write to Titorelli in order to give him the impression that he appreciated his recommendation, and he was already thinking how he could meet Titorelli. If he really thought Titorelli's help would be worthwhile, he would not hesitate to write to him; but it was only when the manufacturer mentioned it that he realised how dangerous this might be. Had he really taken leave of his senses? If he was capable of writing an explicit letter to such a dubious person inviting him to the bank, where only a door separated him from the deputy manager, to ask his advice about the case, was it not possible, even very probable, that he was also overlooking other dangers – or running straight into them? He did not always have someone standing beside him to warn him. And now, just as he should be summoning up all his energy in the conduct of his case, he was having such doubts about his own alertness as he had never had before! Were the problems he was having with his work in the office now affecting his conduct of his case too? At any rate, he could no longer understand how he could possibly have intended to write to Titorelli and invite him to the bank.

He was still shaking his head over this when the messenger came up to him and drew his attention to three gentlemen sitting there on a bench in the anteroom. They had been waiting a long time to see him. They stood up when they saw the messenger talking to K., and each tried to approach K. before the others. Since the bank had been so inconsiderate as to make them waste their time waiting, they had no intention of acting considerately either. 'Herr K.,' one of them began. But K. had already asked the messenger to bring his overcoat, and as he helped him on with it, K. addressed all three of them: 'Forgive me, gentlemen, I'm afraid I cannot see you at the moment. I am very sorry, but I have some very urgent business to do, and I must leave at once. You have seen for yourselves how long I have been held up. Would you be so kind as to come back tomorrow or some other time? Perhaps you would like to discuss matters over the phone? Or could you tell me briefly here and now what your business is, and I will give you a detailed reply in writing? It would of course be best if you could come again before long.' The three men, who now saw that they had waited so long to no purpose, were so astonished that they looked at each other in silence. 'We are agreed, then?' asked K., turning to the messenger, who was now bringing him his hat. Outside, as could be seen through the open door of K.'s office, the snow was falling more heavily; K. pulled up his coat collar and buttoned it right up to his chin.

At that moment the deputy manager came out of the next room, and smiled when he saw K. discussing matters with the three men in his overcoat. 'Are you leaving just now, Herr K.?' he asked. 'Yes,' said K., pulling himself up, 'I have to go out on business.' But the deputy manager had already turned to the three men. 'And these gentlemen?' he asked, 'I believe they have been waiting some time.' 'We have come to an agreement,' said K. But now the men would not be put off; they surrounded K. and protested that they would not have waited for hours unless they too had import-ant business that must be dealt with immediately in great detail and in private. The deputy manager listened to them for a while, then looked at K., who was holding his hat and brushing some dust off it. Then he said: 'Gentlemen, there is a very simple solution. If you are agreeable, I will be glad to take over the negotiations from my colleague. Of course your business must be seen to without delay. We are businessmen like you, and we know very well how valuable your time is. Will you come in?' And he opened the door leading to the anteroom of his office.

The deputy manager certainly knew how to take over everything that K. was forced to give up! But was K. not giving up more than was strictly necessary? While he was going to see an unknown painter with vague and, as he had to admit, very slim hopes, his prestige at the bank was being damaged irreparably. It would probably have been much better if he had taken off his overcoat and tried to make amends, at least with the two men who must still be waiting next door. And K. might still have tried to do that if he had not caught sight of the deputy manager in his room, searching for something in K.'s bookcase as if it were his own. As K. went to the door in a state of agitation, the deputy manager called: 'Ah, you haven't gone yet!' He turned towards K., his heavily-lined face appearing to suggest power rather than age, then immediately resumed his search. 'I'm looking for the copy of a contract,' he said, 'which, according to the firm's representative, should be in your room. Would you help me to find it?' K. took a step forward, but the deputy manager said: 'Thank you, I've got it,' and returned to his own room with a large bundle of papers that must have con-tained not only the copy of the contract, but much more besides.

'I can't cope with him just now,' said K. to himself, 'but once my personal problems are out of the way, I swear he'll be the first to know about it, and he'll be sorry, too.' This thought calmed him a little; he told the messenger, who had been waiting for some

time holding the corridor door open for him, to inform the
manager at the first opportunity that he was out on business and,
feeling almost glad that he could now devote himself for a time
entirely to his case, he left the bank.

He immediately took a cab to the painter, who lived in a suburb
on the other side of the city from the court chambers. It was an
even poorer area; the houses were even more dismal, and the
narrow streets were choked with rubbish floating sluggishly in the
slush from the melting snow. At the entrance to the painter's
house, only one of the double doors was open; at the foot of the
other door a hole had been hacked in the wall, through which, just
as K. approached, poured a revolting yellow, steaming stream of
liquid, driving some rats before it into the nearby canal. At the foot
of the stairs a small child lay on its belly crying; but its cries could
hardly be heard above the deafening noise from a plumber's
workshop on the other side of the entrance. The door of the
workshop was open, and three workmen were standing in a
semicircle hammering at some piece of metalwork. A large sheet
of tin hanging on the wall reflected a pallid light between two of
the workmen that shone on their faces and aprons. K. gave all this
only a fleeting glance; he wanted to get things done here as quickly
as possible, to put a few questions to the painter and return to the
bank at once. If he were to have only the slightest success here, it
would help him in his day's work at the bank.

By the time he reached the third floor he was quite out of breath
and had to slow down; the stairs were long, the house was
surprisingly high, and the painter, he had been told, lived in a
garret at the very top. The air was most oppressive, too; there was
no stairwell, the narrow stairs were enclosed on both sides by walls
that only had a few small windows high above him.

K. stopped for a moment, and just then some young girls ran out
of one of the apartments and rushed up the stairs laughing. K.
followed them slowly, overtaking one of the girls, who had
tripped and fallen behind the others. 'Does a painter called Titorelli live here?' he asked her. The girl, who was scarcely thirteen
and slightly hunchbacked, nudged him with her elbow and leered
up at him. She was already quite depraved; neither her youth
nor her deformity had been able to protect her. She did not even
smile, but gazed at K. intently with a bold inviting look in her

eyes. K. pretended not to notice her behaviour, and asked: 'Do you know Titorelli the painter?' She nodded, then asked: 'What do you want him for?' K. thought he should take the opportunity to learn something about Titorelli. 'I want him to paint my portrait,' he said. 'Paint your portrait?' said the girl. She gaped at him open-mouthed, gave him a gentle slap with her hand as if he had said something unexpected or inappropriate, lifted her skirt, which was already short enough, in both hands and ran as fast as she could after the other girls whose shouts were growing fainter further up the stairs. But round the next turn in the stairs K. ran into them all again; the deformed girl had obviously told them what he was doing there, and they were waiting for him. They stood on either side of the stairs, pressed against the walls so that K. could get past, smoothing their aprons with their hands. All their faces, and the way they lined up against the walls, suggested a mixture of childish innocence and wickedness. Laughing, they clustered behind K.; in front was the little hunchback, who was now leading the way. It was thanks to her that he knew where to go; he was about to continue straight up the stairs, but she indicated that he had to turn off to one side to find Titorelli. The staircase leading to his room was particularly narrow, very long and straight; it was possible to see right to the very top where it ended at Titorelli's door. The door, which in contrast to the rest of the staircase was relatively well-lit by a small skylight above it, was made of unvarnished boards on which the name Titorelli had been written in red paint with broad brushstrokes. K. and his companions were scarcely half-way up when, clearly as a result of the noise of so many feet on the stairs, the door above opened a little, and a man evidently wearing only a nightshirt could be seen through the half-open door. 'Oh!' he cried when he saw the crowd coming towards him, and disappeared. The little hunchback clapped her hands for joy, and the other girls swarmed behind K., driving him on.

They had scarcely reached the top when the painter threw the door open and with a deep bow invited K. to enter; but he turned the girls away and would not let any of them in, however much they pleaded and tried to get past, whether with his permission or not. Only the hunchback managed to slip past under his outstretched arm, but the painter ran after her, grabbed her by her skirts, swung her round and set her down in front of the door with the other girls, who had not dared to venture into the room while the painter was away from his post. K. did not know what to make of all this, for it all seemed to be done in a friendly spirit. The girls at the door craned their necks one behind the other and shouted various droll comments at the painter which K. did not understand; the painter laughed too as he threw the little hunchbacked girl into the air. Then he shut the door, bowed once more to K., put out his hand and said by way of introduction: 'I am Titorelli, the artist.'

K. pointed to the door, behind which the girls were whispering, and said: 'You seem to be very popular in this house.' 'Oh, those rascals!' said the painter, trying unsuccessfully to button up his nightshirt at the neck. Otherwise he was barefoot, and dressed only in a pair of wide yellowish linen trousers secured by a belt with a loose end that flapped about. 'They're a real pest,' he went on. He stopped fiddling with his nightshirt, the top button of which had just come off, brought a chair and made K. sit down. 'I painted one of them once – she's not even with them today – and since then they all chase after me. When I'm here they can only come in if I let them, but when I'm out there's always at least one of them here. They've had a key to my door made, and they lend it to each other. You can't imagine what a nuisance it is. For instance, if I bring home a lady I'm supposed to paint, I open the door and find that hunchback at the table over there painting her lips red with one of my brushes, while her little brothers and sisters she's supposed to be looking after are rushing around and messing up the room. Or I come back late at night, as I did just yesterday – that's why I'm in this state, and why the room is so untidy, please excuse all this – I come back late and get into bed, and something pinches me in the leg; I look under the bed and pull another of these creatures out. Why they pester me like this, I don't know; as you must have noticed just now, I don't encourage them, and of course they distract me from my work. If I didn't have this studio rent-free I'd have moved out long ago.' Just then a small voice behind the door called out gently and pleadingly: 'Titorelli, can we come in now?' 'No,' answered the painter. 'Not even just me?' the voice asked. 'Not even you,' said the painter, going to the door and locking it.

In the meantime K. had looked round the room; it would never have occurred to him to call this wretched little garret a studio. It scarcely measured more than two good paces each way. Everything, the floor, walls, and ceiling, was made of wood, and there were narrow gaps visible between the boards. Opposite K. against the wall was the bed, piled high with bedclothes of various colours. In the middle of the room was a painting on an easel, covered with a shirt, its sleeves dangling to the floor. Behind him was a window through which the snow-covered roof of the neighbouring house could be seen through the mist.

The sound of the key turning in the lock reminded K. that he had meant to leave before long. So he took the manufacturer's letter out of his pocket, handed it to the painter and said: 'This gentleman, an acquaintance of yours, told me about you and advised me to come and see you.' The painter read the letter cursorily and dropped it onto the bed. If the manufacturer had not made it perfectly clear that he knew Titorelli and that he was a pauper who depended on his charity, it would have been quite possible to believe that Titorelli did not know the manufacturer, or at least that he did not remember him. Moreover, the painter then asked: 'Do you want to buy some pictures, or have your portrait painted?' K. looked at the painter, astonished. What did the letter actually say, then? K. had assumed as a matter of course that the manufacturer had explained to the painter in his letter that K. only wanted to ask him about his trial. So he had rushed over here far too quickly without thinking! But he had to give the painter some sort of answer, so he said, looking at the easel: 'Are you working on a picture just now?' 'Yes,' said the painter, and threw the shirt hanging on the easel onto the bed with the letter. 'It's a portrait. A good piece of work, but it's not quite finished.'

This was most fortunate for K.; it gave him a clear opportunity to mention the court, for it was obviously the portrait of a judge. It was, moreover, strikingly similar to the picture in the advocate's study. It was true that this was a quite different judge, a stout man with a full black bushy beard covering his cheeks; that one was an oil-painting, while this one was done sketchily and lightly in faint pastel colours. But everything else was similar; here too the judge was grasping the arms of his chair, about to rise menacingly from his judgement seat. 'But that's a judge,' K. had been about to say;

but he checked himself for the moment and went up to the picture
as if he wanted to study it in detail. There was a large figure
hovering over the back of the chair that he could not make out,
and he asked the painter what it was. He replied that it still needed
to be worked on; he fetched a pastel crayon from a small table and
drew a few strokes at the edges of the figure, but this made it no
clearer to K. 'It is Justice,' the painter said finally. 'Ah, now I
recognise it,' said K., 'this is the blindfold, and these are the scales.
But aren't those wings on her ankles, and is she not flying?' 'Yes,'
said the painter. 'I was commissioned to paint it like that; actually,
it's Justice and the goddess of Victory all in one.' 'That's not a very
happy combination,' said K., smiling. 'Justice must be still, otherwise the scales will waver and no just verdict is possible.' 'I must do
as my clients tell me,' said the painter. 'Yes, of course,' said K.,
who had not intended his remark to cause offence. 'You have
painted the figure just as it really is on the seat of judgement.' 'No,'
said the painter, 'I haven't seen either the figure or the chair, that's
all imagined; but I was told what I had to paint.' 'What?' asked K.,
pretending that he did not fully understand the painter. 'But it is a
judge sitting there, isn't it?' 'Yes,' said the painter, 'but he's not a
senior judge, and he never sat on a chair like that.' 'But he still has
himself painted with such ceremony? He's sitting there like a high
court judge.' 'Yes, they're vain, these gentlemen,' said the painter.
'But they have the authorities' permission to be painted like that.
Everyone is given precise instructions how he may be painted. But
I'm afraid it's not possible to judge the details of the costume or the
chair from this particular picture; pastels are unsuitable for portraits
like this.' 'Yes,' said K., 'it's odd that it's done in pastel.' 'The
judge wanted it like that,' said the painter, 'it's meant for a lady.'

   Looking at the picture seemed to have made him keen to set to
work; he rolled up his sleeves, picked up some crayons, and K.
watched as under the delicate strokes of the crayons a reddish
shadow formed about the judge's head and radiated out towards
the edge of the picture. Gradually the shadows began to play about
the head like a halo or a sign of special distinction. The figure of
Justice, however, remained set against a bright background, except
for a discreet touch of colour. This brightness seemed to highlight
the figure, so that it now scarcely suggested either the goddess of
Justice or the goddess of Victory; it looked exactly like the goddess

of Hunting. The painter's work took up more of K.'s attention than he wished; finally he began to reproach himself for staying here so long without yet having done anything to further his own interests. 'What is this judge's name?' he asked abruptly. 'I'm not allowed to say,' replied the painter. He was hunched over the picture and was clearly ignoring the guest he had received so courteously at first. K. put this down to the painter's mood and felt annoyed because he was wasting his time.

'I suppose you are on familiar terms with the court?' he asked. At once the painter put down his crayons, stood up straight, rubbed his hands together and smiled at K. 'Let's not beat about the bush,' he said. 'You want to learn something about the court – after all, that's what it says in your letter of introduction; but you began by talking about my pictures to win me over. But I don't mind; you weren't to know that's not the way to go about it. No, please!' he said sharply as K. was about to protest. Then he went on: 'Besides, you are perfectly correct, I am on familiar terms with the court.' He paused as if to give K. time to digest this. Now the girls could again be heard outside the door. They were probably crowding around the keyhole; perhaps they could also see into the room through the cracks. K. made no effort to apologise, for he did not wish to distract the painter; but neither did he wish the painter to feel so superior as to be inaccessible. So he asked: 'Is that an official appointment?' 'No,' said the painter curtly, as if the question made him unable to say anything further. But K. wanted him to go on, so he said: 'Well, these unofficial positions are often more influential than the official ones.' 'That is just the case with mine,' said the painter, and nodded, frowning. 'I spoke to the manufacturer yesterday about your case. He asked me if I would help you, and I told him: "Let the man come and see me some time"; and now I'm glad to see you here so soon. The case seems to affect you closely, which of course doesn't surprise me at all. But won't you take your coat off for now?'

Although K. only intended to stay for a short time, the painter's suggestion was most welcome. He had found the atmosphere in the room more and more oppressive, and had frequently cast puzzled glances at a small iron stove in the corner, which was clearly not working; the room was inexplicably stuffy. While he was removing his overcoat and unbuttoning his jacket, the painter said apologetically: 'I must have warmth. It's really very cosy here, isn't it? The room is very well situated in that respect.' K. did not reply. It was not so much the warmth that made him uncomfortable, but rather the stuffy atmosphere that made it difficult to breathe properly; the room had probably not been ventilated for a long time. K.'s discomfort increased when the painter asked him to sit on the bed, while he seated himself in front of the easel on the only chair. Moreover, the painter did not seem to understand why K. stayed perched on the edge of the bed; he urged him to make himself comfortable, and when K. hesitated, came over and pushed him down deep among the bedding and the pillows. Then he returned to his chair and at last put the first relevant question, a question that made K. forget everything else.

'Are you innocent?' he asked. 'Yes,' said K. It gave him real pleasure to answer this question, especially as it was addressed to him in private, and therefore involved no liability. No one so far had asked him so candidly. In order to savour this pleasure, he added: 'I am completely innocent.' 'I see,' said the painter. He bent his head as if in thought. Suddenly he raised his head and said: 'If you are innocent, then the matter is quite simple.' K.'s face fell; this man who claimed to be familiar with the court was talking like an ignorant child. 'My innocence does not make things any simpler,' he said. In spite of everything he had to smile, and shook his head slowly. 'There are many subtleties in which the court gets involved; but in the end it drags some serious form of guilt out of nowhere.' 'Yes, yes, of course,' said the painter, as if K. were interrupting his train of thought unnecessarily. 'But you are in fact innocent?' 'Why, yes,' said K. 'That is the main thing,' said the painter. He could not be persuaded otherwise; but in spite of his decisiveness it was not clear whether he was saying this out of conviction or simply out of indifference. K. wanted to establish which it was, so he said: 'I'm sure you know the court much better than I do; I don't know much more about it than what I have been told, though I have listened to various people. But they were all agreed that frivolous charges are not brought, and that if the court does bring charges it is firmly convinced of the guilt of the accused, and it is very difficult to shake this conviction.' 'Difficult?' cried the painter, flinging his arms into the air. 'The court's view can never be shaken. If I were to paint all the judges here side by side on a canvas, and if you were to defend yourself before this canvas, you would have more success than you would before the real court.' 'Yes,' said K. to himself, forgetting that he had only intended to sound out the painter.

Once again a girl outside the door started up: 'Titorelli, will he be going soon?' 'Quiet!' the painter shouted at the door. 'Can't you see I'm having a discussion with this gentleman?' But the girl would not be put off, and asked: 'Are you going to paint him?' And when the painter did not reply, she added: 'Please don't paint him, he's so ugly.' A confused babble of argument followed. The painter leapt to the door, opened it just a crack, through which the girls' hands could be seen, clasped together and stretched out imploringly, and said: 'If you don't keep quiet I'll throw you all down the stairs. Sit on the steps and behave yourselves.' Apparently they did not obey at once, so he ordered them: 'Sit down on the steps!' Only then was there silence.

'Excuse me,' said the painter as he returned to K., who had scarcely looked towards the door; he had left it entirely to the painter whether and how he wished to protect him. And even then he hardly moved as the painter bent down and whispered into his ear so that those outside could not hear: 'These girls belong to the court, too.' 'What?' asked K., turning to look at the painter, who sat down again in his chair and said, half in jest, half by way of explanation: 'Everything belongs to the court.' 'I had not noticed that before,' said K. shortly; the painter's all-embracing remark had removed any disquiet K. felt at his reference to the girls. Still, for some time K. stared at the door, behind which the girls were now sitting quietly on the stairs, except that one of them had pushed a straw through a crack in the boards and was moving it slowly up and down.

'You don't seem to have any overall picture of the court yet,' said the painter; he had spread his legs wide apart and was tapping his feet on the floor. 'But since you are innocent, you won't need to. I can get you out of this myself.' 'How are you going to do that?' asked K. 'You said yourself just now that the court is quite impervious to evidence.' 'Only to evidence that is submitted to the court,' said the painter, raising his index finger as if K. had not grasped a subtle distinction. 'But what is done outside the public courts, that is in committee rooms, in the corridors, or

even here in my studio for example – that is a different matter.'
What the painter was now saying no longer seemed so incredible
to K., indeed it closely matched what he had also heard from
others. It even gave him cause for hope. If the judges were as
easily influenced by personal relationships as the advocate had
suggested, then the painter's connections with these vain judges
were particularly important; at all events they should not be
underrated. So the painter was a valuable addition to the circle of
helpers K. was gradually gathering around him. His talent for
organisation had been praised in the bank; now that he was
relying on his own resources, it was a good opportunity to show
his talents to the full.

The painter observed the effect of his remarks on K., and
continued rather anxiously: 'Has it not occurred to you that I
almost talk like a lawyer? It's because I am constantly in touch with
the gentlemen of the court. Of course, I profit from it greatly,
though I lose much of my artistic impulse.' 'How did you first
come in contact with the judges?' asked K.; he wanted to gain the
painter's confidence before fully engaging his services. 'That was
very simple,' said the painter, 'I inherited my connections. My
father was painter to the court before me. It's one of those
positions that are always inherited. They can't take on new people
for it; you see, there are so many different rules, complex and
above all secret rules, for the painting of the various grades of
officials, that they are quite unknown except to certain families. In
the drawer there, for example, I have my father's drawings, which
I show to no one; but only someone who knows them is capable
of painting judges. Even if I lost them, I still carry so many rules in
my head that no one can challenge my position. And every judge
wants to be painted just like the great judges of old were painted,
and only I can do that.' 'That's enviable,' said K., thinking of his
position at the bank. 'So your position is unassailable?' 'Yes,
unassailable,' said the painter, drawing himself up proudly. 'That's
why I can occasionally take the risk of helping some poor wretch
with his case.' 'And how do you do that?' asked K., as if he were
not the one the painter had just called a 'poor wretch'. But the
painter went on undeterred: 'In your case, for example, since you
are entirely innocent, I shall proceed as follows.' K. found the
repeated references to his innocence becoming tiresome. At times

such remarks suggested that the painter was only prepared to help him if the successful outcome of his trial were guaranteed — in which case, of course, his help was unnecessary. In spite of these doubts, however, K. controlled himself and did not interrupt. He was determined not to forgo the painter's help, which in any case seemed no more dubious than that of the advocate. Indeed, K. much preferred it to the latter because it was offered more candidly and openly.

The painter had drawn his chair nearer to the bed. He continued in a low voice: 'I forgot to ask you firstly what kind of acquittal you want. There are three possibilities, namely, final acquittal, apparent acquittal, and deferred judgement. Final acquittal is the best, of course; but I have not the slightest influence on this kind of result. In my opinion there is not a single person who could have any influence on final acquittal; probably only the innocence of the accused carries any weight in this instance. Since you are innocent, it would be quite possible for you to rely on your innocence alone; but in that case you do not need my help or anyone else's.'

K. was initially bewildered by this systematic exposition, but then he said in equally hushed tones: 'I think you are contradicting yourself.' 'How is that?' said the painter patiently, leaning back with a smile. His smile made K. feel that he was attempting to discover contradictions not in the painter's argument, but in the legal process itself. But he went on undeterred: 'You stated earlier that the court was impervious to evidence; later you limited that to the public courts, and now you even tell me that an innocent person needs no help before the court. That already contains a contradiction. What's more, you said earlier that the judges can be influenced personally, but now you deny that final acquittal, as you call it, can ever be achieved by personal influence. That is a further contradiction.' 'These contradictions can easily be resolved,' said the painter. 'We are talking about two different things here: what the law says, and what I have experienced personally. You must not confuse the two. The law of course says (though I haven't read it myself) on the one hand that an innocent person will be acquitted; but on the other hand it does not say that judges can be influenced. But I have experienced just the opposite. I don't know of any instance of final acquittal, but I do know of many cases where influence has been brought to bear. Of course, it is possible that in all the cases I know of, no one was innocent. But isn't that improbable? Not one innocent person in so many cases? Even as a child I listened carefully to my father at home when he talked about trials, and the judges who came to his studio talked about the court. People in our circles talk about nothing else; as soon as I had the chance to go to court myself, I always made the most of it. I've listened to countless trials at important stages, and followed them as long as they were public – and I must admit I have never seen a single instance of a final acquittal.'

'I see,' said K., as if he were addressing himself and his own hopes. 'Well, that confirms the opinion I already have of the court. So it is pointless in that respect too; a single executioner could replace the whole court.' 'You must not generalise,' said the painter in annoyance, 'I was only talking about my experiences.' 'But that's quite enough,' said K., 'or have you heard of final acquittals in earlier times?' 'Indeed, it is said that there have been such acquittals,' said the painter, 'but it is very difficult to confirm this. The final verdicts of the court are not published; they are not even available to the judges, and as a result only legends survive about earlier judgements. The majority of these legends do provide cases of final acquittal; they can be believed, but they can't be proved. Nevertheless, one should not ignore them; they are sure to contain a certain amount of truth, and they are very beautiful. I have myself painted some pictures based on these legends.' 'Mere legends do not alter my opinion,' said K. 'I don't suppose one can invoke these legends before the court?' The painter laughed. 'No, that's not possible,' he said. 'Then it is pointless to talk about them,' said K.

For the time being, K. was willing to accept the painter's views, even if he found them implausible or if they contradicted other accounts. He did not have time just now to check the truth of everything the painter said, let alone to refute it; the most he could achieve was to persuade the painter to help him in some way, even if it should turn out to lead nowhere. So he said: 'Leaving final acquittal aside, you mentioned two other possibilities.' 'Apparent acquittal and deferred judgement. These are the only options,' said the painter. 'But before we discuss that, won't you take your jacket off? I'm sure you're feeling warm.' 'Yes,' said K. So far he had given his whole attention to the painter's explanations; but now that he was reminded of the warmth of the room, his forehead streamed with sweat. 'It is almost intolerable.' The painter nodded, as if he understood K.'s discomfort very well. 'Couldn't you open the window?' asked K. 'No,' said the painter, 'it's just a fixed pane of glass, it can't be opened.' Now K. realised that all the time he had been hoping that either he or the painter would suddenly go over to the window and fling it open. He was even prepared to breathe in the fog through his open mouth. The thought that he was here completely cut off from the fresh air made him feel dizzy. He patted the bedclothes beside him feebly and said in a faint voice: 'But that's uncomfortable and unhealthy.' 'Oh no,' said the painter in defence of his window, 'although it's only a single pane, if it can't be opened the heat here is kept in better than with a double window. If I need ventilation, which isn't really necessary, because draughts get through between all the boards, I can open one of my doors, or even both.' K., somewhat reassured by this explanation, looked around for the second door. The painter noticed and said: 'It is behind you, I had to block it with the bed.'

Only now did K. see the small door in the wall. 'This is all just far too small for a studio,' said the painter, as if to forestall K.'s disapproval. 'I had to arrange it as best I could. Of course, the bed is in a very bad place in front of the door. For instance, the judge I'm painting at the moment always comes in by the door behind the bed, and I've given him the key to that door so that he can wait in the studio if I'm not here. But then he usually comes early in the morning while I'm still asleep, and so it drags me out of a deep sleep when he opens the door by the bed. You would lose all respect for the judges if you could hear how I curse him when he climbs over my bed early in the morning. I could take the key away from him, of course, but that would only make things worse; it only needs the slightest effort to break open all the doors here.'

All the time the painter was speaking, K. was thinking whether he should take off his jacket; but he eventually realised that if he did not, he would be incapable of staying here any longer. So he took it off, but kept it over his knees so that he could put it back on when the interview was over. He had hardly taken it off when one of the girls cried: 'He's taken his jacket off now!' They could all be heard as they scrambled to look through the cracks in the door to see the spectacle for themselves. 'You see,' said the painter, 'the girls think you're undressing because I'm going to paint you.' 'I see,' said K., not much amused, for he did not feel much better than before, though he was sitting there in his shirtsleeves. Almost irascibly he asked: 'What did you say the other two options were?' He had already forgotten the terms. 'Apparent acquittal and deferred judgement,' said the painter. 'It's up to you which you choose. I can help you achieve either of them, though of course it will take some effort. The difference is that apparent acquittal requires brief but intense effort, while deferred judgement requires much less but more protracted effort. First of all, apparent acquittal: if that is what you wish, I write a statement of your innocence on a sheet of paper. The text of such a statement was handed down to me by my father, and cannot be contested. With this statement I then go round all the judges I know. For instance, I shall start by submitting it this evening to the judge I am painting at the moment when he comes for a sitting. I shall show him the statement, explain to him that you are innocent and myself testify to your innocence. This testimony is not superficial, it is real and binding.'

The painter's expression seemed to suggest he was reproaching K. for burdening him with such a testimony. 'That would be very kind,' said K. 'And the judge would believe you and still not fully acquit me?' 'As I have told you,' replied the painter. 'Besides, it is by no means certain that they would all believe me; for example, some judges will demand I take you to them in person. In that case, you would just have to come along with me; still, if that happens, the case is already half won, especially since I would of course tell you beforehand exactly how to conduct yourself before that particular judge. It's much worse with the judges who turn me down from the start – that can happen, too. Although I shall not fail to make several approaches, we shall have to do without those judges; but we can afford to do that, because individual judges cannot affect the outcome. Then when I have a sufficient number of judges' signatures on this statement, I take it to the judge who is conducting your trial. It may be that I have his signature too, in which case everything will proceed rather more quickly than otherwise. Generally, there are no further obstacles after that, and this is when the confidence of the accused is at its highest. It is remarkable, but true, that during this time people are more confident than after their acquittal. Now no further effort is needed; the presiding judge has in the statement the testimony of a number of judges, he can acquit you without any trouble, which he will undoubtedly do as a favour to me and his other colleagues, though there will be various formalities to complete. And you walk from the court a free man.'

'So then I am free,' said K. uncertainly. 'Yes,' said the painter, 'but you are only apparently free, or more accurately, provisionally free. You see, the lowest judges, who are among those I know, do not have the right to pronounce a final acquittal; only the very highest court, which is inaccessible to you, to me, to all of us, has that right. What goes on there we do not know, and between you and me we don't want to know. So though our judges do not have the supreme right to free the accused from the charges against him, they do have the right to release him from those charges. That is, if you are acquitted in this way, you are released from the charges for the time being, but they remain hanging over you and can be brought against you as soon as the order comes from above. Because I am in such close contact with the court, I can also tell you the difference between final acquittal and apparent acquittal in purely procedural terms, according to the regulations issued to the court chambers. In the case of final acquittal, the files relating to the case must be struck from the record, they are completely eliminated; not only the charges, but the trial and even the acquittal, are destroyed, everything is destroyed. With an apparent acquittal it is different. The files are unchanged, except that the declaration of innocence, the acquittal, and the reasons for it, are added to the record. Moreover, they remain in the system; as the ongoing business of the court requires, they are forwarded to the highest courts, referred down to the lowest ones, and so they shuttle to and fro, sometimes rapidly and expeditiously, at other times subject to shorter or longer delays. These processes are incalculable. Seen from the outside, it can sometimes seem that everything has been long forgotten, that the files have been lost and the acquittal has been made final. No one who knows how the courts work will believe that, however. No file gets lost; the court does not forget. One day, when no one expects it, some judge will examine a file more carefully, realise that in this case the charge still stands, and will order an immediate arrest. I am assuming here that a long time has elapsed between the apparent acquittal and the second arrest; that is possible, and I know of such cases, but it is equally possible that the person acquitted comes home from the court and finds officers waiting there to re-arrest him. That of course is the end of his freedom.'

'So the trial starts all over again?' asked K. almost incredulously. 'Indeed,' said the painter, 'the trial starts all over again, but again there is the possibility, just as before, of obtaining an apparent acquittal. Again, one must summon up all one's energy and not give in.' It may be that the painter spoke these last words because he saw K. slump in dejection. 'But,' asked K., as if he wished to forestall any of the painter's revelations, 'isn't it more difficult to obtain a second apparent acquittal that the first one?' 'It is imposs-ible to be certain,' the painter replied. 'I suppose you mean that because of the second arrest the judges might be biased against the accused? That is not the case. You see, the judges anticipated this arrest when they issued the acquittal, so that hardly affects things. However, for countless other reasons, the attitude of the judges as well as their legal judgement of the case might well have changed, and any efforts to obtain a second acquittal must be adapted to the different circumstances, and must be every bit as strenuous as for the first acquittal.' 'But then this second acquittal is not final either,' said K., shaking his head in disbelief. 'Of course not,' said the painter. 'The third arrest follows the second acquittal, the fourth arrest follows the third acquittal, and so on. That is in the nature of an apparent acquittal.'

K. was silent. 'Obviously you don't think there is any advantage in a provisional acquittal,' said the painter. 'Perhaps deferred judgement would suit you better. Shall I explain what deferment means?' K. nodded. The painter had sprawled back in his chair, his nightshirt was wide open; he had shoved a hand inside and was rubbing his chest and sides. 'Deferment,' he said, staring in front of him for a moment as if he were searching for an exact explanation, 'deferment means that the trial is permanently restricted to the initial stages. To achieve this, the accused and his adviser, but especially the adviser, must constantly keep in personal touch with the court. As I said, it is not necessary to invest so much effort in this as it is for a provisional acquittal, but it requires much closer attention. You must visit the appropriate magistrate at regular intervals and on specific occasions, and make every effort to keep

him well disposed towards you. If you do not know him personally, you must try to influence him through other magistrates you
know; but this should not lead you to neglect direct interviews
with him. If you spare no efforts in this respect, you can be fairly
certain that the trial will not progress beyond its initial stage. The
trial goes on, but the accused is almost as safe from being sentenced
as if he were free. Deferment has the advantage over provisional
acquittal that the defendant's future is less uncertain, he is pro-
tected from the shock of sudden arrest, and he has no cause to fear
that he might, perhaps when other circumstances make it least
convenient for him, have to put up with the stresses and strains
involved in obtaining a provisional acquittal. However, deferment
does have certain disadvantages for the accused that must not be
underestimated. I don't mean so much that in this instance the
accused is never free, because he is not really free if he is provisionally acquitted either. There is a further disadvantage. The
trial cannot be suspended unless there are at least ostensible reasons
for doing so; something must be seen to be happening. So from
time to time various processes have to be gone through, the
accused has to be interrogated, investigations carried out, and so
on. The trial must constantly move within the small circle to
which it has been arbitrarily restricted. That, of course, involves
certain disagreeable aspects for the accused; but you must not
imagine that these are too unpleasant. It is all for form's sake; the
interrogations for example are quite brief, and if you have no time
or if you do not want to attend, you can make your excuses. With
some magistrates you can even agree the arrangements far in
advance; what it amounts to essentially is that as a defendant you
must report to your magistrate from time to time.'

Before the painter had finished speaking, K. had folded his jacket
over his arm and stood up. Immediately a shout came from outside
the door: 'He's getting up now!' 'Are you leaving already?' asked
the painter, who had also got to his feet. 'I'm sure it's the stuffiness
in here that's driving you away. I'm sorry; I could tell you a lot
more. I had to be brief, but I hope I made myself clear.' 'Oh yes,'
said K., whose head ached from the strain of forcing himself to
listen. In spite of K.'s assurance, the painter said by way of
summary, as if he wanted to reassure K. as he left: 'Both methods
have one thing in common − they prevent the conviction of the

accused.' 'But they also prevent his actual acquittal,' said K. quietly, as if he were ashamed to have recognised this. 'You have grasped the nub of the matter,' said the painter shortly. K. picked up his overcoat, but could not even bring himself to put on his jacket; he would have preferred to bundle everything up and rush out into the fresh air. Even the girls outside could not make him put them on, although they were shouting to each other, prematurely, that he was getting dressed.

The painter was eager to gauge K.'s feelings, so he said: 'I dare say you haven't reached a decision yet about what I have told you. I think that's right. In fact, I would have advised you not to make an immediate decision. There is a very fine line between the pros and cons. You must consider everything very carefully; but you should not lose too much time either.' 'I shall come again soon,' said K. Making a sudden decisive effort, he put on his jacket, threw his overcoat over his shoulders and hurried to the door; the girls outside started to shriek. K. thought he could see them through the door. 'You must keep your word,' said the painter, who had not followed him, 'otherwise I shall come to the bank and find out for myself.' 'Won't you open the door?' said K., tugging on the handle, which he realised the girls outside were holding firmly shut. 'Do you want to be pestered by those girls?' asked the painter. 'Use this way out instead.' He pointed to the door behind the bed. K. agreed and leapt towards the bed. But instead of opening the other door, the painter crawled under the bed and asked from there: 'Just a moment; wouldn't you like to see a picture I might sell you?' K. did not wish to be impolite. The painter had really taken an interest in him and promised to help him further; moreover, because of K.'s forgetfulness no mention had been made of any payment for his help, so he could not refuse him. Though he was trembling with impatience to get out of the studio, he agreed to see the picture.

The painter pulled a pile of unframed pictures from underneath the bed, which were so thick with dust that when he tried to blow it off the top one, the dust swirled around K. for some time, making it difficult for him to breathe. 'A moorland scene,' said the painter, handing the picture to K. It showed two scrawny trees growing some distance apart in dark green grass. In the background was a colourful sunset. 'Fine,' said K., 'I'll buy it.' Inadvertently, he had spoken so curtly that he was glad when the painter, instead of taking offence, picked up another picture. 'This is a companion piece to that one,' he said. It might have been intended as a companion piece, but there was not the slightest difference to be seen between them; here were the trees, there was the grass, and there was the sunset. But it mattered little to K. 'They are very nice landscapes,' he said, 'I'll buy both of them and hang them in my office.' 'You seem to like the subject,' said the painter, picking up a third picture, 'so you're lucky I've got another similar one here.' But it was not a similar one; it was exactly the same. The painter was making the most of this opportunity to sell off his old pictures. 'I'll take that one too,' said K., 'how much do all three cost?' 'We'll discuss that another time,' said the painter. 'You're in a hurry now, and we'll keep in touch. I must say I'm glad you like the pictures. I'll give you all the ones I have down here. They're all moorland scenes. I've painted so many of them. Some people don't like them because they're too gloomy, but some people like gloomy scenes best of all, as you do.'

But just then K. had no wish to listen to the professional views of the mendicant painter. 'Pack them all up!' he cried, interrupting him. 'I will send a messenger tomorrow to collect them.' 'That won't be necessary,' said the painter, 'I hope I can find you a porter who will come with you right away.' At last he leaned over the bed and unlocked the door. 'Don't be afraid of stepping on the bed,' said the painter, 'everyone who comes in here does that.' Even without this invitation, K. would not have hesitated; he had already put one foot on the middle of the bed when he looked through the open door and drew his foot back again. 'What is this?' he asked the painter. 'What are you surprised at?' the painter asked, surprised in his turn. 'These are the court chambers. Didn't you know there are court chambers here? They are in almost every attic, why shouldn't they be here as well? In fact, my studio is part of the court chambers, but the court has let me use it.' What alarmed K. was not so much that he had discovered court chambers here too; what alarmed him most was his own ignorance of court matters. A fundamental rule for an accused person, it seemed to him, was always to be prepared, never to be caught off guard, not to look unsuspectingly the other way when a magistrate was standing next to him — and it was this rule that he constantly violated.

Before him stretched a long corridor from which wafted a thick fug compared to which the air in the studio was refreshing. Benches stood on either side of the corridor, just like the waiting-room of the chambers that were dealing with K.'s case. It seemed there were exact prescriptions for the furnishing of chambers. At the moment there were not many clients here. A man was slumped on one bench, his face buried in his arms, seemingly asleep; another man stood in the gloom at the end of the corridor. K. climbed over the bed, and the painter followed with the pictures. They soon met a court attendant – K. could now recognise all court attendants by the gold button they all wore on their everyday clothes alongside their ordinary buttons – and the painter instructed him to accompany K. with the pictures. K. staggered rather than walked, holding his handkerchief pressed to his mouth. They had almost reached the way out when the girls rushed towards them; so he had not escaped them after all. They had evidently seen that the second door to the studio had been opened, and had gone all the way round to get in this side. 'I can't come with you any further!' cried the painter, laughing among the crush of girls. 'Goodbye! And don't take too long to think about it!'

K. did not even give a backward glance. When he reached the street, he took the first cab that came along. He was keen to get rid of the attendant, whose gold button constantly caught his eye, though probably no one else noticed it. In his eagerness to be of service the attendant tried to sit next to the driver, but K. ordered him to step down. It was long past noon when he arrived back at the bank. He would rather have left the pictures in the cab, but feared he might some time have to show the painter he had kept them. So he had them taken to his office and locked them away in the bottom drawer of his desk, so that at least for the next few days they would be safe from the eyes of the deputy manager.

CHAPTER EIGHT

The Corn Merchant – Dismissal of the Advocate

K. had finally decided to take his case out of the advocate's hands. He could not entirely rid himself of doubts as to whether this was the right thing to do; but these were overridden by his conviction that it was necessary. On the day he was to go and see the advocate, this decision had distracted K. from his work, which took him so long that he had to stay late in his office, and it was past ten o'clock when he at last reached the advocate's door. Before he rang the bell he reflected whether it might not be better to dismiss the advocate over the telephone or by means of a letter; a personal interview would certainly be very embarrassing. But in the end K. did not wish to forego an interview. Dismissal by any other means would be met by silence or a few formal words, and unless Leni could find out something about it, K. would never know how the advocate had taken his dismissal, or what the consequences might be for K. in the not unimportant opinion of the advocate. But if the advocate were sitting opposite K., and if he were to be surprised at his dismissal, then even if the advocate gave little away K. would easily be able to infer everything he wanted to know from his expression and his demeanour. It was even quite possible that he could be persuaded to leave his defence in the advocate's hands and that he would withdraw his dismissal.

As usual, there was no response the first time he rang at the advocate's door. 'Leni could be a little quicker,' K. thought. But at least no other person interfered, as usually happened, whether it was the man in the nightshirt or someone else. As K. pressed the bell a second time, he looked back at the other door; but this time it remained shut. At last a pair of eyes appeared at the hatch of the advocate's door; but they were not Leni's. Someone unlocked the door but still held it shut, called back into the apartment: 'It's him!' and only then opened the door wide. K. had pushed at the door when he had heard the key turn quickly in the door of the other apartment, so when the door in front of him was finally opened, he burst straight into the hall just in time to see Leni as she ran down the corridor between the rooms in her nightdress. It was to her that the man who opened the door had shouted a warning. K. looked after her for a while and then turned to the man. He was a small, scraggy man with a beard, and was holding a candle. 'Are you employed here?' asked K. 'No,' the man replied, 'I am a visitor, the advocate is representing me. I am here on a legal matter.' 'Without a jacket?' asked K., indicating the man's state of undress. 'Oh, I'm sorry!' said the man, looking at himself by the light of the candle as if he had only just noticed the state he was in. 'Are you Leni's lover?' K. asked curtly. He stood with his legs a little apart, his hands clasped behind his back, holding his hat. Simply because he was wearing a heavy overcoat he felt very superior to this skinny little man. 'Good God, no!' said the man, raising one hand to his face in a gesture of alarm and denial, 'no, whatever are you suggesting?' 'You look like a man of your word,' said K. with a smile, 'even so – come along.' He waved him on with his hat and let him lead the way. 'So what is your name?' asked K. as they went. 'Block. I'm a corn merchant,' said the little man, turning round to introduce himself; but K. did not let him stand still. 'Is that your real name?' asked K. 'Of course,' came the answer, 'why do you doubt it?' 'I thought you might have some reason to conceal your name,' said K. He felt at ease, as one does only when speaking to one's inferiors in a foreign country, keeping one's own affairs to oneself and flattering them by taking a casual interest in them while being able to dismiss them at will.

K. stopped at the door of the advocate's study, opened it, and called to the merchant, who had obediently followed him: 'Not so fast! Bring the light over here!' K. thought Leni might have hidden in here; he made the merchant search every corner of the room, but it was empty. In front of the judge's portrait K. held the merchant back by his braces. 'Do you know him?' he asked, pointing up at it. The merchant lifted the candle, peered up at the portrait, and said: 'It's a judge.' 'A senior judge?' asked K., stepping to one side to observe the impression the portrait made on the merchant. He looked up with awe. 'He is a senior judge,' he said. 'You haven't much idea,' said K. 'Of all the junior judges, he is the lowest.' 'Now I remember,' said the merchant, lowering the candle, 'I have heard that too.' 'But of course,' cried K., 'I was forgetting, of course you must have heard.' 'But why, though, why?' asked the merchant as K. pushed him with both hands towards the door. Outside in the hall K. asked: 'Do you know where Leni is hiding?' 'Hiding?' said the merchant. 'No, she's probably in the kitchen making soup for the advocate.' 'Why didn't you tell me that straight away?' asked K. 'I was going to take you there, but you called me back,' replied the merchant. He seemed confused by these conflicting instructions. 'I suppose you think you're very clever,' said K. 'Take me there, then!'

K. had never been in the kitchen, which was surprisingly large and well-equipped. The stove alone was three times as big as a normal one; of the rest only a few details could be made out, for the kitchen was lit simply by a small lamp hanging by the entrance. Leni stood at the stove in her usual white apron, tipping eggs into a pan over a spirit burner. 'Good evening, Josef,' she said, glancing sideways at him. 'Good evening,' said K., gesturing to the merchant to sit in a chair to one side, which he did. K., however, went to stand close behind Leni, leaned over her shoulder and asked: 'Who is this man?' Leni put one arm around K., stirring the soup with her other hand, pulled him towards her and said: 'He's a pathetic creature, a poor merchant called Block. Just look at him.' They both looked round. Block was sitting in the chair as K. had indicated; he had blown out the candle that was no longer needed, and was pinching the wick between his fingers to stop it smoking. 'You were in your nightdress,' said K., taking her head in his hand and turning it back towards the stove. She said nothing. 'Is he your lover?' asked K. She tried to reach for the soup-bowl, but K. took hold of both her hands and said: 'Answer me!' 'Come into the study,' she replied, 'I will explain everything.' 'No,' said K., 'I want you to tell me here.' She clung to him and tried to kiss him, but K. pushed her away and said: 'I don't want you to kiss me now.' 'Josef,' said Leni, looking at K. pleadingly but candidly, 'you're surely not going to be jealous of Herr Block?' Then she turned to the merchant and said: 'Rudi, help me, you can see he suspects me, leave that candle alone.' One might have thought Block had not been paying attention, but he knew exactly how things stood. 'I don't know why you should be jealous,' he said humbly. 'Actually, I don't know either,' said K., smiling at the merchant. Leni burst out laughing. While K.'s attention was diverted she slipped her arm into his and whispered: 'Let him be, you can see what he's like. I've looked after him a bit because he's one of the advocate's best clients, for no other reason. What about you? Do you want to see the advocate today? He's very poorly today, but I'll tell him you're here if you like. You'll stay the night with me, for sure. You haven't been to see us for so long; even the advocate has been asking after you. Don't neglect your case! I've found out various things to tell you about, too. But first of all, take your coat off!'

She helped him off with his hat and coat, dashed into the hall to hang them up, then hurried back to keep an eye on the soup. 'Shall I announce you now, or take him his soup first?' 'Tell him I'm here,' said K. He was annoyed. He had originally intended to discuss his business closely with Leni, especially the matter of dismissing the advocate; but the presence of the merchant put him off. He now thought the whole thing was too important for this little man to be allowed to interfere, perhaps decisively, and so he called back Leni, who was already in the hallway. 'No, take him his soup first,' he said, 'it will give him some energy for the interview with me; he'll need it.' 'So you're one of the advocate's clients too,' said the merchant quietly from his corner, as if wishing to confirm this. His question was not well received. 'What business is that of yours?' said K., and Leni added: 'Will you be quiet. – I'll take him his soup first, then,' she said to K., and poured the soup into a bowl. 'The only problem is that he might fall asleep, because he often goes to sleep soon after a meal.' 'What I have to tell him will keep him awake,' said K. He wanted everything he said to convey the impression that he had important business with the advocate; he wanted Leni to ask him about it and then to seek her advice. But she simply did exactly as she was told. As she passed him with the bowl of soup, she nudged him gently and whispered: 'When he's had his soup I'll announce you straight away so that I'll get you back as soon as possible.' 'Get on,' said K., 'just get on with it.' 'Don't be so rude,' she said, turning round in the doorway with the bowl of soup.

K. looked after her; it was now finally settled that the advocate was to be dismissed. It was probably better, too, that he could

CORN MERCHANT — DISMISSAL OF ADVOCATE   129

not talk to Leni about it beforehand; she scarcely had sufficient knowledge of the whole matter, and would certainly have advised against it. She might even have prevented K. from dismissing him just then; he would have remained in a state of doubt and anxiety, and in the end he would still have done what he had decided, for he was quite determined. The sooner it was done, moreover, the less damage would be done. Perhaps the merchant would have something to say about it.

K. looked round; as soon as the merchant noticed him, he began to get up. 'Stay there,' said K., pulling up a chair beside him. 'Are you an old client of the advocate?' he asked. 'Yes,' said the merchant, 'a very old client.' 'How long has he been acting for you?' asked K. 'It depends what you mean,' said the merchant. 'In business affairs — I am a corn merchant — the advocate has been my lawyer since I took over the business, that's about twenty years; but in my trial, which you're presumably referring to, he has represented me from the beginning, that's more than five years. Yes, well over five years,' he added, pulling out an old pocket-book. 'I've written it all in here; I can tell you the exact dates if you like. It's hard to remember everything. My trial has probably been going on much longer — it began shortly after my wife's death, and that's more than five and a half years ago.' K. moved his chair closer. 'So the advocate also takes on ordinary cases too?' he asked. He found this relationship between the criminal court and civil legal practice oddly reassuring. 'Certainly,' said the merchant, then whispered to K.: 'He is said to be better at civil cases than at others.' But then he seemed to regret what he had said. He put a hand on K.'s shoulder and said: 'I beg of you, please don't give me away.' K. patted his leg reassuringly and said: 'No, I don't betray confidences.' 'You see, he's vindictive,' said the merchant. 'Surely he won't do anything to a faithful client like you,' said K. 'Oh yes, he will,' said the merchant, 'when he's upset he makes no allowances; in any case, I'm not really faithful to him.' 'How is that?' asked K.

'Can I trust you?' asked the merchant doubtfully. 'I think you can,' said K. 'Well,' said the merchant, 'I'll tell you part of it; but you must tell me a secret of yours, so that we stick together against the advocate.' 'You are very cautious,' said K., 'but I will tell you a secret that will reassure you completely. So how have you been unfaithful to the advocate?' 'I have,' said the merchant hesitantly, as if confessing to something dishonourable, 'I have another advocate besides him.' 'But that's nothing so terrible,' said K., a little disappointed. 'It is here,' said the merchant; since he made his confession he had been breathing heavily, but gained in confidence after K.'s remark. 'It is not allowed. And what is allowed least of all is to take on hole-in-the-corner advocates as well as an official advocate. And that's just what I have done; apart from him I have five hole-in-the-corner advocates as well.' 'Five!' cried K., astonished by the number alone. 'Five advocates besides this one?' The merchant nodded. 'I'm negotiating with a sixth one just now.' 'But why do you want so many advocates?' asked K. 'I need them all,' said the merchant. 'Will you explain why?' asked K. 'Certainly,' said the merchant. 'Above all, I don't want to lose my case, that goes without saying. And so I can't ignore anything that might help me; even if there's very little hope of any advantage in a particular instance, I can't reject it. That's why I've spent everything I have on my case. For example, I have taken all the money out of my business; my premises used to occupy almost a whole floor; now I manage with a small room at the back where I work with an apprentice. Of course, this decline is not just due to the withdrawal of the funds, but more to the fact that I had to give up my work. If you want to do something for your case, you can't devote yourself to very much else.' 'So you work at the court yourself?' asked K. 'That's just what I would like to know about.' 'I can't tell you much about that,' said the merchant. 'I did try at first, but I soon gave it up. It's too exhausting, and it doesn't get you very far. For me, at least, it proved quite impossible to work there. It's a great effort just sitting there and waiting. You know for yourself how stuffy the atmosphere is in those chambers.'

'How do you know I've been there?' asked K. 'I was in the waiting-room when you went through.' 'What a coincidence!' cried K., so engrossed now that he had quite forgotten how ridiculous the merchant had seemed earlier. 'So you saw me! You were in the waiting-room when I walked through. Yes, I did pass through once.' 'It's not such a coincidence,' said the merchant, 'I'm there almost every day.' 'And now I shall probably have to attend more often,' said K., 'but I don't suppose I shall be received as respectfully as I was then. Everyone stood up; I expect they thought I was a magistrate.' 'No,' said the merchant, 'we were greeting the court attendant. We knew you were a defendant. News like that travels fast.' 'So you knew me even then?' said K. 'Perhaps you thought I was behaving arrogantly. Didn't anyone comment on it?' 'No,' said the merchant, 'on the contrary. But it's all nonsense.' 'What is all nonsense?' asked K. 'Why do you want to know?' said the merchant impatiently. 'You don't seem to know the people there yet; you might get the wrong impression. You must realise that in this situation many matters constantly arise that are beyond understanding, one is simply too tired and too distracted to do very much, and people fall back on superstition instead. I'm talking about the others, but I'm no better myself. One of these superstitions, for example, is that many believe you can predict the result of a case from the defendant's face, especially from the lips. So these people claimed that judging by your lips you would definitely be convicted before long. As I said, it's a ridiculous superstition, and in most cases it turns out to be quite unfounded; but when you mix with people like that it's difficult to get away from these ideas. Just imagine what an effect these superstitions can have. You spoke to one of them, didn't you? But he was scarcely able to answer you. Of course, there were plenty of reasons for his confusion, but one of them was the sight of your lips. He told us later that he believed he had seen a sign of his own sentence on your lips.'

'On my lips?' asked K., taking out a pocket mirror and looking at himself. 'I can't see anything peculiar about my lips. Can you?' 'No, I can't,' said the merchant, 'nothing at all.' 'How superstitious these people are!' cried K. 'Didn't I tell you?' said the merchant. 'So do they have so much to do with each other and discuss things among themselves?' said K. 'I've kept to myself so far.' 'As a rule they don't have much to do with each other,' said the merchant, 'that wouldn't be possible, there are so many of them. And they have very little in common. Occasionally some of them might think they have found a common interest, but it soon turns out to be a mistake. As a body they cannot act against the court. Each case is examined individually; the court is most meticulous. So nothing can be done through combined action; just occasionally an individual might achieve something covertly. But the others only get to know about it when it has been done;

no one knows how it happened. So there is no common cause; people meet now and again in the waiting-rooms, but not much is discussed there. These superstitious beliefs have existed for ages and just proliferate.' 'I saw the men in that waiting-room,' said K., 'it seemed to me that they were waiting pointlessly.' 'Waiting is not pointless,' said the merchant. 'Only individual intervention is pointless. As I told you, I now have five advocates as well as this one. You might think – I thought so myself at first – that I could leave the matter entirely to them now. But that would be quite wrong; I can't leave it to them any more than I could if I only had one. You don't understand that, I suppose?' 'No,' said K. He laid his hand reassuringly on the merchant's in order to stem his all too rapid flow of talk. 'I would just ask you to speak a little more slowly; all these things are of great importance to me, and I can't quite follow you.' 'I'm glad you reminded me,' said the merchant, 'of course you are a newcomer, a beginner. Your case is six months old, isn't it? Yes, I've heard about it – your case is in its infancy! But I have already thought these things through countless times, I just take them as a matter of course.' 'I suppose you're glad your case is so far advanced?' asked K. He did not wish to ask straight out how the merchant's affairs stood, nor was he given a very clear answer. 'Yes, I've been pushing my case along for five years,' said the merchant, bowing his head. 'That's no small achievement.' Then he fell silent for a while.

K. listened to hear whether Leni was coming back. On the one hand he did not want her to come, for he still had many questions, and did not want her to find him in this confidential discussion with the merchant; but on the other hand he was annoyed that while he was here she was spending so much time with the advocate, far longer that she needed to serve his soup. 'I remember the time very clearly,' the merchant resumed; K. at once gave him his full attention. 'I remember when my case was about as far on as yours is now. Then I only had this advocate, but I wasn't very satisfied with him.' Now I shall find out everything, thought K., and nodded eagerly as if this would encourage the merchant to tell him everything that was worth knowing. 'My case,' continued the merchant, 'made no progress, although hearings were being held. I went to all of them, too; I collected evidence, handed over all my business ledgers to the court, which, as I learned later, was not even necessary. I went to see the advocate time and time again, and he submitted various pleas . . . ' 'Various pleas?' asked K. 'Yes, of course,' said the merchant. 'This is most important to me,' said K. 'He is still working on my first submission. So far he has done nothing; I see now that he is neglecting me disgracefully.' 'There may be several good reasons why the submission is not ready yet,' said the merchant. 'In any case, my submissions later turned out to be quite worthless. I even read one of them myself through the good offices of a court official; it was very learned, but lacked any substance. In particular, there was a great deal of Latin, which I cannot understand, then whole pages of general appeals to the court, then flattery of certain individual officials who, although they were not named, could easily be identified by anyone in the know, then words of praise for the advocate from himself as he fawned on the court like a dog, and finally studies of ancient cases that were supposed to be similar to mine. These studies, as far as I could follow them, were certainly made with great care. All this is not meant as a criticism of the advocate's work, and the submission I read was only one of many; at all events, though, as I shall explain, I could not see that my case had made any progress at that point.'

'What sort of progress were you expecting?' asked K. 'That is a perfectly sensible question,' said the merchant with a smile. 'You only rarely see any progress in these proceedings, but I did not know that then. I am a merchant, and I was much more so then than now; I wanted to see real progress, I wanted to get the whole thing over, or at least see the case advance properly. Instead of that there were only interviews, most of which followed the same course; I had the answers ready like a litany. Several times a week messengers came from the court to my office, my apartment, or wherever they could find me. Of course, it was a nuisance – nowadays at least it's much better in that respect, a telephone call is less of a nuisance. And rumours began to spread about my case among my business colleagues, and especially among my relatives, so a great deal of harm was done all round; but there was not the slightest sign to suggest that even the first court hearing would take place in the near future. So I went to the advocate and complained. He explained things at great length, but he firmly refused to do anything I put to him; no one, he said, had any

influence on when a hearing should be held – to insist on this in a
submission, as I had wanted to, was unheard of and would ruin us
both. I thought to myself: if this advocate won't or can't do
anything, another one will and can. So I looked for another
advocate, but I'll tell you this straight away, none of them ever
requested a date for the main hearing, none of them ever obtained
one; that is quite impossible (though there is one exception I will
tell you about). So in this respect the advocate did not mislead me;
but otherwise I had no reason to regret having engaged other ones.
You may well have heard quite a lot from Dr Huld about hole-in-
the-corner advocates; he has probably described them as beneath
contempt, and in fact they are. However, when he talks about
them and compares them with himself and his colleagues, he
always makes a small mistake which I will point out in passing: he
always draws a distinction between them and the advocates in his
circle, whom he calls the "great" advocates. That is wrong; of
course, anyone can call himself "great" if he likes, but only court
convention decides these things. And according to this convention
there are, apart from the hole-in-the-corner advocates, lesser and
greater advocates. However, this advocate and his colleagues are
only lesser advocates; the great advocates, of whom I have only
heard and have never seen, are incomparably higher in rank than
the lesser advocates – as high above them as *they* are above the
despised hole-in-the-corner advocates.'

'The great advocates?' said K. 'Who are they, then? How can
they be reached?' 'So you have never heard of them?' said the
merchant. 'There is hardly a defendant who doesn't dream about
them for some time after he has been told about them. But you
should not be tempted to do that. I don't know who the great
advocates are, and I don't suppose they can ever be reached. I
don't know of a single case of which it could be said with
certainty that they had intervened. They do defend some people,
but that can't be achieved at your own request; they only defend
those they wish to defend. But the cases they take on must have
gone further than the lower court. Apart from that, it is better not
to think about them, because if you do, you find your consult-
ations with the other advocates, their advice and their proposals,
so off-putting and useless – I've experienced it myself – that all
you want to do is give it all up, take to your bed and forget all

about it. But of course that would be completely stupid, because even in bed you wouldn't get any peace for very long.' 'So you didn't consider going to the great advocates at the time?' asked K. 'Not for very long,' said the merchant with another smile. 'Unfortunately you can't get them out of your mind completely, and such thoughts come to you at night especially. But at the time I wanted immediate results, so I went to these hole-in-the-corner advocates.'

'So you've got your heads together!' cried Leni, who had returned with the soup-bowl and was standing in the doorway. They were indeed sitting so close to each other that at the slightest movement they would have bumped their heads together; the merchant, who was in any case very small, was hunched up so that K. was forced to bend low in order to hear everything. 'Just a moment!' cried K., motioning to Leni with an impatient wave of his hand, which was still resting on the merchant's. 'He wanted me to tell him about my case,' the merchant said to Leni. 'Go on, then, tell him all about it,' she said. She spoke condescendingly but affectionately to him. K. was annoyed; he now recognised that the man was of some value to him, at least he had some experience and was perfectly able to pass it on. Leni had probably misjudged him. He looked on with irritation as Leni took the candle from the merchant, who had been holding on to it all this time, wiped his hand with her apron and then knelt down beside him to scrape off some wax that had dripped onto his trousers. 'You were about to tell me about the hole-in-the-corner advocates,' said K., pushing Leni's hand away without further comment. 'What are you after?' Leni asked, giving K. a gentle slap and going about her work. 'Yes, the hole-in-the-corner advocates,' said the merchant, rubbing his brow as if in thought. K. tried to prompt him: 'You wanted quick results, so you went to the hole-in-the-corner advocates.' 'Quite right,' said the merchant, but he did not continue. 'Perhaps he doesn't want to talk about it in front of Leni,' thought K. He restrained his impatience to hear any more just now, and did not press the merchant any further.

'Have you announced me?' he asked Leni. 'Of course,' she replied. 'He's waiting for you. Leave Block alone now, you can talk to Block later, he's staying here.' K. still hesitated. 'Are you going to stay here?' he asked the merchant. He wanted him to answer for himself, and did not want Leni to talk about the merchant as if he were not there. Today he was filled with suppressed anger against Leni. Again it was Leni who spoke: 'He often sleeps here.' 'He sleeps here?' cried K. He had imagined the merchant would wait here for him while he quickly concluded his interview with the advocate, and that they would then both leave and discuss everything thoroughly without being disturbed. 'Yes,' said Leni, 'it's not everyone who is allowed to see the advocate any time he likes as you are, Josef. You don't seem in the least surprised that he will see you at eleven o'clock at night in spite of his illness. You just take everything your friends do for you far too much for granted. Well, your friends do it willingly, at least I do. I just want you to be fond of me; I don't ask for any other thanks, and don't need any either.' 'To be fond of you?' was K.'s first thought; only then did he think to himself: 'Well, yes, I am fond of her.' Nevertheless, putting all this aside, he said: 'He will see me because I am his client. If I needed anyone else's help to see him, I would be pleading with them and thanking them all the time.'

'Isn't he awful today?' Leni asked the merchant. 'Now I'm the one who is being ignored,' thought K., and almost felt angry with the merchant too when he said, falling in with Leni's rudeness: 'That's not why the advocate will see him. It's because his case is more interesting than mine. What's more, his case is still in the early stages, so it's probably not in such a muddle, so the advocate is glad to take it up. Later it will be different.' 'Get away with you,' said Leni, laughing at the merchant, 'what nonsense! You see,' she said, turning to K., 'you can't believe a word he says. He's very nice, but he chatters so much. Perhaps that's why the advocate can't stand him. At any rate, he only sees him when he's in a good mood. I've gone to a lot of trouble to alter things, but it's impossible. Just think – sometimes I announce Block, but he only sees him three days later. But if Block isn't there when he's called, he's lost his chance and I have to announce him all over again. That's why I allowed Block to sleep here; he's even rung for him in the middle of the night. So Block is ready to see him during the night, too. But then it sometimes happens that when the advocate sees Block is there, he changes his mind and won't see him.'

K. looked questioningly at the merchant, who nodded and said with the same candour as he had shown to K. earlier – perhaps his embarrassment had confused him – 'Yes, later on you come to depend on your advocate very heavily.' 'He's only making a show of complaining,' said Leni. 'He likes sleeping here, as he has often admitted to me.' She went to a small door and pushed it open. 'Do you want to see his bedroom?' she asked. K. went over and from the door looked into the low, windowless room; there was just enough space for a narrow bed, which could only be reached by climbing over the end of it. At the head of the bed was a recess in the wall in which stood, neatly arranged, a candle, a pen, an inkwell, and a bundle of papers – probably papers relating to the merchant's case. 'You sleep in the maid's room?' asked K., turning back to the merchant. 'Leni made it up for me,' he replied, 'it's very convenient.' K. took a good look at him. Perhaps his first impression of the merchant had been correct; he had a lot of experience, but he had paid dearly for it.

Suddenly K. could no longer stand the sight of the merchant. 'Put him to bed!' he cried to Leni, who did not seem to understand him. But he wanted to go to the advocate and dismiss him, thus liberating himself not only from the advocate, but from Leni and the merchant too. However, before he reached the door, the merchant addressed him in a low voice: 'Sir.' K. turned, frowning angrily. 'You have forgotten your promise,' said the merchant, holding out his arms imploringly to K. from his chair. 'You were going to tell me your secret.' 'So I was,' said K. with a glance at Leni, who was watching him attentively. 'Well, listen; it's scarcely a secret any more. I'm going to see the advocate now to dismiss him.' 'He's dismissing him!' cried the merchant. He jumped up from his chair and ran round the kitchen waving his arms in the air. 'He's dismissing the advocate!' Leni tried to rush at K., but the merchant got in her way, so she hit him with her fist. Then, her fists still clenched, she ran after K., but he was well ahead of her. He had already reached the advocate's room when she caught up with him; he had almost shut the door behind him, but Leni, holding the door open with her foot, seized his arm and tried to pull him back. But he gripped her wrist so tightly that she gasped and let him go. She did not dare to enter the room, but K. turned the key in the lock anyway.

'I have been waiting for you for a very long time,' said the advocate from his bed. He laid a document he had been reading by candlelight onto his bedside table and put on a pair of spectacles through which he looked at K. severely. Instead of apologising, K. said: 'I shall not be staying very long.' Since it was not an apology, the advocate ignored K.'s remark and said: 'I shall not admit you again at such a late hour.' 'That suits my purposes,' said K. The advocate looked at him inquiringly. 'Take a seat,' he said. 'If you wish,' said K., pulling a chair up to the bedside table and sitting down. 'It seems that you have locked the door,' said the advocate. 'Yes,' said K., 'it was because of Leni.' He did not intend to spare anyone. But the advocate asked: 'Has she been making a nuisance of herself again?' 'Making a nuisance of herself?' asked K. 'Yes,' said the advocate, laughing. He had a fit of coughing, then when he had recovered, began to laugh again. 'You have surely noticed how forward she is?' he asked, and tapped K.'s hand; in his distraction he had let his hand rest on the bedside table, but now withdrew it quickly. 'So you don't take much notice of it,' said the advocate when K. did not reply. 'All the better. Otherwise I might have had to apologise to you. It is one of Leni's peculiarities that I have long since forgiven her; I would not mention it if you had not locked the door just now. You are the last person I should have to explain this to, but since you look so dismayed, I will. It is Leni's peculiarity that she finds most defendants attractive. She becomes attached to all of them, she loves them all, and indeed all of them seem to love her. Sometimes, if I let her, she tells me about it to entertain me. It is a remarkable phenomenon, almost a law of nature. Of course, it is not as if there is any clear or definable alteration in their appearance as a result of being accused. It is not like other court cases; most of them carry on with their normal lives and are not hindered by their trial if they have a good advocate who looks after them. Nevertheless, those with experience of these things are able to pick out defendants, one by one, from any crowd, however large. How do they do this, you will ask. My answer will not convince you; it is because the accused are the most attractive ones. It cannot be their guilt that makes them attractive, since – at least, I have to say this as an advocate – they are not all guilty; nor can it be the appropriate punishment that makes them attractive at this stage, because they are not all punished. So it can only be because proceedings have been taken against them; somehow this clings to them. Some of them are especially attractive; but they are all attractive, even that miserable creature Block.'

When the advocate had finished, K. was completely calm. He had even nodded vigorously at these last words, thus confirming his previous opinion that the advocate was once again, as always, distracting him by making general observations that were quite irrelevant and deflected attention from the main question, namely, what he had actually achieved in K.'s case. The advocate evidently noticed that K. was more determined than usual, for he fell silent in order to give K. a chance to speak. Then, when K. said nothing, he asked: 'Did you come here today with a specific purpose in mind?' 'Yes,' said K., shielding his eyes from the light of the candle with his hand in order to see the advocate better. 'I wanted to tell you that as from today I am dispensing with your services.' 'Do I understand you correctly?' asked the advocate, half rising from the bed and supporting himself on the pillow. 'Presumably,' said K., who was sitting bolt upright as if on guard. 'Well, we can also discuss this plan,' said the advocate after a pause. 'It is no longer a plan,' said K. 'Perhaps,' said the advocate, 'but all the same, we don't want to be too hasty.' He used the word 'we' as if he had no intention of letting K. go, as if he intended to remain as his adviser even if he could not represent him. 'I am not being over-hasty,' said K. He stood up slowly and went to stand behind his chair. 'I have thought it over carefully, perhaps even too long. My decision is final.'

'Then allow me to say just a few more words,' said the advocate, lifting the quilt and sitting on the edge of the bed. His bare legs covered in white hairs were shivering with cold. He asked K. to pass him a blanket from the sofa. K. fetched the blanket and said: 'You are quite unnecessarily risking a chill.' 'The matter is important enough,' said the advocate, as he wrapped the quilt around himself and covered his legs with the blanket. 'Your uncle is my friend, and I have grown fond of you, too, in the course of time. I admit that freely; I do not need to be ashamed of it.'

K. found the old man's sentimental words most unwelcome, for they forced him to give a more detailed explanation, something he would rather have avoided; besides, as he had to admit to himself, they distracted him too, though of course they could never make him go back on his decision. 'I am grateful for your kindness,' he said. 'I also recognise that you have helped me in my case as far as you could, and as it seemed to you to be in my interests. However, I have recently become convinced that this is not sufficient. Of course, I shall never attempt to convert an older and so much more experienced man as you to my way of thinking. If I have at times unwittingly tried to do so, please forgive me; but the matter, as you say yourself, is important enough, and I am convinced it is necessary to pursue the case much more forcefully than hitherto.' 'I understand,' said the advocate. 'You are impatient.' 'I am not impatient,' said K. with some irritation, not choosing his words very carefully. 'You may have noticed that on my first visit to you with my uncle I was not too concerned about my case; indeed, unless I was reminded of it rather forcefully, I forgot all about it. But my uncle insisted that I should engage you, and I did it to please him. After that, one might have expected that the case would have concerned me even less than before, since one engages an advocate in order to take some of the burden of the case from one's own shoulders. But the opposite happened; I had never worried about my case so much until the moment I engaged you to represent me. When I was on my own, I did nothing about my case, I was scarcely aware of it; but now that I had someone to represent me, everything was set for something to happen. At every moment, and with ever greater expectation, I waited for you to act; but you did not. To be sure, I received from you various communications about the court, which I could not perhaps have had from anyone else. But that is insufficient now that the case, which is being conducted entirely in secret, is affecting me more and more closely.'

K. had pushed his chair away and was now standing there upright, his hands in his pockets. 'From a certain stage in the conduct of a case,' said the advocate calmly and quietly, 'nothing really happens any more. How many clients have stood before me like you at a similar stage in their case and have said something similar!' 'Then all these similar clients,' said K., 'were just as right as I am. That does not prove me wrong at all.' 'I do not wish to prove you wrong,' said the advocate, 'but I wished to add that I would have expected more judgement from you than from the others, especially as I have given you more insight into the court and into my activities than I usually do to my clients. And now I am forced to realise that in spite of everything you do not have sufficient confidence in me. You are not making it easy for me.'

How the advocate was humbling himself before K. – and without any regard for the dignity of his position, which is surely at its most sensitive on this point! And why did he do this? By all appearances he was a busy advocate, and a rich man too; neither the loss of income nor the loss of a client could in themselves mean very much to him. Moreover, he was ailing and should be taking good care to shed some of his work. But still he clung to K.! Why? Was it a personal attachment to his uncle, or did he really regard K.'s case as so extraordinary, and hope to gain prestige from it, either in K.'s eyes or – and this possibility could not be excluded – in the eyes of his friends in the court? Nothing could be gathered from his demeanour, however searchingly K. studied him. One might almost suppose that he was deliberately masking his expression in order to assess the effect of his words. But he clearly interpreted K.'s silence only too much in his own favour when he continued: 'You will have noticed that although I have a large practice, I do not employ any assistants. Once it was otherwise, there was a time when some young lawyers worked for me; but now I work alone. This is partly due to the changes in my practice, in that I restrict myself more and more to cases such as yours, and partly to the more profound experience I have of these cases. I found that I was unable to let anyone else do this work without violating my obligations to my clients and to the duties I had taken on. But the decision to do all the work myself had the natural consequence that I had to refuse almost all those who asked me to represent them, and was only able to accept those I had a personal interest in – and there are enough poor wretches, indeed some not far from here, who are glad to snap up any scraps I throw them. On top of that, I became ill from overwork; but still I did not regret my decision. Perhaps I should have refused to take on more cases than I did; but it turned out that it was absolutely necessary for me to devote myself fully to the cases I accepted, and this was justified by their successful outcomes. I once read a document that expressed very well the difference between representing a client in ordinary legal cases and cases such as these. It said that one advocate leads his client on a thread to the verdict, while another lifts his client straight onto his shoulders and carries him, without once putting him down, to the verdict and beyond. It is so. But I was not quite right when I said that I never regret this hard work. When it is so completely misunderstood, as in your case, well, then I almost regret it.'

Far from convincing K., these words only made him more impatient. He rather imagined that he could gather from the advocate's tone what he could expect if he relented: the assurances would begin all over again, references to the progress of his plea, to the improved mood of the court officials, but also to the huge difficulties to be faced – in short, everything he was all too familiar with would be trotted out in order to delude him with vague hopes and torment him with vague menaces. This had to be prevented once and for all, so he said: 'What do you intend to do in my case if your services are retained?' The advocate submitted even to this insulting question, and answered: 'I would continue to do what I have already done for you.' 'I knew it,' said K., 'anything further you have to say is superfluous.' 'I will make one more attempt,' said the advocate, as if K.'s anxieties were his rather than K.'s. 'You see, I suspect you have not only misjudged the legal support I have given you, but that you have been misled into behaving as you do because, although you are a defendant, you have been too well treated – or, to be more accurate, you have been leniently treated, or so it seems. I have good reason for suspecting this; it is often better to be in chains than to be free. But I would like to show you how other defendants are treated; perhaps you might learn a lesson from it. I will now summon Block; unlock the door and sit here by the bedside table.' 'With pleasure,' said K., doing as the advocate told him; he was always willing to learn. But to avoid any misunderstanding, he added: 'You realise that I am removing you from my case?' 'Yes,' said the advocate, 'but you still have time to reverse that decision.' He got back into bed, drew the quilt up to his chin and turned towards the wall. Then he rang the bell.

Almost immediately Leni appeared. She glanced round the room quickly, trying to gather what had been going on; she seemed reassured that K. was sitting calmly by the advocate's bed. She nodded at K., smiling, but he looked at her blankly. 'Fetch Block,' said the advocate. But instead of going to fetch him, Leni went only as far as the door and called: 'Block! The advocate wants you!' – and then, no doubt because the advocate remained facing the wall and was paying no attention, she slipped behind K.'s chair. Then she began to pester him by leaning over the back of the chair or, very gently and carefully, running her hands through his hair and stroking his cheeks. Eventually K. had to stop her by seizing one of her hands, which with some reluctance she surrendered to him.

Block had appeared as soon as he was called; but he stood outside the door and appeared unsure as to whether he should come in. He raised his eyebrows and cocked his head, as if he were listening for the advocate's summons to be repeated. K. could have encouraged him to come in, but he had made up his mind to break off all relations not only with the advocate, but with everything and everybody in this house; so he did not stir. Leni, too, said nothing. Block, noticing that at least no one was driving him away, came in on tiptoe, his face tense and his hands clasped tight behind his back. He had left the door open as a possible avenue of escape. He did not give K. a glance, looking only at the piled quilt under which the advocate, who had rolled over close to the wall, was not even visible. But then his voice was heard: 'Is Block here?' Block had by now advanced some way into the room; the question seemed to have the effect of a blow to his chest, and then another in his back. He staggered, stood bending low, and said: 'At your service.' 'What do you want?' asked the advocate, 'this is a most inconvenient time.' 'Wasn't I called?' asked Block, more to himself than to the advocate; he held up his hands to protect himself, and stood ready to run away. 'You were called,' said the advocate, 'but it is still an inconvenient time.' After a pause he added: 'You always come at an inconvenient time.'

As soon as the advocate began to speak to him, Block stopped looking towards the bed; instead he stared at a corner of the room and simply listened, as if the sight of the speaker were too dazzling to bear. But even listening was difficult for him, because the advocate talked towards the wall, and he spoke quietly and rapidly. 'Should I go away?' asked Block. 'Now you're here,' said the advocate, 'stay here!' One might have thought that the advocate, instead of granting Block's wish, had threatened him with a beating, because now Block really began to shake. 'Yesterday,' said the advocate, 'I was with my friend the third judge, and I gradually brought the conversation round to you. Do you want to know what he said?' 'Oh, yes please,' said Block. When the advocate did not reply immediately, Block repeated his plea and bent down as if he were about to fall to his knees. But K. shouted at him: 'What are you doing?' – and because Leni had tried to stop him calling out, he seized her other hand, too. It was not with a lover's touch that he held her; she sighed several times and tried to escape his grasp. But Block was made to suffer for K.'s outburst, for the advocate asked him: 'Who is your advocate?' 'You are,' said Block. 'And who else apart from me?' asked the advocate. 'No one else,' said Block. 'Then don't take advice from anyone else,' said the advocate.

Block assented wholeheartedly; he scowled angrily at K. and shook his head at him violently. These gestures, if translated into words, would have expressed coarse abuse. And this was the man K. had tried to engage in a friendly discussion of his own case! 'I won't interrupt you again,' said K., leaning back in his chair, 'you can kneel or crawl on all fours if you wish, it won't bother me.' But Block still had his self-respect, at least towards K., for he went up to him, shook his fists and shouted as loud as he dared in the advocate's presence: 'You are not to speak to me like that, it's not right. Why are you insulting me here in front of the advocate, where both of us, you and I, are tolerated only out of the goodness of his heart? You are no better than I am, you are also a defendant with a case on your hands. If you still think you're a gentleman, I'm a gentleman too just as much as you, if not more so. And I will be treated like a gentleman, especially by you. If you think you are superior because you can sit here and listen calmly while I, as you put it, crawl around on all fours, I'll remind you of the old legal maxim: movement is better for the suspect than staying still, because those who are still might be on the scales being weighed along with their sins.'

K. said nothing; he could only stare in amazement at this crazed man. What a change had come over him in the last hour! Was his case causing him such confusion that he failed to distinguish friend from foe? Could he not see that the advocate was deliberately humiliating him, and was now seeking only to impress K. with his power, and thereby perhaps to dominate him too? But if Block was not capable of realising this, or if he was so afraid of the advocate that even this realisation could not help him, how was it that he was cunning or bold enough to deceive the advocate and conceal from him that he had other advocates working for him? And how did he dare to attack K., who after all could betray his secret there and then? But he dared to do more than that; he approached the advocate's bed and began to complain about K. 'Sir,' he said, 'have you heard how this man spoke to me? His case has only been going for a few hours, and he is trying to give advice to me, someone whose case has been running for five years. He even abused me. He knows nothing and abuses me, who to the best of my poor abilities have studied closely all that decency, duty and the customs of the court demand.' 'Pay no attention to anyone,' said the advocate, 'and do what seems right to you.' 'Certainly,' said Block, as if to give himself courage, and after glancing briefly to one side kneeled down close to the bed. 'I am on my knees, your Honour,' he said. But the advocate said nothing. Block cautiously stroked the quilt with one hand.

In the ensuing silence Leni freed herself from K.'s grasp, saying: 'You are hurting me. Let me go, I want to be with Block.' She went over and sat on the edge of the bed. Block was delighted by this, and immediately begged her with silent but lively gestures to plead with the advocate on his behalf. He obviously needed the advocate's advice very urgently, but perhaps only in order to make use of it through his other lawyers. Leni evidently knew exactly how to approach the advocate; she pointed to his hand and put out her lips as if for a kiss. At once Block kissed the advocate's hand and, encouraged by Leni, did it twice more. But still the advocate said nothing. Then Leni leaned over the advocate, revealing the lovely form of her body as she stretched, and bending down close to his face she stroked his long white hair. This did force an answer from him. 'I hesitate to tell him,' said the advocate; one could see him shaking his head gently, perhaps the better to feel the touch of Leni's hand. Block listened, his eyes lowered as if by listening he was transgressing some law. 'Why do you hesitate?' asked Leni. K. had the feeling that he was listening to a well-rehearsed conversation that had often been repeated and would often be repeated in the future, one that only for Block would never lose its novelty. 'How has he behaved today?' asked the advocate instead of replying. Before Leni answered, she looked down at Block and watched for a short while as he raised his hands towards her, wringing them imploringly. At last she nodded gravely, turned to the advocate and said: 'He has been quiet and hard-working.' An elderly merchant, a man with a long beard, was pleading with a young girl for a favourable report! Whatever Block's ulterior motive might be, nothing could justify his behaviour in the eyes of a fellow human being.

K. did not understand how the advocate could have imagined that this spectacle would win him over. If K. had not dismissed him already, this performance would have made him do so; it almost degraded the onlooker. So this was the effect of the advocate's method, to which K. had fortunately not been exposed for too long: the client finally forgot the whole world and could only drag himself along this illusory path to the end of his trial. He was no longer a client; he was the advocate's dog. If the advocate had ordered Block to crawl under the bed as if into a dog kennel and bark, he would have done it willingly. K. listened intently but with detachment, as if he had been commissioned by a higher authority to take careful note and to submit an eye-witness account and full report of everything that was said here. 'What did he do all day?' asked the advocate. 'I locked him in the maid's room so he couldn't disturb me in my work,' said Leni. 'That's where he usually stays anyway. Now and again I took a look through the hatch to see what he was doing. He was kneeling on the bed all the time; he had spread out the documents you lent him on the windowsill and was reading them. That made a good impression on me, because the window only opens onto a ventilation shaft and lets in hardly any light. The fact that he was reading in spite of this showed me how obedient he is.' 'I am pleased to hear that,' said the advocate, 'but did he understand what he was reading?'

During this exchange Block was constantly moving his lips; clearly he was formulating the answers he hoped Leni would give. 'Well, of course,' said Leni, 'I can't say definitely. At any rate, I saw that he was reading very carefully; he spent the whole day on one page, and as he read he followed the words with his finger. Whenever I looked in he sighed, as if reading was a great effort. I suppose the documents you gave him are hard to understand.' 'Yes,' said the advocate, 'they certainly are. And I don't believe he understands them either. They are meant to give him some idea of what a hard struggle it is to defend him. And who is it I struggle like this for? It's almost absurd to say it – for Block. He must learn to understand what that means, too. Did he study without a break?' 'Almost without a break,' Leni answered. 'Just once he asked me for a drink of water, so I handed him a glass through the hatch. Then at eight I let him out and gave him something to eat.' Block glanced sideways at K., as if what Leni was saying was greatly to his credit and ought to impress K. Now he seemed to have high hopes, he moved more freely and shuffled to and fro on his knees.

It was all the more noticeable, then, how he froze at the advocate's next words. 'You are praising him,' said the advocate, 'but that only makes it hard for me to tell him. The fact is, the judge has not given a favourable opinion, either on Block or on his case.' 'Not favourable?' asked Leni. 'How is that possible?' Block looked at her with such a tense look on his face, as if he believed she could, even now, turn the judge's opinion, which had been given so much earlier, to his advantage. 'Not favourable,' said the advocate. 'He was even unpleasantly surprised when I started to talk about Block. "Don't talk about Block," he said. "He is my client," I replied. "He is taking advantage of you," said the judge. "I do not regard his case as hopeless," I said. "He is taking advantage of you," he repeated. "I don't think so," I said, "Block works hard on his case and follows it closely. He almost lives with me so that he can keep up with it. One does not always see such zeal. It is true he is personally unattractive, he has disgusting manners, and he is dirty; but in the conduct of his case he is exemplary." When I said exemplary, I was deliberately exaggerating. Then he said: "Block is just cunning. He has gained a lot of experience and knows how to drag out his case. But his ignorance is much greater than his cunning. What do you think he would say if he discovered his case has not started, if he were told that the bell has not even been rung to mark the beginning of his trial?" Be still, Block!' said the advocate, for Block had just begun to stand up shakily, and clearly wanted to ask for an explanation. This was the first time the advocate had addressed himself directly to Block. With weary eyes he looked vacantly down at Block, who under the advocate's gaze sank slowly back to his knees.

'This pronouncement by the judge is of no significance to you,' said the advocate. 'Do not be alarmed by every word I say. If this happens again, I won't confide in you any more. I can't open my mouth without you looking at me as if you were about to be sentenced. You should be ashamed to act like that in front of my client! And you're destroying the confidence he has in me. What more do you expect? You're still alive, you're still under my protection. Your anxiety is pointless! You have read somewhere that in some cases the final verdict comes unexpectedly, from any source at any time. With many reservations that is in fact true; but it is equally true that your anxiety repels me, and that I see it as a lack of necessary confidence. What have I said, then? I have repeated the words of a judge. You know that various opinions spring up in the course of proceedings until they become impenetrable. This judge, for example, understands the case as starting at a different point from my understanding of it. It's a difference of opinion, that's all. At a certain stage of the trial, according to an old custom, a bell is rung. In the opinion of this judge the trial begins at that point. I can't give you just now all the arguments against this view, and you wouldn't understand them; it's sufficient for you to know that there are many arguments against it.' Embarrassed, Block rang his fingers over the surface of the blanket; for the moment, his anxiety at the judge's words made him forget his own inferior position vis-à-vis the advocate; he thought only of himself and turned the words over and over in his mind. 'Block,' Leni cautioned him, pulling him up by his collar, 'leave the blanket alone and listen to the advocate.'

CHAPTER NINE
In the Cathedral

A very important Italian business associate of the bank was visiting the town for the first time, and K. had been instructed to show him some of the local monuments. It was a task that at any other time he would have considered an honour; but now that it was such a great effort to maintain his own position at the bank, it was one he accepted unwillingly. Every hour spent away from the bank caused him anxiety; although he could not take advantage of his time at the office nearly as much as he could before – he spent many hours in the feeblest pretence of doing any real work – he worried all the more when he was not there. He imagined that the deputy manager, who had always watched him closely, would come into his office now and again, sit down at his desk and look through his papers, or receive clients with whom K. had for years been almost on terms of friendship and turn them against him, or even that he might discover mistakes he had made; for K. now felt threatened on every side by mistakes made at work, mistakes he could no longer avoid. And so whenever he was instructed to go out and meet clients, or even to make a short business trip, however much of an honour this might be – and quite by chance, such assignments had recently come his way more frequently – he still had the suspicion that he was being removed from the office for a while so that his work could be checked, or at least that he was regarded as quite dispensable. He could have refused most of these assignments without difficulty, but he did not dare to do so; for if his suspicions were even remotely justified, to refuse would be to admit his fears.

For this reason he accepted the assignments with apparent calm; he even concealed a severe cold when he was asked to go on a strenuous two-day business trip, simply in order to avoid the risk of having to call it off because of the prevailing wet autumnal weather. When he returned from the journey with a raging headache, he learned that he was expected to show the Italian business associate around the next day. The temptation to refuse just this once was very strong, especially since this assignment had nothing directly to do with business, though it was no doubt important enough to fulfil this social obligation to a colleague; but it was not important to K., who knew very well that he could only maintain his position through success at work, and that if he did not achieve this it would do him no good even if, against all expectations, he were to charm the Italian. He did not wish to be absent from his work, even for a day, for his fear that he might not be allowed back was too great. He knew perfectly well that this fear was exaggerated, but still it oppressed him. In any case, on this occasion it was almost impossible to invent an acceptable excuse; his knowledge of Italian was not great, but it was adequate. More decisive was the fact that he had earlier acquired some knowledge of the history of art – an expertise that had become known at the bank, although it was a wholly exaggerated impression, because for a while K., if only for reasons to do with business, been a member of the Society for the Preservation of Ancient Monuments. Now it happened, or so rumour had it, that the Italian was an art lover, so the choice of K. as his companion was perfectly obvious.

It was a very wet and windy morning when K., extremely annoyed at the prospect of the day in front of him, arrived at the office at seven o'clock so that he could at least do some work before his visitor made him leave it all. He was very tired, for he had spent half the night studying an Italian grammar by way of preparation. The window, at which he had recently been in the habit of sitting far too often, attracted him far more than his desk, but he resisted the temptation and sat down to work. Unfortunately, at that moment the messenger appeared and told him that the manager had sent him to see whether Herr K. had arrived yet; if he had, would he kindly step over to the reception area because the gentleman from Italy was already there. 'I'm coming right away,' said K. He put a small dictionary into his pocket, picked up a folder of places of interest in the town that he had put together for the visitor, put it under his arm and went through the deputy manager's office into the reception room. He was very pleased that he had come in so early that he was available at once, which no one could seriously have expected. The deputy manager's office was of course as still and empty as if it were the middle of the night; the messenger was no doubt supposed to have summoned him to the meeting, but without success.

As K. entered the reception room the two men rose from their deep armchairs. The manager gave him a friendly smile; he was obviously very pleased that K. had arrived. He introduced K. at once; the Italian shook K.'s hand firmly and with a smile referred to someone as an early riser. K. did not at first understand what he meant; it was a strange word, the sense of which he only guessed after a while. He replied with some polite phrases that the Italian also received with a smile, frequently passing his hand nervously over his bushy grey-blue moustache. It was evidently scented; K. almost felt tempted to go up to him and smell it. When they were all seated and had exchanged a few introductory words, K. was most put out to find that he only understood fragments of what the Italian was saying. When the man spoke calmly he understood him almost perfectly, but this happened only occasionally; mostly the words came pouring out of his mouth as he shook his head with delight. But when he talked like this he regularly lapsed into some form of dialect that K. did not recognise as Italian, but which the manager not only understood but also spoke. K. could of course have anticipated this, for the visitor was from southern Italy, where the manager had also lived for some years. At all events, K. realised that there was little possibility of communicating with the Italian, whose French was also difficult to understand; moreover, his moustache concealed his lip movements, which might have helped K. to follow him.

K. began to foresee many problems; for the time being he gave up trying to understand the Italian – it would have been an unnecessary effort while the manager was there because he understood him so easily – and confined himself to watching morosely as the Italian sat back comfortably in his armchair. He tugged frequently at his short close-fitting jacket, and at one point tried, by raising his arms and flapping his wrist, to express something that K. could not grasp, although he leaned forward in order not to lose sight of these gestures. Eventually K., who had desultorily and mechanically followed the exchanges with his eyes, became overwhelmed by his

earlier weariness, and to his horror only checked himself, fortunately just in time, as in his confused state of mind he been about to
stand up, turn round and leave. At last the Italian looked at the
clock and jumped up. When he had said goodbye to the manager
he approached K., but he came up so close that K. had to push
back his armchair in order to move. The manager, who could
clearly read in K.'s eyes the desperate situation he found himself in
with this form of Italian, joined in the conversation so tactfully and
discreetly that he appeared merely to be offering scraps of advice,
while in fact he was succinctly explaining to K. all that the Italian,
who was constantly interrupting him, had to say.

K. learned that the Italian first had some business to see to, that
he would unfortunately have only a little time, and that he had
no intention whatever of rushing round all the sights, but had
decided – of course, only if K. was agreeable, it was his decision
alone – to visit just the cathedral; but he wished to do this
thoroughly. He was exceptionally delighted, he said, to do this in
the company of such a learned and amiable man – by which he
meant K., who was intent on ignoring what the Italian was saying
and trying to follow the manager's words. He asked K., if it was
convenient to him, to meet him in the cathedral in two hours'
time, say, at ten o'clock. For his part, he was confident that he
could be there by then. K. said a few words in reply, the Italian
shook the manager by the hand, then K., then the manager once
more, and made to leave, still in full flow but only half turning
towards them as they followed him to the door. K. stayed behind
for a while with the manager, who looked particularly unwell
today. The manager felt he ought to apologise to K., and confided
to him (they were standing very close to each other) that he had
initially intended to accompany the Italian himself, but then – he
gave no further reason – he had decided to send K. instead. If he
did not at first understand the Italian, he should not be put out, he
would soon pick it up, and even if he did not understand very
much at all, that was no bad thing, because it did not matter very
much to the Italian whether he was understood or not. Besides,
K.'s Italian was surprisingly good, and the manager was sure he
would cope very well. With these words he let K. go.

K. spent the rest of the time left to him writing out from the
dictionary some unfamiliar terms he would need for a tour of the

cathedral. It was a most irksome task. Messengers brought in the post, clerks came in with various inquiries and, when they saw that K. was busy, stood around at the door and would not leave until he had heard what they had to say. The deputy manager did not miss this opportunity to interrupt him; he came in frequently, took the dictionary from him and flicked through the pages, clearly quite aimlessly. Even clients appeared in the gloom of the waiting room when the door was opened and bowed hesitantly, wishing to attract his attention, but uncertain whether they were visible. All this went on around K. as if he were at the hub of it, while he drew up a list of the terms he needed, then looked them up in the dictionary, wrote them out, practised pronouncing them, and finally tried to learn them by heart. But his once reliable memory seemed to have deserted him, and at times he felt so furious with the Italian who was the cause of all this effort that he buried the dictionary under a pile of papers with the firm intention of doing no more preparation; but then he realised that he could not simply walk around the cathedral with the Italian in silence, and took out the dictionary again feeling even more furious.

At half past nine, just as he was about to leave, the telephone rang. Leni wished him good morning and asked how he was. K. thanked her hastily and told her he could not possibly talk to her, as he had to go to the cathedral. 'To the cathedral?' asked Leni. 'Yes, yes, to the cathedral.' 'Why do you have to go to the cathedral?' said Leni. K. tried to explain briefly, but he had hardly begun when Leni suddenly said: 'They are hounding you.' K., who could not bear anyone feeling sorry for him unexpectedly or gratuitously, broke off abruptly with just two words; but as he hung up the receiver he said, half to himself and half to the distant woman who could no longer hear him: 'Yes, they are hounding me.'

Now it was getting late; he was in danger of not being on time. He took a cab – at the last minute he had remembered the folder; he had not had the chance of handing it over before, so he took it with him now. He held it on his knees and drummed his fingers on it nervously for the whole journey. The rain had eased, but it was damp, cool and dark; they would be able to see very little in the cathedral, and K.'s cold would undoubtedly get much worse there by standing around on the cold flagstones. The square in front of the cathedral was quite empty; K. remembered that it had

always struck him even as a small child that in the houses on this
narrow square almost all the window blinds were always down. Of
course, this was more understandable than usual in weather like
this. The cathedral too seemed deserted; clearly, no one would
think of coming here today. K. walked along both side aisles, but
saw only an old woman wrapped warmly in a shawl kneeling in
front of an image of the Virgin and gazing at it. Some way away he
also saw a sacristan with a limp disappearing through a door in the
wall. K. had arrived punctually; just as he walked in it had struck
ten, but the Italian was not there. He went to the main porch,
stood there for a while undecided, then walked around the outside
of the cathedral in the rain to see whether the Italian might be
waiting at a side entrance. He was nowhere to be seen. Had the
manager perhaps been mistaken about the time? How could one
understand this man properly? Whatever the case, K. would have
to wait half an hour for him anyway. He felt tired and wanted to sit
down, so he went back into the cathedral and on a step found a
small scrap of carpet-like material. With his foot he pulled it over
to a nearby bench, wrapped himself more closely in his overcoat,
pulled up his collar and sat down. To pass the time he opened the
folder and glanced through it, but soon had to stop because it was
getting so dark that when he looked up he could scarcely make out
any details in the nearby aisle.

In the distance a large pyramid of candles flickered on the high
altar; K. could not have said for sure whether he had noticed them
before. Perhaps they had only just been lit. Sacristans go about
their work stealthily, they go unnoticed. K. happened to turn
round, and not far behind him also saw a candle burning, a tall,
thick candle fixed to a pillar. Beautiful as it was, it was quite
inadequate to light the altarpieces, most of which hung in the
obscurity of the side-chapels; indeed, it only increased the gloom.
The Italian's discourtesy in not coming was matched by his good
sense; there would have been nothing to see, and they would have
had to be content with inspecting a few pictures inch by inch by
the light of K.'s pocket lamp. In order to find out what might be
achieved by this, K. went to a nearby side-chapel, climbed a few
steps to a low marble balustrade and, bending over it, shone his
torch onto the altarpiece. The sanctuary light glowed in front of it,
interrupting his view. The first thing K. saw, partly by guesswork,

was a tall knight in armour at the very edge of the picture. He was leaning on his sword, which he had thrust into the bare earth in front of him; only a few blades of grass emerged here and there. He seemed to be watching attentively something that was going on in front of him. It was astonishing that he stood there like that and did not move closer. Perhaps he was meant to be standing guard. K., who had not looked at any pictures for a long time, looked at the knight for quite a while, though he constantly had to strain his eyes because of the weak greenish light of his torch. As he shone it over the rest of the picture, he found a conventional portrayal of the Burial of Christ; moreover, it was a modern painting. He put his torch away and returned to his seat.

By now it was probably pointless to wait for the Italian; it was sure to be pouring with rain outside, and since it was not as cold in the cathedral as K. had expected, he decided to stay for the time being. Nearby was the great pulpit; on its small round canopy were fixed two crosses, slanted so that their tips over-lapped. The outer wall of the balcony and the area between it and the supporting pillar consisted of carved green foliage to which small angels were clinging, some in movement, some at rest. K. stepped up to the pulpit and examined it from all sides; the stone carving was most delicate, the deep shadow between and behind the foliation seemed to have been caught and held there. He put his hand into one of the gaps in the foliage and felt the stone carefully. He had not previously been aware of the existence of this pulpit. Then K. happened to notice the sacristan behind the nearest row of benches; he was standing watching him in a long black flowing gown and holding a snuff-box in his left hand. What does the man want? thought K. Does he find me suspicious? Does he want a tip? When the sacristan saw that K. had noticed him, he pointed with his right hand, in which he was still holding a pinch of snuff between two fingers, in a vague direction. His behaviour was almost incomprehensible; K. waited for a while, but the sacristan continued to indicate something with his hand, emphasising the gesture by nodding his head. 'What does he want?' muttered K. to himself; he did not dare to call out loud in here. Then he took out his wallet and pushed along the next row of benches to reach the man; but he immediately held out his hand to stop K., shrugged his shoulders and limped off. His rapid

limping gait was similar to that with which K. as a child had tried
to imitate a horseman. 'A silly old man,' thought K., 'with just
enough wits to serve in a church. Look how he stops when I stop
and peers at me to see whether I am coming.' Smiling, K. followed
the old man the whole length of the aisle almost as far as the high
altar. The man kept pointing at something, but K. deliberately
refrained from looking round; all this pointing was only meant to
stop K. following him. Finally he let him go; he did not wish to
alarm him too much, nor to frighten him away completely, just in
case the Italian turned up after all.

As he returned to the nave to find the seat on which he had left
his folder, he noticed against a pillar very close to the choir-stalls a
small, quite simple side-pulpit of pale bare stone. It was so small
that from a distance it looked like an empty niche intended for the
statue of a saint. A preacher could certainly not take a full step back
from the balustrade. Moreover, the stone vaulting over the pulpit
began unusually low down and, though it was not decorated, rose
in such an abrupt curve that a man of average height could not
stand upright there, but would have to lean forward over the
balustrade all the time. It was as if the whole thing were designed
for the discomfort of the preacher; it was incomprehensible why
this pulpit was needed when the other one, which was large and so
finely decorated, was available.

K. would certainly not even have noticed this small pulpit if a
lamp had not been fixed over it, as is usually done shortly before
a sermon. Was a sermon about to be delivered? In the empty
church? K. looked towards the foot of the steps clinging to the
pillar, which led up to the pulpit and were so narrow that they
seemed designed not for people, but only to decorate the pillar.
Then K. smiled in astonishment – the priest was in fact standing at
the foot of the pulpit steps; his hand was on the rail ready to climb
them, and he was looking at K. Then he gave a little nod of the
head, and K. crossed himself and genuflected, something he should
have done before. The priest pulled himself up by the rail and
climbed to the pulpit with short, quick steps. Was a sermon really
about to begin? Had the sacristan not been quite such a fool, had
he meant to guide K. towards the preacher – a very necessary
expedient in the empty church? And yet there was still an old
woman somewhere in front of an image of the Virgin who should

have been here too. And if a sermon was about to begin, why was there no organ music to introduce it? But the organ remained silent and only gleamed faintly out of the gloom high above.

K. wondered whether he should not make a hasty exit just then; if he did not go now, there would be no chance of leaving during the sermon, and then he would have to stay as long as it lasted. He was losing so much time he could have spent at the office, and he was no longer obliged to wait for the Italian. He looked at his watch; it was eleven. But could there really be a sermon now? Could he be the only one in the congregation? What if he had been a stranger who only wanted to visit the church? That was essentially the case. It was absurd to imagine a sermon was about to be delivered now, at eleven o'clock on a weekday in this appalling weather. The priest – he was undoubtedly a priest, a young man with a smooth, dark face – was obviously only going up there to extinguish the lamp that had been lit by mistake.

But this was not the case. Instead, the priest examined the lamp and turned it up a little, then he turned slowly to the balustrade and grasped the front edge with both hands. He stood like that for a while, and without moving his head looked around. K. had moved quite a long way back and leaned his elbows on the first row of benches. Somewhere he could dimly make out, without being able to identify the exact spot, the sacristan, slumped at rest as if his task had been done. What silence reigned now in the cathedral! But K. had to disturb it; he had no intention of staying here. If it was the priest's duty to preach at a particular time whatever the circumstances, let him do so; he would manage without K.'s support, just as K.'s presence would not enhance the effect. So K. slowly began to move; on tiptoe he felt his way along the bench, reached the broad central gangway and walked down it quite undisturbed, except that the stone floor rang with his lightest footstep, continuously echoing and re-echoing from the vaults in a faint but regularly repeated rhythm as he walked. He felt rather isolated as he walked alone between the empty benches; perhaps the priest was watching him, and the vastness of the cathedral seemed to him to border on the limits of what a human being could endure. When he reached his earlier seat where he had left the folder he did not stop, but just snatched it up and took it with him. He had almost reached the end of the rows of benches and was approaching the open space between them and the way out when he heard the priest's voice for the first time. It was a powerful, well-trained voice; how it rang through the expectant spaces of the cathedral! But it was not a congregation the priest was addressing. There was no mistaking it, and no escaping it; he was calling 'Josef K.!'

K. stopped and looked at the floor. He was still free for the moment; he could still go on and get away through one of the small, dark wooden doors not far from him. It would simply indicate that he had not understood, or that he had indeed understood but was paying no heed. But if he turned round, he was caught, for that would be to admit he had understood very well that he had been the one addressed, and that he would obey the summons. If the priest had called him again, K. would certainly have left; but since all remained silent while K. waited, he turned his head a little to see what the priest was doing. He was standing in the pulpit as before, but it was clear that he had seen K.'s head turn. It would have developed into a child's game of peek-a-boo if K. had not now turned round completely. As he did, the priest beckoned him with his finger. Since everything could now be done openly, K. ran – both out of curiosity and in order to cut things short – with long, raking strides towards the pulpit. When he reached the first row of benches he stopped, but the priest seemed to think he was still not close enough; he stretched out his hand and pointed his forefinger straight down towards a spot right in front of the pulpit. K. followed this instruction too, though from here he had to bend his head right back in order to see the priest.

'You are Josef K.,' said the priest, lifting one hand from the balustrade in a vague gesture. 'Yes,' said K. He thought how freely he used to give his name; for some time now it had been a burden to him. Moreover, people he met for the first time knew it; he thought how much better it was when they did not know his name until he had introduced himself. 'You have been accused,' said the priest in a particularly low voice. 'Yes,' said K., 'so I have been informed.' 'Then you are the man I am looking for,' said the priest. 'I am the prison chaplain.' 'I see,' said K. 'I have had you called here,' said the priest, 'to talk to you.' 'That is not what I understood,' said K. 'I came here to show an Italian round the cathedral.' 'That is beside the point,' said the priest. 'What are you holding in your hand? Is it a prayer book?' 'No,' replied K., 'it is a collection of places to visit in the city.' 'Put it down,' said the priest. K. threw it away so violently that it burst open and slid across the floor, its pages crumpled. 'Do you know that your case is going badly?' asked the priest. 'That is my impression too,' said K. 'I have taken a great deal of trouble, but so far without success. However, I have not yet submitted my plea.' 'How do you think it will end?' asked the priest. 'At first I thought it would end well,' said K., 'but now I sometimes have doubts. I don't know how it will end. Do you?' 'No,' said the priest, 'but I fear it will end badly. You are thought to be guilty. Your case might never get any further than a lower court. Your guilt is thought to be proven, at least provisionally.' 'But I am not guilty,' said K., 'it is a mistake. How can any human being be guilty – we are all human after all, every one of us.' 'That is correct,' said the priest, 'but all guilty men talk like that.' 'Are you biased against me too?' asked K. 'I am not,' said the priest. 'I am grateful to you,' said K., 'but all the others involved in the case are biased against me. They also influence those who are impartial. My position is becoming increasingly difficult.' 'You misinterpret the facts,' said the priest. 'The verdict is not arrived at all at once, the proceedings move gradually towards a verdict.'

'So that is how it is,' said K., bowing his head. 'What do you intend to do next in the matter?' asked the priest. 'I shall seek help,' said K., raising his head to see how the priest would react, 'there are still certain possibilities I have not explored yet.' 'You seek too much help from others,' said the priest disapprovingly, 'especially from women. Can you not see that this is not true help?' 'In some cases, indeed in many cases, I would agree with you,' said K., 'but not in every case. Women have great power. If I could persuade some women I know to work together for me, I would surely succeed – especially in this court, which consists almost entirely of womanisers. If the examining magistrate sees a woman on the other side of the room, he will trample over the bench and the defendant to get at her.' The priest bent his head over the balustrade; only now did the canopy of the pulpit seem to press down on him. K. wondered what the weather might be like outside; it was no longer a gloomy day, it was deepest night. Not all the stained glass in the great window could cast a single gleam of light to relieve the darkness – and the sacristan chose that moment to extinguish the candles on the high altar one by one. 'Are you angry with me?' K. asked the priest. 'Perhaps you do not know what sort of a court you serve.' He received no answer. 'These are only my own experiences,' said K. Still no answer came from above. 'I did not mean to offend you,' said K. At this the priest shouted at K.: 'Can you not see what is right in front of your eyes?' It was a shout of anger, but at the same time it was that of a man who sees someone falling and, because he is himself alarmed, shouts involuntarily and spontaneously.

Neither spoke for some time. The priest could certainly not see K. at all clearly in the darkness below, while K. could see the priest distinctly by the light of the small lamp. Why did the priest not come down? He had not delivered a sermon, but had only given K. some information which, if he took full account of it, would probably do more harm than good. And yet K. did not doubt the priest's good intentions; it was not impossible that if he were to come down, they would see eye to eye. It was not impossible that he could give K. some crucial and welcome advice which would, for example, show him, not perhaps how his trial could be influenced, but how he could escape from it, how it could be circumvented, how he could live beyond the reach of the court. This possibility must exist; K. had recently given it much thought. But if the priest knew of such a possibility, would he reveal it to him if he were asked to, even though he belonged to the court himself, and when K. had attacked the court, had suppressed his mild nature and had even shouted at K.?

'Won't you come down?' said K. 'You are not going to preach a sermon. Come down here to me.' 'I can come down now,' said the priest; perhaps he regretted shouting at K. As he unhooked the lamp, he said: 'I had to talk to you at first from a distance. Otherwise, I can be too easily influenced and forget my duty.'

K. waited for him at the foot of the steps. As he came down, the priest held out his hand from one of the steps above. 'Can you spare me a little time?' asked K. 'As much time as you need,' said the priest, handing him the small lamp to carry. Even when he was close to K., he still retained a certain solemnity. 'You are very kind to me,' said K. as they walked up and down the dark aisle together. 'You are an exception among all those who belong to the court; I trust you more than anyone else I have met. I can speak frankly to you.' 'Do not be deluded,' said the priest. 'How should I be deluded?' asked K. 'You are deluding yourself about the court,' said the priest. 'In the preamble to the law, this is what it says about that delusion:

'Before the law stands a doorkeeper. A man from the country comes to this doorkeeper and asks to be admitted to the law. But the doorkeeper tells him he cannot grant him admittance to the law now. The man considers this, and asks whether he can be admitted later. "It is possible," says the doorkeeper, "but not now." Since the door to the law is standing open as it always does, the man stoops to look inside through the door as the doorkeeper steps to one side. When the doorkeeper sees this he laughs and says: "If you are so keen, try to get in against my orders. But take note of this: I am powerful, and I am only the lowest doorkeeper. But in one hall after another there are more doorkeepers, each more powerful than the last. Even I cannot bear to look at the third one." The man from the country did not expect such difficulties. The law should be accessible to everyone at all times, he thinks; but now that he looks more closely at the doorkeeper in his fur coat, with his great hooked nose and long, thin, black Tartar's beard, he decides he would rather wait until he gets permission to enter. The doorkeeper gives him a stool and lets him sit down to one side of the door. He sits there for days and years. He makes many attempts to be admitted and wearies the doorkeeper with his pleas. The doorkeeper often asks him a few questions, asks him about where he comes from and all sorts of other things; but they are casual questions, like those asked by important people, and in the end he tells him once again that he cannot admit him yet. The man, who has made great provision for his journey, gives up everything, however precious, to bribe the doorkeeper, who accepts everything; but as he does, he says: "I am only accepting it so that you don't think you have neglected anything." During these many years the man watches the doorkeeper almost continuously. He forgets about the other doorkeepers, this first one seems to him the only obstacle to his admission to the law. He curses his unhappy fate, in the first years out loud, but later, when he is old, he only mutters to himself. He becomes childish, and because after years of observing the doorkeeper he has even become familiar with the fleas in his fur collar, he appeals to the fleas to help him change the doorkeeper's mind. In the end his eyesight grows weak, and he cannot tell whether it is really getting darker around him or whether his eyes are deceiving him. But he does now notice an inextinguishable radiance that streams from the entrance to the law. By now he does not have very long to live. Before he dies, everything that he has experienced during all this time focuses in his mind into one question that he has not asked the doorkeeper before. He beckons him, for he can no longer lift his stiffening body. The doorkeeper has to bend low to hear him, for the difference in their height has increased, much to the disadvantage of the man. "What is it you want to know now?" says the doorkeeper. "You are insatiable." "Everyone aspires to the law," says the man, "so how is it that in all these years no one except me has demanded admittance?" The doorkeeper realises that the man is finished, and so that the dying man's ears can catch his words, he roars at him: "No one else could be admitted here; this door was meant only for you. Now I am going to shut it." '

'So the doorkeeper deceived the man,' said K. immediately, much taken by the story. 'Don't be over-hasty,' said the priest, 'do not accept another's opinion uncritically. I told you the story according to the letter of the text. It says nothing about deception.' 'But it's clear,' said K., 'and your initial interpretation was quite correct. The doorkeeper only spoke the words of deliverance when it was too late to help the man.' 'He had not been asked before,' said the priest. 'Remember, he was only a doorkeeper, and as such he fulfilled his duty.' 'What makes you believe he fulfilled his duty?' asked K. 'He did not. It was perhaps his duty to deter all strangers, but he ought to have admitted this man, since the door was meant for him.' 'You do not have enough respect for the text, and you are altering the story,' said the priest. 'The story contains two important statements by the doorkeeper about admittance to the law, one at the beginning, one at the end. The one is that he cannot admit him now, and the other is that this entrance was meant only for him. If there were a contradiction between these two statements, you would be right, and the doorkeeper would have deceived the man. But there is no contradiction. On the contrary, the first statement even implies the second. One could almost say the doorkeeper exceeded his duty by holding out the prospect that the man might be admitted at some time in the future. At first, it seems, it was his duty only to refuse to admit the man, and indeed many interpreters of the text express surprise that the doorkeeper hinted at such a possibility, for he seems keen to be precise and performs his official duties punctiliously. Over many years he does not leave his watch, and only shuts the door at the very end; he is very conscious of the importance of his duty, for he says: "I am powerful". He has respect for his superiors, for he says: "I am only the lowest doorkeeper". He is not talkative, for during all those years he only puts, as the text has it, "casual questions"; he is not corruptible, for he says about a gift: "I am only accepting it so that you don't think you have neglected anything". As for fulfilling his duty, he is not to be moved by pleas or entreaties, for it says of the man that "he wearies the doorkeeper with his pleas". Finally, even his appearance indicates his punctilious nature, the great hooked nose and the long, thin, black Tartar's beard. Can there be a more dutiful doorkeeper?

'The doorkeeper, however, also has other characteristics which are very favourable to anyone who seeks admittance and which help to explain why he exceeded his duty somewhat in suggesting the possibility of future admittance; for it cannot be denied that he is rather simple-minded and therefore rather conceited. Even if his statements about his own power and that of the other doorkeepers, and about their fearsome appearance which even he cannot bear – as I say, even if all these statements are correct in themselves, the manner in which he expresses them indicates that his perceptions are clouded by naïvety and conceit. The commentators say to this: "Truly to understand something and to misunderstand the same thing are not entirely mutually exclusive". Nevertheless, we must assume that such naïvety and conceit, in however trivial a form they are expressed, still impair his ability to guard the entrance; they are defects in the character of the doorkeeper. In addition to this, the doorkeeper seems to have a kind nature, he is by no means an official through and through. In the very first moments he laughs and invites the man to enter in spite of the express and strictly enforced ban on admittance; then he does not send him away, but, as the text says, gives him a stool and lets him sit down to one side of the door. The patience with which he tolerates the pleas of the man during all those years, the brief questions he asks him, his acceptance of the gifts, the courtesy with which he allows the man beside him to curse the unhappy fate that has placed the doorkeeper here – all this suggests that he feels pity for the man. Not every doorkeeper would have acted like that. And finally he bends right down when the man beckons him to give him the chance to put his last question. He expresses only faint impatience – the doorkeeper knows, after all, that it is all over with the man – in the words: "You are insatiable". Some go even further in this interpretation, and believe the words "you are insatiable" express a sort of kindly admiration, though they are not free from condescension. At all events, the figure of the doorkeeper emerges in a different light from how you see it.'

'You know the story better than I do, and you have known it for longer,' said K. They were silent for a while. Then K. said: 'So you believe the man was not deluded?' 'Don't misunderstand me,' said the priest. 'I am only giving you the opinions that have been expressed. You must not pay too much attention to opinions. The text is unalterable, and opinions are often only an expression of bewilderment. In this connection there is even a view that it is the doorkeeper who is deluded.' 'That is a far-fetched view,' said K. 'How is that justified?' 'It is based,' said the priest, 'on the naïvety of the doorkeeper. The argument is that he does not know what lies beyond the entrance to the law; he knows only the area he must patrol in front of the entrance. His notions of what is inside are held to be childish, and it is assumed that he himself is afraid of the very things he describes in order to frighten the man. Indeed, he is more afraid than the man is, for the man is still eager to be admitted even when he hears of the fearsome doorkeepers inside; the doorkeeper, on the other hand, has no wish to enter – at least, we are told nothing of this. Of course, others say he must have been inside, because he has after all been appointed as a servant of the law, and that, they say, can only have taken place inside. Against that it can be argued that he might well have been appointed as doorkeeper by a call from inside, and in any case he cannot have been very far inside, because he could not even bear

the sight of the third doorkeeper. Moreover, there is no indication
that during all those years he said anything about what was inside,
except for his remark about the doorkeepers. He might have been
forbidden to enter; but he says nothing about this. From all this, it
is inferred that he knows nothing about the appearance or the
significance of the interior, and is deluding himself about it. But he
is also thought to be deluding himself about the man from the
country, for he is inferior to this man and does not know it. That
he treats the man as his inferior is clear from many details that you
will no doubt remember; but according to this view it should be
just as clear that he is in fact inferior to the man. Above all, a free
man is superior to a man in service. Now, the man is indeed free,
he can go wherever he wishes; only entrance to the law is
forbidden him – and this, moreover, only by one individual, the
doorkeeper. When he sits on a stool to one side of the door and
stays there for the rest of his life, he does this voluntarily; the story
does not mention any compulsion. The doorkeeper, on the other
hand, is bound to his post by his office; he may not move away
from the entrance, but apparently he may not go inside either,
even if he wanted to. Moreover, although he is in the service of
the law, he only serves at this entrance, so he is there only for this
man, for whom alone this entrance is intended. For this reason too
he is inferior to the man. We must assume that for many years,
perhaps for a whole lifetime, his service has in a certain sense been
fruitless, for we are told that a man arrives. The man is an adult; so
the doorkeeper must have had to wait a long time in order to
perform his duty, that is, as long as it suited the man, because he
came voluntarily. But the length of his service is also determined
by the death of the man, so he remains subordinate to him right to
the end. And it is emphasised time and again that the doorkeeper
knows nothing of all this. But this is seen as nothing remarkable,
for in this view the doorkeeper is even more gravely deluded in
the matter of his service. At the end he refers to the door and says:
"I am now going to shut it"; but at the beginning the text says
that the door to the law stands open as it always does. Now, if it
always stands open – always, that is, irrespective of the life-span of
the man for whom it is intended – then the doorkeeper will not
be able to shut it. Opinions are divided on whether the doorkeeper, when he announces that he is going to shut the door, is

simply answering a question, whether he is emphasising his devotion to duty, or whether he is trying to cause the man sorrow and regret at his very last moment. But many agree that he will not be able to shut the door, they even believe that he is, at least at the end, inferior to the man also in what he knows; for the man sees the radiance streaming from the entrance to the law, while the doorkeeper, as is his duty, presumably stands with his back to the entrance and says nothing to suggest that he has noticed anything new.'

'That is well argued,' said K., who had been repeating to himself some passages from the priest's explanation under his breath. 'It is well argued, and I also now believe that the doorkeeper is deluded. But that still doesn't change my earlier opinion, for the two views coincide to some extent. The decisive factor is not whether the doorkeeper is deluded or otherwise. I said the man was deceived. If the doorkeeper sees correctly, one might doubt this; but if the doorkeeper is deluded, then his delusions must necessarily be shared by the man. In that case, the doorkeeper is not deceiving the man; but he is so naïve that he ought to be dismissed from office at once. You must take account of the fact that the delusion the doorkeeper suffers from does him no harm, whereas it harms the man enormously.' 'There is an argument against that,' said the priest. 'Many say that the story gives no one the right to judge the doorkeeper. However he may seem to us, he is a servant of the law, so he belongs to the law, hence he is beyond human judgement. In that case one cannot believe that the doorkeeper is inferior to the man. Being bound to his service, even if it is only at the entrance to the law, is incomparably better than living freely in the world outside. When the man comes to the law, the doorkeeper is already there. He is a servant appointed by the law; to doubt his status would be to doubt the law.' 'I do not agree with that,' said K., shaking his head. 'If we take that view, we must accept that everything the doorkeeper says is true. But you yourself have demonstrated in detail that this is not possible.' 'No,' said the priest, 'we must not accept everything is true, we must only accept it is necessary.' 'A dismal thought,' said K., 'it makes untruth into a universal principle.'

K. said this by way of conclusion, but it was not his final judgement. He was too tired to consider all the implications of the story; it led him into unfamiliar trains of thought, unreal notions that were more suitable for discussion by an assembly of court officials than for him. The simple story had become confused, he wanted to be rid of it, and the priest, who now showed great delicacy of feeling, accepted this and made no reply to K.'s comment, although he cannot have agreed with it.

They walked on for a time in silence. K. kept close to the priest, not knowing where they were. The lamp in his hand had long since gone out. Once the silver statue of a saint shone with a whitish gleam just in front of him, then was immediately lost in the darkness. K. did not wish to remain wholly dependent on the priest, so he asked him: 'Are we not near the main porch?' 'No,' said the priest, 'we are a long way from it. Do you want to leave?' Although it had not been in K.'s mind just then, he said immediately: 'Of course, I must go. I am a senior official in a bank, I am expected back. I only came here to show a foreign business associate round the cathedral.' 'Well,' said the priest, 'go then.' 'But I cannot find my way alone in the dark,' said K. 'Go left as far as the wall,' said the priest, 'then keep to the wall, and you will find a way out.' The priest was only a few steps away, but K. called out: 'Please wait!' 'I am waiting,' said the priest. 'Is there anything else you want from me?' asked K. 'No,' said the priest. 'You were so kind to me earlier,' said K., 'and explained everything to me. But now you dismiss me as if I meant nothing to you.' 'But you have to go,' said the priest. 'Yes, I do,' said K., 'you must understand that.' 'You must first understand who I am,' said the priest. 'You are the prison chaplain,' said K., moving closer to the priest; his immediate return to the bank was not as necessary as he had made out, he could well stay here for a while. 'So I belong to the court,' said the priest. 'Why then should I want anything from you? The court wants nothing from you. It receives you when you come, and it releases you when you go.'

Chapter Ten

End

On the eve of his thirty-first birthday – it was towards nine in the evening, the time when the streets fall silent – two men in frock coats came to K.'s apartment; they were pale and plump, with top hats clamped firmly on their heads. After some formalities at the front door concerning who should enter first, the same formalities were repeated more elaborately at K.'s door. Although the visit had not been announced, K. sat in a chair near the door, also dressed in black, slowly pulling on new gloves that fitted tightly over his hands, in the attitude of someone who was expecting guests. He stood up at once and looked at the men with curiosity. 'So you have come for me?' he asked. The men nodded, each pointing to the other with top hat in hand. K. admitted to himself that he had been expecting different visitors. He went to the window and looked out into the dark street. Almost all the windows on the far side were dark; in many of them the blinds were lowered. In one of the lighted windows on the block, small children were playing behind a window grille; they were still too small to move around, but reached out to each other with tiny hands. 'They are sending ageing second-rate actors for me,' K. said to himself, and looked round to confirm this impression. 'They are trying to get rid of me cheaply.' He suddenly turned to them and asked: 'Which theatre are you appearing at?' 'Theatre?' one of them turned to ask the other, the corners of his mouth twitching. The other acted like a deaf mute struggling to control an unmanageable disability. 'They are not trained to answer questions,' said K. to himself and went to fetch his hat.

On the staircase the men tried to hold K. by the arms, but he said: 'Not until we are on the street. I am not ill.' But just as they reached the door they took hold of him in a way no one had done before. They kept their shoulders close behind his, and without bending their arms held his tight along their full length, grasping his hands in an expert, practised, irresistible grip. K., held rigid, walked between them; the three of them formed such a close unit that if one of them had been knocked over, the others would have followed. It was the kind of unity that only inanimate forms can achieve.

Under the street lamps K. frequently attempted, difficult though it was when he was being held so closely, to see his companions more clearly than had been possible in the dim light of his room. 'Perhaps they are tenors,' he thought, looking at their heavy double chins. Their shiny faces nauseated him; he could easily imagine the hand reaching to wipe the corners of the eyes, rubbing the upper lip, smoothing out the folds of the chin.

When K. thought of this, he stopped. The others stopped too; they were at the edge of a deserted open space with some flower-beds. 'Why did they have to send you!' he cried out rather than asked. The men appeared to have no answer; they waited with their free arms hanging down, like medical orderlies pausing for the invalid to take a rest. 'I am not going any further,' K. ventured. The men did not bother to answer; without slackening their grip they tried to drag him off, but he resisted. 'I shall not need my strength much longer, I shall use it all now,' he thought. He was reminded of flies that tear off their wings struggling to free themselves from a fly-paper. 'These gentlemen will have to work hard.'

At that moment Fräulein Bürstner emerged into the square from a small flight of steps leading from a lane below. It was not quite certain that it was Fräulein Bürstner, but the resemblance was very close. But it did not matter to K. whether it was or not; all he was aware of just then was the futility of resistance. He would be doing nothing heroic if he resisted, if he caused trouble for these men, if by defending himself he attempted to enjoy a last glimmer of life. He set off again, and some of the pleasure this gave the men communicated itself to him too. They now allowed him to choose which way they went; he led them in the direction Fräulein Bürstner was taking, not because he wanted to catch up with her, nor because he wanted to keep her in view as long as possible, but only so that he would not forget the rebuke she represented for him. 'The only thing I can do now,' he said to himself, and the steady rhythm of his steps and those of his companions confirmed his thoughts, 'the only thing I can do now is to keep calm and marshal my thoughts rationally. I always wanted to rush headlong at things, not always for the best reasons. That was quite wrong. Am I now to show that not even a case that has lasted a whole year could teach me anything? Am I to leave the world as a man who is impervious to argument? Are people to say of me that when my case started, I wanted to finish it, and now that it is finishing I want to start it again? I don't want them to say that. I am grateful that I have been given these inarticulate, ignorant companions, and that it has been left to me to tell myself what has to be said.'

The young woman had meanwhile turned off into a side-street; but K. could now do without her and let his companions lead him. All three now walked with one accord across a bridge in the moonlight. The men willingly yielded to K.'s slightest movement; if he swerved slightly towards the parapet, they also wheeled round in that direction. The water, glinting and shimmering in the moonlight, flowed round a small island on which trees and shrubs crowded together in a dense mass of foliage. Underneath them, invisible now, ran gravel paths with comfortable benches where K. had stretched himself out and relaxed during many a summer. 'I didn't want to stop,' he said to his companions, embarrassed by their ready compliance. One of them seemed to reproach the other mildly behind K.'s back for this misunder-standing, then they went on.

They climbed through narrow streets in which policemen stood here and there or walked up and down, some in the distance, others very close. One, with a bushy moustache, his hand grasping the hilt of his sabre, approached this not wholly innocent-looking group, it seemed with intent. The men hesitated, and the police-man seemed about to open his mouth, but K. used all his strength to pull the men on. Several times he turned round cautiously to see whether the policeman was following them; then as soon as they turned a corner, he began to run, and the men had to keep up with him, gasping for breath.

They quickly left the town, which on this side soon gave way to open fields. A small quarry, bleak and deserted, lay near a house that looked just like a town house. Here the men paused, perhaps because this place had been their destination from the start, perhaps because they were too exhausted to go any further. Then

they let K. go. He waited in silence; they removed their top hats
and mopped the sweat from their brows with their handkerchiefs
while they looked round the quarry. The moonlight lay over the
whole scene with the natural serenity no other light has.

After an exchange of polite formalities concerning who was to
perform the following task – the men seemed not to have been
given separate instructions – one of them went up to K. and
removed his coat, his waistcoat and finally his shirt. K. shivered
involuntarily, at which the man gave him a light, reassuring pat on
the back. Then he folded the clothes carefully, as if they might still
be needed, though not perhaps in the immediate future. In order
to give K. some exercise to protect him from the night air, which
was cold enough, he took him by the arm and walked him up and
down for a time, while the second searched the quarry for a
suitable spot. When he had found it, he beckoned, and the first
man led K. to it. It was close to the quarry face; a stone that had
broken loose lay there. The men sat K. on the ground, laid him
against the stone and cushioned his head on the top. In spite of all
the trouble they took, and in spite of all K.'s cooperation, his
posture was still most awkward and unnatural, so one of them
asked the other to leave the positioning of K.'s body to him; but
that made things no better. Finally they left him in a position that
was not even the most comfortable of those they had already tried.
Then one of the men unbuttoned his frock-coat, and from a sheath
hanging from a belt around his waistcoat he took a long, thin,
double-bladed butcher's knife and held it up in the moonlight to
judge its sharpness. Again they started their dreadful courtesies; the
one handed the knife to the other, who handed it back again. K.
now knew perfectly well that it should have been his duty, as the
knife was passed from hand to hand over him, to take hold of it and
plunge it into himself. But he did not; instead he turned his head,
which was still free, and looked about him. He could not bring
himself to do it; he would not relieve the authorities of all their
duties. The responsibility for this final failing lay with those who
had deprived him of the remaining strength he needed.

His eyes fell on the upper storey of the house that stood near the
quarry. Like a flash of light, the windows there flew open, and a
man, indistinct and tenuous at that distance and elevation, suddenly
leaned out and stretched out his arms still further. Who was he? A

friend? A good man? Someone who cared? Someone who wanted to help? Was it one man? Was it all men? Was there still help? Were there objections that had been overlooked? Certainly there were some. Logic is unshakeable, but it cannot prevail against a man who wishes to live. Where was the judge he had never seen? Where was the high court he had never had access to? He raised his hands and spread out all his fingers.

But one of the men took K. by the throat while the other plunged the knife deep into his heart and twisted it twice. As his sight failed, K. could still see them in front of his face, leaning together cheek by cheek as they watched the final moment. 'Like a dog!' he said; it was as if the shame was to outlive him.